THE
HOMECOMING
TRILOGY

LUCY DANIELS

Illustrated by
Trevor Parkin

Hodder
Children's
Books

a division of Hodder Headline Limited

Also by Lucy Daniels

THE
BETRAYAL

This edition of *The Betrayal*, *The Sacrifice* and *The Homecoming*
first published in 2002.

ISBN 0 340 85239 9

10 9 8 7 6 5 4 3 2 1

The Betrayal

Special thanks to Helen Magee

Text copyright © 1999 Working Partners Limited
Series created by Ben M. Baglio, London W6 OQT
Illustrations copyright © 1999 Sheila Ratcliffe

First published as a single volume in Great Britain in 1999
by Hodder Children's Books

Typeset by Avon Dataset Ltd, Bidford-on-Avon, Warks

Printed and bound in Great Britain by
The Guernsey Press Co. Ltd, Vale, Guernsey, Channel Islands

Hodder Children's Books
a division of Hodder Headline Limited
338 Euston Road
London NW1 3BH

1

'We're going to have a great party tonight, Jess!' Jenny Miles said, as she gazed up at the towering bonfire, which was waiting to be lit.

Jess, her black and white Border collie, looked up at her, his head to one side, and Jenny laughed. 'OK, I know what you're waiting for,' she said, picking up a stick. 'Go find, boy!'

Jenny tossed the stick high in the air for him. The young sheepdog scampered off across the field as Jenny watched the stick arc high in the blue November sky. From up here, above Windy Hill, her family's farm in the Scottish borders, Jenny could see Puffin Island, lying like a green jewel off the coast, its cliffs sparkling in the morning sun. The wind from the sea blew her shoulder-length fair hair across her eyes and caught at the stick she had thrown. It sailed over the drystone wall that separated Windy Hill's land from Dunraven, the neighbouring farm.

Jenny spotted a tall dark-haired girl and a little boy walking down the track on the other side of the wall. It was Fiona McLay and her brother, Paul. Toby, his brown and black Border terrier, was at his side. 'Oh no!' Jenny gasped. 'Watch out!'

The stick fell, just grazing Fiona's arm. She immediately turned towards Jenny, her mouth set in an angry line. 'You did that deliberately, Jenny Miles,' she accused, as Jenny ran over towards them. Fiona McLay's father owned Dunraven. He and Fraser Miles, Jenny's father, had never been friends and Fiona tried to pick fights with Jenny whenever she could.

'I didn't, Fiona,' Jenny protested. 'I'm sorry. Are you hurt?'

'As if you care!' Fiona replied.

'It was an accident, Fiona,' Paul put in. 'Jenny didn't mean to hit you.'

Fiona glanced down at her eight-year-old brother. 'Don't interfere, Paul,' she snapped. Then she turned on her heel and walked off down the track. 'Come on, Paul!'

Paul looked after her, his wide grey eyes unhappy. 'I want to talk to Jenny about the bonfire party,' he called.

Fiona whirled round. 'Oh, yes – the famous Windy Hill bonfire party,' she scoffed, nastily. 'Don't expect *me* to come. I know you only invited me because you *had* to!'

'I don't want you to come anyway!' Jenny called after her. She was so angry at Fiona's rudeness that she spoke without thinking.

'Are you all right?' Paul asked, scrambling over the wall, Toby following at his heels. 'Did Fiona upset you?'

Jenny smiled at the little boy. 'It's all right, Paul, it's not your fault,' she said, stroking Jess's head. She picked up the stick and threw it for the collie.

Jess and Toby immediately scampered after it.

'Doesn't Jess run fast?' said Paul. 'He's faster than Toby now, even *with* his bad leg!'

Jenny nodded and smiled. Jess had been born with a badly twisted leg. Fraser Miles had thought that putting the puppy down would be kindest, since he would never make a working dog, but Jenny had pleaded for Jess's life and nursed him through an operation to straighten his leg.

Jenny's dedication and Jess's courage had paid off. Now Jess was as lively as any other dog, and he had proved a great help with the lambing last spring. Even Jenny's father admitted that Jess had been worth saving.

Paul's eyes shifted across the field to the wood pile that was to be the bonfire. 'Wow!' he said. 'It's enormous! Have you got a guy as well?'

Jenny nodded. 'We've just got to finish making him,' she said. 'We'll put him on the top of the bonfire just before we light it.'

'I know all about Guy Fawkes Night and why we have bonfires and fireworks and guys,' Paul said proudly. 'We learned a rhyme about it at school: "Remember, remember, the fifth of

November, gunpowder, treason and plot!" '

Jenny laughed. 'Did you learn what the plot was?' she asked.

Paul nodded. 'Hundreds of years ago some men who didn't like the government tried to blow up the Houses of Parliament with a barrel of gunpowder. And they were led by a man called Guy Fawkes.'

Jenny nodded, smiling. She looked at the two dogs, chasing each other round the bonfire. 'You mustn't bring Toby tonight, Paul,' she warned him.

Paul shook his head. 'The fireworks would scare him. I'll leave him at home. Who else is coming to the party?'

'Matt's coming home,' Jenny told him. 'He's bringing his new girlfriend with him. She's on the same course as him.' Matt was Jenny's nineteen-year-old brother. He was away at agricultural college, but he came home as often as he could to help on the farm. 'And lots of my new friends from school are coming too,' Jenny went on. She had recently started senior school in Greybridge, the local market town. 'You'll like them.'

'Fiona doesn't like them,' Paul announced. 'She says she hates the new school.'

Fiona was in the same class as Jenny at Greybridge School, but they had little to do with each other.

'She's got a project to do,' Paul went on. 'It's all about drawing a map of where you live with routes marked to all your friends' houses. She says she can't be bothered with it.'

Jenny was surprised. 'That's our Geography project,' she explained. 'Most people are really enjoying it. It's fun.'

'Fiona doesn't think so,' Paul said. He looked round and whistled for Toby. 'I'd better go. Fiona will be angry if she has to wait for me.'

Jenny sighed as she watched Paul and Toby run off. Fiona *was* difficult. She had scared Paul so badly when he had needed to go into hospital for an ear operation that the little boy had run away. Jess had found Paul at Darktarn Keep further up the hill and had then helped rescue the little boy when he had fallen into the river below. At first Fiona had been so relieved that Paul was all right that she'd made a special effort to be nice to him. But it hadn't lasted long and now it seemed she was back to her old self, bossing Paul around.

Jenny sighed and whistled for Jess. The collie came racing across the short grass towards her. 'Come on, boy,' she cried. 'We've got work to do! And Matt is coming home!'

A motorbike was drawing up in the farmyard as Jenny and Jess hurtled down the track. Matt! But two leather-clad figures sat astride the bike. Who was with him? Matt parked the bike and took off his helmet. He put out a hand to help his companion off the back of the bike, before turning to unload a couple of bags out of the side-paniers. Jenny raced across the farmyard and threw herself at her brother.

'Hi, Jen,' Matt laughed, dropping the bags on the cobbles of the yard and giving his sister a bear hug. He stood away from her and ruffled her hair – his way of affectionately teasing his younger sister. Behind him, a slim girl was taking off her helmet and smoothing down her fair hair. Matt looked back at her and smiled. 'How about saying hello to Vicky, Jen?'

Jenny turned to the girl and held out her hand. 'Hi, Vicky,' she said. 'Welcome to Windy Hill!'

Vicky took Jenny's hand and shook it firmly, then she looked down at Jess. Tail wagging, the Border collie leaped up at her.

'Down, Jess!' Jenny commanded.

Vicky laughed. 'Oh, I don't mind,' she said, her bright hazel eyes twinkling. 'I've heard all about the famous Jess from Matt. He really is a gorgeous dog.'

Jenny beamed at Vicky. Nothing pleased her more than people complimenting Jess – and Jess obviously liked Vicky.

The farmhouse door opened and Fraser Miles strode across the cobbled yard towards them. He held out his hand to Vicky in greeting and then hugged his son. With his dark colouring and startling blue eyes, he and Matt were very alike. Two black and white sheepdogs trotted at Fraser's heels.

'That's Jake and Nell,' Matt told Vicky. 'They're the best working dogs in the Borders – but their greatest claim to fame as far as Jenny's concerned is that they're Jess's parents!'

Vicky laughed as Jess barked then raced up to the two older dogs and began to run around them, wagging his tail. Jake and Nell butted him playfully but they didn't chase him. They were working dogs and they behaved like working dogs. Jess scampered off towards the kitchen door just as Mrs Grace, the housekeeper, came out into the yard.

'What do you think of the lambing barn now that it's finished and painted, Matt?' she asked, after the introductions had been made.

Matt swung round to look at the new barn his father had built with the profits from the last lambing. Its fresh green paint sparkled in the sun. 'It looks great,' he said approvingly. 'Last time I was here it still needed its roof putting on. It looks a lot better than the old one.' Matt turned to Vicky. 'The old lambing barn had been falling to bits for years,' he explained. 'It finally blew down in a gale, last winter. This one is much better.'

Fraser Miles looked pleased. 'It's going to be really useful to us this winter,' he said. 'I've got some of the young pregnant ewes in there already. And it will make the lambing so much easier.'

Fraser Miles had a thousand Scottish Blackface sheep on his farm. He had put the rams into the fields with the ewes in October and now most of the flock were pregnant. Scottish Blackfaces were a hardy hill breed and their thick coats were perfectly suited to the harsh Border winters but, even so, pregnant ewes, especially those expecting lambs for the first time, needed a lot of looking after.

'I bet this spring's lambing is going to be even better than last year's,' Jenny said, looking at her father.

'If it's as good as the last lambing, I'll be happy,' Fraser responded. 'Things are certainly looking good so far.'

Jenny smiled, delighted to see her father so optimistic. Sheep farming was Fraser Miles's whole life. It was a hard life but he loved it.

'Come and have something to eat,' Mrs Grace urged them. 'I've been baking for two days for this bonfire party, so there's plenty.'

'You don't have to ask twice,' Matt joked, heading for the kitchen door.

'Carrie arrived not long ago, too,' Mrs Grace said to Jenny. 'She's gone over to the shearing shed to help Ian with making the guy. They're bound to be hungry.'

Jenny grinned. 'Ian's always hungry,' she said, as she and Jess made for the shearing shed. Ian Amery was Ellen Grace's nephew. He had come to stay with his aunt when his parents had gone to Canada. Ellen and Ian had come to live at Windy Hill when Calum McLay had turned Ellen out of the cottage she had rented on Dunraven land.

'Hi, Jen,' Carrie said. 'Look at this. It's going to be the best guy in the world!' she announced as she stuffed straw into the sack that made up the guy's body.

Jenny smiled. Carrie had come to live in Cliffbay, a nearby fishing village, the previous year. She was now Jenny's best friend.

'Can you hold the bottoms of the trouser legs, while I tie some string round them, Jen?' Ian said. 'We don't want the straw falling out.'

Jenny held the bottoms of the old pair of trousers as Ian tightened the string and knotted it. 'Mrs Grace says we've to come in for something to eat,' she said.

Ian looked up. 'Great!' he said. 'I'm starving. We can finish the guy later. We've got loads of

time before tonight – and have you *seen* the piles of food Aunt Ellen has made?'

The big farmhouse kitchen was bright with winter sunlight. Red checked curtains hung at the window and the blue and white crockery on the dresser gleamed. The flagged floor was bright with warm rag rugs and Jess's basket was tucked away in one corner, his favourite blue woollen blanket folded inside. Smells of baking filled the air and the Aga gave off a comforting heat after the chill of the sea wind.

'I'm really going to miss your cooking when I go to Canada for Christmas, Aunt Ellen,' Ian said, as he sat down at the big kitchen table. 'But at least I'm going to learn to ski – that'll be great.'

'Skiing,' Jenny sighed. 'I've never been skiing.'

Ian grinned at her. 'I'll teach you when I come back from Canada,' he promised. 'We can go up by Darktarn Keep if there's enough snow this winter.'

'Tell me about a winter when there hasn't been plenty of snow in these parts,' Mrs Grace joked.

'We had a bad winter on our farm too,' Vicky said.

Fraser looked at her in surprise. 'Matt didn't tell us you came from a farming family,' he said.

'I told her to keep quiet about it,' Matt laughed. 'I warned her she'd get dragged in to help if she admitted to being a farmer's daughter.'

Jenny gave him a dig in the ribs as he sat down at the table beside her. Vicky told Fraser and the others about the farm her parents owned.

'A sheep farm – like this?' Ian exclaimed.

'But on the other side of the border,' Vicky said with mock seriousness. 'The English side.'

'Uh-oh,' said Carrie. 'That means you and the Mileses are probably old enemies. Your ancestors probably stole each other's sheep.'

Vicky laughed. 'I suppose we did,' she said.

Jenny looked round the table. Everyone was talking and laughing and having a great time – and tonight at the bonfire there would be even more people.

'By the way, Mum is bringing loads of toffee apples for the party,' Carrie said.

'That'll be a help,' Mrs Grace approved. 'With

all the school friends you two have invited, we'll need them.'

Jenny smiled. 'Amy Jarrow says she hasn't had an invitation to any other bonfire parties so she'll come.'

'Charming!' said Ian.

Carrie spluttered with laughter. 'Amy is always putting her foot in it,' she said. 'She doesn't mean to sound rude. She's nice, really.'

'Her dad is going to drive a crowd of them over from Greybridge,' Jenny said.

A warm, wet tongue licked her hand and Jenny looked down. Jess was gazing up at her with soulful eyes. 'All right,' she whispered. 'Just this once.' She fed him a chunk of scone from her plate.

Jess gulped it down, then he laid his head on Jenny's lap. 'Oh, Jess,' Jenny said. 'It's such a pity you'll have to miss the bonfire tonight, but the fireworks would frighten you. I'll save you some sausages, though – I promise.'

Fraser Miles looked up and smiled at her. 'Do you remember how much your mum loved bonfire night?' he asked softly.

Jenny nodded. 'Everyone is really glad we've

decided to hold our traditional bonfire party again. They missed having it last year. Mum made it famous . . .' Jenny felt a sudden wave of sadness, remembering why there hadn't been a Windy Hill bonfire party the previous year. Her mother, Sheena Miles, had been killed in a riding accident a few months before.

Tonight's celebration, the first without Sheena, wouldn't be quite the same. But Jenny had asked her father specially if they could have a bonfire party. She was sure her mother would have liked that.

'I reckon we'll have to keep its reputation up then,' Matt put in, squeezing Jenny's arm.

Jenny smiled and nodded. 'We'll make it the best bonfire night ever!'

2

Jenny dashed up to her bedroom early that evening to fetch her old padded jacket. Her father had given her a new jacket for her birthday two weeks earlier but she didn't want to get it all smoky from the bonfire.

She cast a glance round her bedroom. Its yellow painted walls were covered with posters but, in pride of place above her bed, was the sketch Carrie's mother had drawn of Jess when he was just a few months old. He looked so appealing, with his front leg still in the plaster cast he'd worn after his operation.

Jenny picked up her woolly hat and scarf and opened the wardrobe door to look for her jacket. Just then, her bedroom light went out.

'It's all right, it's probably just a fuse blown,' Matt called from downstairs. 'I'll have it fixed in a moment.'

Jenny rummaged in the wardrobe but it was so dark, she couldn't see a thing. Then she had an idea. 'My candles!' she exclaimed, feeling her way across to her desk by the window. The desk was piled with papers for her Geography project. Jenny reached across them to the windowsill and felt around for the fat pink candle and box of matches she knew was there. Striking a match, she lit the candle and smiled ruefully. Matt had given her the candle-making kit for her birthday. Her initial attempts at candle making hadn't been too successful, to say the least! The first one had collapsed all over the kitchen table. This one was a *little* better. Jenny cleared a space and set it in the middle of the desk. She had just found her jacket when the light went on again and she heard feet on the stairs. Her father popped his head round her bedroom door.

'Come on, lass,' he said. 'People are beginning to arrive! Don't forget to put that candle out.'

Jenny hastily blew out the candle and made for the door. She couldn't wait for the bonfire party to start!

Jess was already out in the yard, tail wagging, greeting the guests. Jenny smiled as she saw the fuss everyone made of him.

Tom Palmer, the vet who had looked after Jess when he was a puppy, rubbed the collie's ears. 'How's my favourite sheepdog?' he said as Jess leaped up at him.

The Turners' car drew into the yard and Jess was off again, leaping up at Pam and Gordon Turner, Carrie's parents, as they unloaded boxes of toffee apples from the boot.

Amy Jarrow's father was the last to arrive, and a crowd of youngsters spilled out of the back of his minibus.

'I don't think I'll ever get Jess inside,' Jenny laughed, as Amy and the others began to play with him.

'You'll have to, lass,' her father said. 'We can't

have him outside with fireworks around.'

Jenny nodded and called to Jess. The Border collie came running towards her, barking excitedly. 'Come on, boy,' Jenny said. 'Time to see you safely inside.'

Fraser was organising everyone into teams to shift the provisions from the kitchen to the jeep. 'Ready, Jenny?' he called as he loaded the portable barbecue.

Jenny shook her head. 'I just want to make sure Jess is all right,' she said. 'He's quite excited with all these people around. I'll wait and see that he's settled. You go on ahead. I'll catch up.'

Mr Miles nodded.

'I've checked on Jake and Nell,' Matt said, walking up to the jeep with Vicky. 'They're safely shut in the stable with Mercury.'

'And the breeding ewes?' Mr Miles asked.

Matt nodded. 'They're all in the pens in the lambing barn.' He turned to Jenny. 'Don't be too long, Jen,' he called as he and Vicky climbed into the jeep. 'You don't want to miss any of the fun!'

'I won't,' Jenny called back. She waved as Matt and Vicky drove off in the jeep, following the road round to the top field where the bonfire stood, waiting to be lit.

Fraser, Mrs Grace, Carrie, Ian and the others cut across the fields on foot. It was dark but her father led the way and they all had torches.

Jenny led Jess into the kitchen and settled him down in his basket. He was still excitable and it took quite a while to calm him down. 'I know you want to come with me, Jess,' she said. 'But, really, this is for your own good. I'll come down and see you in a little while.'

Jess whined and put a paw on Jenny's knee, looking up at her pleadingly. 'I'll be back,' she promised, backing out of the door. Feeling a little guilty, she closed the door carefully behind her.

Turning towards the track, Jenny switched on her torch. The bright beam lit up the way ahead. Jenny snuggled into her jacket, pulling her scarf up round her ears. The wind had dropped but the air smelt frosty and crisp. Perfect weather for a bonfire, she said to herself as she set off for the top field.

'I've got the barbecue going,' Matt announced

as Jenny arrived. 'It's just about ready for cooking.'

'Time for me to get started,' Mrs Grace said. 'Hand me that plastic container, Jenny, and I'll get the sausages on.'

Carrie and Ian had unloaded the boxes of food on to a table next to the barbecue.

'Wow!' said Ian, looking at the array of sandwiches and rolls. 'There's enough here to feed an army.'

'You'll be all right then, Ian,' Pam Turner joked, as she dumped a box of toffee apples on the table.

Ian grinned. 'I've just got a healthy appetite, that's all,' he said.

'Time to light the bonfire, Jenny,' Fraser Miles shouted over.

Carrie was dancing with impatience. 'Come on, Jen!' she called. 'Everyone's waiting!'

Jenny hurried over to join the dozens of people huddled round to watch the lighting of the bonfire. Matt and Vicky had put the guy on top of the pile of old fence posts and wood and it looked magnificently eerie. Fraser took a box of matches and lit a long taper. He held it out to

Jenny. 'Would you like to do it?' he asked, smiling.

Jenny nodded and took the taper. She felt a lump in her throat as she thought of her mother and how much she would have enjoyed this.

Mr Miles pointed to a heap of white blocks nestled in paper and tucked into the bonfire. 'Put the taper just there,' he advised. 'Those are firelighters so they should get the fire started pretty easily.'

Jenny's hand shook a little as she touched the taper to the firelighters. At once a blue flame sprang up and swept throughout the bed of paper and twigs. It reached the smaller branches and began to crackle as the flames caught and ran like red and yellow tongues through the middle of the bonfire. There was a cheer, followed by clapping from the assembled crowd as the fire took hold and the bonfire leapt into life.

'Well done, Jenny,' Gordon and Pam Turner called out to her.

Jenny smiled and shoved her hands in her pockets. She cast a look around all their guests as they stood happily watching the bonfire flames reach up into the sky.

'How's Jess?' Matt asked as he and Vicky came to stand beside Jenny. Matt had his arm round Vicky's shoulder and she snuggled close to him, smiling up at him. It was good to see Matt looking so relaxed and happy.

'He wasn't too pleased to be left at home,' Jenny replied. 'But I'll go down and see him in a while – just to make sure he doesn't feel left out. Poor thing, he couldn't understand why I had to lock him in the kitchen.'

'He must wonder what's going on,' Vicky said sympathetically.

'He'll forgive you – if you take him some sausages,' Matt said with a twinkle in his eye.

'Make that *lots* of sausages,' Carrie put in.

'I'm going to take some for Nell and Jake too,' said Jenny.

'Will you have a look at Mercury while you're there?' Matt asked.

'Sure thing,' Jenny said, 'and I'll take him an apple.'

'How about giving Mrs Grace a hand with the barbecue, first?' Carrie suggested. 'She looks pretty busy.'

'Good idea,' agreed Jenny. She sniffed as they walked towards the barbecue. 'It smells great already.'

'We've come to help,' Carrie said as they approached Mrs Grace.

Ellen Grace smiled at them and scooped a load of sausages off the barbecue and on to a large platter. 'Right, girls, you can start passing these around!'

'I'll just test one,' Carrie announced, taking a bite of sausage. 'Whoo! It's hot!' she said, frantically fanning her mouth. 'But really good!'

'I'm glad they've got the seal of approval,' Mrs Grace laughed, putting more sausages on to the barbecue. 'Don't forget to leave some for the others.'

'Food's up!' Jenny called. 'Is anybody hungry?'

She didn't have to repeat the question. Matt and Vicky handed out paper plates and everyone started to help themselves from the table. Some of Jenny's school friends helped to pass round cans of coke and other drinks as well as bowls of crisps and popcorn. Soon the barbecue was crowded with people laughing, talking and eating.

Mrs Grace was kept busy refilling the platters and, after the first rush, Jenny and Carrie managed to fill a plate for themselves.

'These are yummy!' Jenny congratulated Mrs Turner as she took a bite of her toffee apple.

'They're certainly going down well,' Carrie's mum agreed as young Paul McLay ran up to them, a toffee apple clutched in each hand.

'One of these is for Mum,' he explained breathlessly. 'She's just coming now.'

'Hello, everyone! Sorry I'm late.' Anna McLay, Paul's mother, made her way over to them. 'Well, this looks delicious,' she said, as she took the toffee apple her son offered her.

'Matt, your dad says it's time to start the fireworks,' Ian called over.

'Right!' Matt replied. 'What are we waiting for?' Taking Vicky's hand, he led her over to help.

Jenny watched as Matt and Vicky set off with Ian towards the corner of the field. Fraser had insisted that the fireworks be kept at a safe distance from the spectators.

'It was really good of you to ask us all to the party,' Anna McLay said to Jenny, who was helping Mrs Grace to put potatoes wrapped in tinfoil around the edges of the barbecue.

'Oh, that's OK,' Jenny said as she picked up another potato. 'I met Fiona this morning. She told me she didn't want to come,' she added.

Anna McLay looked embarrassed. 'Well, she had lots of schoolwork she had to finish,' she said lamely. 'And Calum is very busy at the moment, too . . .' Her voice trailed off.

Jenny guessed that, like Fiona, Calum McLay had refused to come to Windy Hill. It seemed that there was just too much bad history between Fraser Miles and Calum McLay for the two men ever to be friends.

'Maybe Fiona will come later when she sees the fireworks,' Ellen said, as a shower of sparks from the bonfire lit up the night and the people nearest to it backed away.

'I don't think so,' Mrs McLay said sadly. 'Fiona has been really difficult recently. I think she's been feeling a bit left out. Paul's operation was such a great success that maybe we made too much fuss of him and neglected Fiona a little. I am trying hard to make it up to her, but it isn't easy.'

Jenny and Carrie, who were listening, looked

at each other. 'No wonder Mrs McLay is having a hard time,' Carrie said to Jenny softly. 'Fiona is bad enough normally. She must be a real misery when she sulks.'

Jenny nodded, her eyes on Paul as he danced round the bonfire, his face alight with laughter. 'Paul is so different,' she said to Carrie. 'He's always cheerful – just like his mum.'

Jenny smiled at Paul who was waving a sparkler in the air. It left trails of light in the darkness. Suddenly there was a great whoosh from the bonfire and a shower of sparks burst upwards.

'Look! The guy's going up!' Carrie called.

Jenny watched as the straw-stuffed guy blazed like a beacon. For a few moments it seemed to come to life, its arms waving in the flames. Then, at the top end of the field a Catherine wheel began to whirl, sending out showers of light. Fraser had started the firework display!

Paul whooped with delight and Jenny watched as Mrs McLay moved towards her son. 'I thought Fiona had changed after Paul nearly drowned,' Jenny said to Carrie and Ellen. 'She seemed so sorry about frightening Paul into running away. It seemed like she'd turned over a new leaf. But then she was really mean to Jess this morning. She threw a stick at him.'

'If you ask me, Fiona will never change,' Carrie sniffed.

Jenny sighed. She had to agree but she wasn't going to worry about sulky Fiona McLay tonight. Tonight she was going to concentrate on enjoying herself. She and Carrie walked over to the crowd round the bonfire. A brilliant shower of sparks burst in the night sky, bathing the whole scene in its light. A rocket followed and another until the sky seemed filled with whistling fireworks exploding in the darkness.

As everyone ooh-ed and aah-ed, Jenny noticed that up on the hill, Darktarn Keep was illuminated, its broken walls looking even more dramatic than usual as coloured lights exploded all over the sky.

'Wow! Look at that one, Mum!' Paul cried, as a huge rocket burst open, showering the surrounding countryside in brilliant red and green stars.

Jenny grinned then turned to Carrie. 'I'm going to take some sausages down to Jess now,' she said. 'Do you want to come?'

Carrie shook her head. 'No, I think I'll stay here to see the last of the fireworks.'

Jess threw himself at Jenny as soon as she opened the kitchen door. He licked her face ecstatically and the only way she got him to stop was by producing the sausages. She watched him gobble up four in a row and laughed. 'Honestly, Jess,' she scolded him. 'Anyone would think I never fed you.'

Jess looked at her, his head on one side and his big dark eyes pleading.

'No,' Jenny said firmly as he butted the pocket of her jacket. 'Those are for Jake and Nell.' Jenny had wrapped some more sausages in foil and put them in her pocket, out of sight. Trust Jess to sniff them out.

Jenny stayed with him for a while, concerned in case the sound of the fireworks was upsetting him. But he seemed fine. From inside the house you could hardly hear the distant explosions and the curtains were safely drawn against the bright lights from the hill.

'I've got to go now, Jess,' she told him at last.

'I've got to check on Mercury and Jake and Nell.'

Jess whined as Jenny backed out of the door and closed it firmly behind her. Jenny made her way across the farmyard and pushed open the stable door. It felt warm and snug in the stables. Mercury whickered softly and the two sheepdogs trotted towards her, tails wagging. Jenny bent to fondle them.

'Good dogs,' she said softly, as Jake and Nell rubbed themselves against her legs. She stroked their rough coats then produced the treats she had brought for them, watching happily as they gobbled up the sausages, licking their lips afterwards and looking for more.

'That's all,' she told them, making her way to Mercury's box. She pulled an apple out of her pocket and held it out on the palm of her hand. The big black horse nuzzled at her hand as he took the apple from it. Jenny reached up her other hand and stroked his mane while Jake and Nell settled down once more.

'You aren't frightened, are you, Mercury?' she whispered.

Mercury whinnied and Jenny put an arm

round his neck. He felt warm and seemed perfectly calm. Jenny listened. She could hear only dull thuds as the fireworks exploded far away up the hill. The animals would be perfectly safe.

Jenny gave the sheepdogs a quick pat then opened the stable door. The night air blew in, cold and clear. She shut the door gently behind her.

As she was crossing the farmyard a rocket lit up the sky and Jenny increased her pace and turned for the top field. It was time she got back to her friends.

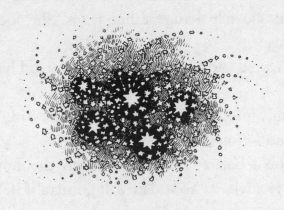

3

'That's the last firework,' Paul sighed, as a golden starburst exploded in the sky.

Jenny sighed too. 'Dad saved the best one until last,' she said.

'Brilliant!' Carrie chimed in, her face still bathed in the glow from the showering sparks.

All around them, friends and neighbours were cheering and clapping. Matt, Ian and Fraser appeared and jokingly took a bow to the assembled company. Jenny was applauding them when she felt a tug at her jeans. She looked down.

'Cripes!' said Carrie. 'It's Jess! How did he get out?'

Jenny gulped. 'I don't know,' she said. 'I'm certain I closed the door after me.'

'You'd better get him back to the house,' Carrie advised. 'Your dad will go mad if he sees Jess.'

Jenny nodded. 'I'll take him back right away,' she said, taking hold of his collar. But Jess kept on tugging, looking up at her intently. 'There's something wrong with him,' Jenny said. 'He won't stop pulling at me.'

'You're right,' Carrie agreed. 'He seems to want to move faster.'

Jess pulled forward again, almost pulling her off balance. Jenny put a hand on the dog's head but he wouldn't be distracted. He *was* acting oddly. Something was wrong.

'I don't know what's got into him,' Jenny said, puzzled.

'I'd better come with you,' Carrie said briskly. The girls slipped away as quietly as they could.

Jess ran in front of them, turning every so often to urge them on. They were halfway across the field, out of the range of the bonfire's light, when a dark shadow raced up to them.

Jenny swung her torch and switched it on. 'Ian!' she exclaimed.

'Why are you leaving?' Ian asked as Jess scampered back to them. He looked down. 'And what's Jess doing here?'

'He got out somehow,' Jenny explained hurriedly. 'He came to fetch me. We're just going to check that everything is OK down there.'

'I'll come too,' Ian said at once. 'OK, Jess, lead the way!'

At once Jess was off like the wind, skimming across the short-cropped grass, vanishing into the darkness. Jenny swung her torch beam wide, lighting the way in front of them. Jess leapt up on the drystone wall that bordered the field and turned back to them, barking urgently.

'We're coming, Jess,' Jenny gasped as they sped over the field towards the farm. 'What *is* the matter with you?'

Jess was moving faster than ever now, running like the wind towards the farmhouse. Jenny cast a quick look at Ian and Carrie. They were out of breath too, but they carried on, pelting after the young sheepdog, into the farmyard. Jess stood in the middle of the cobbled yard, barking furiously.

Ian sniffed. 'I smell smoke,' he said, urgently.

They stood for a moment, looking round.

Jenny looked up at the first floor of the farmhouse. 'That's odd,' she said. 'I don't remember leaving my bedroom window open.' Then her breath caught in her throat. Smoke was drifting out of her bedroom window, and a flickering orange glow was coming from inside the room. 'Oh, no!' she cried, pointing. 'The farmhouse is on fire!'

Suddenly one of the curtains burst into flames and flapped in the wind, blazing. Bits of burning material drifted across the farmyard. Jenny's eyes went to the stables. There was a scattering of straw on the ground at the base of the stable door. A burning fragment settled on to the straw and it caught alight. A small trail of flames worked its way along the straw and under the gap at the bottom of door, into the stables.

Jenny swung round. Ian was already halfway

across the yard. 'I'll go and fetch help!' he yelled. 'I'll be as fast as I can!'

Jenny nodded. 'I'll see to the animals!' she shouted back. 'We've got to get them out.'

'I'll help you,' Carrie called, following Jenny towards the stables. The straw on the ground was well alight now.

Jenny kicked the burning straw away and wrenched open the stable doors, but it was too late – the fire was already spreading inside. 'Come on, Carrie, we've got to work fast!' she yelled, coughing as a cloud of smoke hit her face. The wood shavings that littered the floor of the stables caught alight as the wind came through the door, fanning the flames. In the far corner Jenny could see flames beginning to lick round a loosebox door.

Just then, two black and white shapes came out through the open doorway and threw themselves on to the cobbled courtyard, panting in the cool night air. It was Jake and Nell. Jenny breathed a sigh of relief, but Jess sniffed round them worriedly.

'They've probably inhaled some smoke,' Carrie said. 'But they're safe now.'

Jenny could hear Mercury whickering nervously in his stall. Suddenly a line of fire raced along the top of a loosebox and burst into flames as it met a rack of hay. There was a terrified whinnying sound. 'Mercury!' Jenny cried. 'Hold on,' she gasped, 'I'm coming!'

Jenny drew her scarf up over her mouth and nose. 'Hang on to Jess out here, Carrie,' she said. 'I might need you to guide me out.'

She went into the stables. Dense smoke billowed round her. Her breath caught in her throat, choking her. Desperately fumbling her way over to Mercury's stall, Jenny tugged at the door. For a horrifying moment she thought the door had jammed. Inside, the big black horse neighed, kicking the walls and rolling his eyes in terror.

Jenny's eyes were smarting so much from the smoke that tears were running down her cheeks, making it virtually impossible to see. As the door opened, she immediately reached in and fumbled for the rope that tethered Mercury. It seemed like an age before it came loose and she was able to get the terrified horse out of the stall.

'Jenny, hurry!' Carrie called, anxiously. 'The doorway's going to catch fire!'

Jenny turned to see flames flickering near the door of the stable. Her way out would be cut off any second. Willing Mercury to keep calm, Jenny urged the terrified horse towards the exit. Mercury tossed his head in panic as flames found their way across the floor of the stable. Jenny's breath rasped in her throat and she felt her own panic rising. The smoke made it almost impossible to concentrate. She dragged the scarf back up over her face but it didn't make her breathing any easier.

Then Jenny became aware of a furious barking. 'Jess!' she cried out. At once, Jess was by her side. The collie pulled at her coat, then ran round to the other side of Mercury, urging him along, reassuring the nervous horse, as he had done on other occasions. Jenny realised that Jess was crouching low. Of course! Nearer the ground the air was fresher and clearer. Clever Jess! Jenny crouched low and immediately found it easier to breathe.

Mercury tossed his head again, then haltingly, followed Jess through the doorway and out to safety. At last Jenny emerged into the open, coughing and choking. Carrie caught her as she stumbled, supporting her while she pulled down her scarf from her face and dragged in great lungfuls of cool, fresh air.

As Jenny recovered, she looked up at her friend, and her heart sank as she saw the dismayed expression on Carrie's face. 'What is it?' she asked.

'The new lambing barn,' Carrie told her. 'It's caught fire.'

Jenny wheeled round to see for herself. 'The ewes are in there,' she cried, her voice hoarse with smoke. 'We have to get them out!'

'No you don't,' a familiar voice said and she found herself in her father's arms.

Jenny looked up at him through eyes smarting with tears. 'Dad! The ewes,' she croaked.

Her father strode across the yard, holding her tightly to his side. 'You're more important than the ewes,' he said, looking anxiously down at her. 'You need to get some more air into those lungs.'

Fraser Miles led Jenny to the far side of the yard and sat her gently down, her back propped against the wall of the farmyard. Jenny's eyes were still streaming but her breathing was getting easier.

Mrs Grace hurried towards them, and bent towards Jenny. 'I'll look after her, Fraser,' she said. 'You'd better try and get those ewes out.'

Fraser nodded, then looked back down at Jenny. 'Are you sure you're all right?' he asked.

Jenny smiled up at him weakly. 'I'm feeling much better already, Dad,' she assured him. 'Now, go!' she urged him. Then she started to cough again.

'Don't try to talk, lass,' Mrs Grace advised her. 'Just breathe deeply.'

Jenny did as she was told. She watched her father run towards the lambing barn. The roof was already well alight and more sparks were drifting on the wind from the burning house all the time. The stone walls of the stables would withstand the fire better than the barn's wooden ones. Matt was there already and the yard seemed to be full of people now. Surely there was a hope that they could save Windy Hill.

Carrie and Ian appeared and crouched down beside her.

'How are you feeling?' Ian asked.

'Fine,' Jenny croaked.

Carrie smiled. 'Liar,' she joked but her face was strained and worried looking.

Jenny tried to smile. Nell was standing beside Ian. The sheepdog shook her head and licked Jenny's hand.

'Nell seems all right now,' Carrie said.

Jenny clutched Carrie's arm. 'Where's Jess?' she asked anxiously.

'He's right here,' Mrs Grace assured her, leading Jess over. 'You just needed a moment to recover.'

'Oh, Jess,' Jenny cried as Jess rushed up to her, licking her face. She put her arms round his neck. 'You got us out of there,' she said softly. 'You're the best dog in the world, Jess.'

Ian looked across at the lambing barn. 'Your dad and Matt are starting to release the ewes now,' he told Jenny. 'I just hope they've got time.'

Jenny nodded. She and Ian both knew that it wasn't a good idea to let all the ewes out at once. They would panic and stampede and the weaker ones would get trampled. They watched as Fraser, Matt and several neighbours began to herd the sheep out of the barn.

Mr Turner had uncoiled the high-pressure hose her father used for cleaning the cobbled farmyard from its wheel on the wall and, as Jenny watched, he turned the tap and pointed the hose at the stables. A great whoosh of water flooded out of the hose, creating billows of steam as the jet sprayed the burning stalls. Then he shifted position and began to douse the roof of the lambing barn.

Jenny looked towards the house. The upstairs was glowing red now; the flames were really taking hold.

'What about the house?' Jenny asked. 'Why doesn't he spray the house?'

'Because there are still animals in the lambing barn,' said Ian. 'They know what they're doing, Jenny.'

Jenny watched the sparks drifting on the air towards the lambing barn and nodded. The house would have to wait. The animals were more important. Jenny could see her father and Matt working frantically to herd the sheep out of the barn. The yard was a confusion of noise as the terrified animals tried to get away from the smell and heat of the burning lambing barn, making Fraser and Matt's job even more difficult.

Vicky and Carrie raced across the farmyard and began to help, guiding the panicking ewes towards the gate at the bottom of the yard. Jake seemed to be everywhere, running between the ewes, forcing them to move in the right direction.

As Matt drove the last of the ewes from the barn, there was a tremendous cracking sound. Jenny watched in horror as the roof creaked, and sagged, threatening to collapse.

'Get out of there, Dad!' Matt yelled. 'Now!'

Jenny saw her father drag one last terrified ewe out of the barn. Then, as if in slow motion, the roof fell in on itself. The fresh wood of the lambing barn, newly primed and painted, had no resistance to the flames. It exploded as the fire hit it. With a great tearing sound the rafters collapsed and Jenny lifted her arms to her face to ward off the heat.

Matt, Vicky and Carrie had the sheep rounded up hard against the far gate, ready to drive them into the lower field. Jenny looked all around her.

The fire was raging through the farmhouse and outbuildings too. Only the shearing shed with its corrugated iron roof seemed to be escaping the flames. A sob tore at her throat as she saw everything she loved go up in the blaze.

'At least they got the sheep out,' Ian said, trying to comfort her.

Mrs Grace put an arm round Jenny's shoulder. 'That's right,' she said. 'After all, the pregnant ewes are Windy Hill's future. That's what's important. And the shearing shed should be all right.'

Jenny turned to Mrs Grace. She knew the housekeeper was only trying to comfort her. 'But look at it,' she cried, the tears coursing down her cheeks. 'Windy Hill is ruined!'

4

'Come on,' Ian said. 'Let's go and see if we can help – if you feel up to it.'

Jenny watched as her father organised a human chain. She saw the silhouettes of all their friends, dark against the blaze beyond them. They were passing buckets from hand to hand. Fraser Miles was encouraging them, directing their efforts where they were most needed.

She dashed her tears away. 'Of course I do,' she said, as she started to follow Ian across the yard.

Mrs Grace laid a hand on her arm. 'Why don't you try to get the sheep into the field?' she said. 'If they stampede we could have an even worse situation on our hands.'

Jenny nodded and turned to Jess. 'Here, boy,' she said. 'We've got work to do.' She looked at Jake and Nell. 'You too,' she said.

All three collies came to heel immediately. Jenny called over to her father. 'We'll get the sheep into the field, Dad,' she told him.

Fraser gave her a critical look. 'You all right?' he asked.

Jenny nodded. Fraser turned to Matt. 'Come on, Matt,' he called. 'We've got to keep the fire at bay until the fire brigade arrives.'

Jenny whirled round as Matt and her father got back to work. 'The fire brigade!' she shouted to them. 'Where are they?'

'We got them on the mobile phone,' Matt said. 'But it's bonfire night, the busiest night of the year for them. It could take them an hour or more to get here. We have to do what we can ourselves to save our home.'

Vicky and Carrie came over. 'Let's get these sheep sorted out, shall we?' Carrie said. Jenny nodded.

'I'll take Mercury out of the way, first,' Vicky said. 'I'll be back as soon as I can to help with the sheep.'

Jenny pushed open the gate. With Ian and Carrie's help she began herding the sheep through. The three sheepdogs moved as one, circling the ewes, keeping them in line.

It seemed to take a long time to get the terrified animals out of the yard and on to the track. Vicky had joined them shortly afterwards and was a great help. Jenny could hear the shouts from the farmyard above the anxious bleating of the sheep. Her father's voice came clearly to her as she closed the gate behind her and started off down the track towards the field gate. Jenny knew that if anyone could save Windy Hill, it would be her father.

Afterwards, as the four of them trudged back up the track, Jenny could see that the whole of the upper storey of the house was now on fire. Her father had the farmyard hose trained on it, desperately trying to keep the fire from spreading. Black wisps of smoke were still rising from the stable but the fire there was out. At least the stables would be saved.

Matt ran towards them, his face streaked with smoke and dirt. 'Grab a bucket!' he yelled as he passed, a bucket in each hand. 'We've got to try and keep the house as wet as possible.'

'Over here,' Vicky called, as she ran for a heap of buckets in the corner of the yard.

Jenny, Ian and Carrie followed her, grabbing a bucket each, dashing back to the standpipe to wait their turn. It seemed a desperately slow process, filling the buckets, passing them on, hoping against hope that they would be able to stem the blaze.

Jenny looked down the line at the row of helpers. Gordon Turner was at the end of the line, directing where the water should be thrown. The fire flickered on faces, blackened by smoke but intent on their work. Jenny heaved her full bucket off the ground and passed it to Ian who was next in line. A small figure ran up behind her.

'Paul!' she cried.

'I'm bringing down the empty buckets,' the little boy told her, then he was off back up the line to wait for the next one.

Jenny swallowed hard and swung the next bucket on down the line. Even little Paul was trying to save Windy Hill.

Half an hour later, her arms aching, and feeling as if she couldn't lift even one more bucket of water, Jenny looked towards the farmhouse. It didn't seem to her as if they were making any difference.

'It isn't any good, is it?' she said to Ian.

Ian shook his head. 'We aren't putting the fire out, if that's what you mean,' he said. 'But we're keeping it at bay. We should be able to salvage stuff from the house and outbuildings even if we can't save the farmhouse.'

Jenny swung her full bucket up the line, suddenly angry. 'Where is the fire brigade?' she cried.

At that moment, she heard the wail of sirens and a cheer went up from the weary line of workers. Fraser Miles turned too but only to encourage them.

'Not long now,' he called, as he held the hose

trained on the upper storey of the farmhouse. 'Just try and hang on.'

As two fire engines rumbled up the track and into the farmyard, the Miles's friends and neighbours set down their buckets one by one. Jenny rubbed her arms as the firemen leaped down from the fire engines.

A fire officer in a white helmet strode across the yard as Fraser handed the hose to Matt and went to meet him. Jenny watched as the firemen, with incredible swiftness, attached their hoses to the tanks on the engines and turned them on. A great arc of water showered down on the burning farmhouse as a line of firemen directed its powerful stream on the building. Then, another group of firemen turned their hose on the lambing barn. The air was filled with the sounds of rushing water and hissing as the flames began to subside beneath the sheer force of water.

Jenny took a deep breath. 'Look at all that water,' she said in wonder. 'That'll put the fire out now.'

'They'll use the water in their tanks until they find another source,' Matt said behind her. 'The

THE BETRAYAL

man in the white helmet is the one in charge.'

Jenny watched as Fraser Miles showed the fire officer the standpipe.

'Stand well back, please,' a fire officer in a yellow helmet urged, making his way round the yard.

Obediently everyone dropped back and watched in relief as the firemen worked. Jenny stood against the farmyard wall with Ian and Carrie and the three sheepdogs. Matt was close to them, his arm round Vicky's shoulders. Vicky looked exhausted and Jenny realised that her own knees were weak and throbbing with pain. She slid down the wall and sat with her back to it. Jess snuggled close to her and licked her hand as she settled back against the wall. Carrie and Ian sat down too.

'To think this all started out as the best bonfire night ever,' Carrie sighed. 'What do you think happened?'

Jenny frowned. 'I haven't the faintest idea.'

'The fire could have started in your bedroom,' Ian said. 'Remember, we saw your window wide open and smoke coming from it. The curtains were on fire.'

Jenny shook her head. 'But it couldn't have started there,' she said. 'How could a fire start in my bedroom?'

Fraser Miles came to stand beside them. Mrs Grace was with him. Fraser looked exhausted, his face grey with strain. 'You shouldn't have gone into the stables, Jenny,' he scolded her gently.

'But I had to,' Jenny protested. 'The animals were trapped inside. And anyway, Jess showed me the way out.'

'But you could have been killed, Jenny,' her father insisted.

'Now, now, Fraser,' Mrs Grace said. 'Jenny's had a very upsetting time tonight – we all have. If you're going to give her a telling off, leave it until tomorrow.'

Fraser Miles ran a hand through his hair. 'I suppose I should be grateful you're all right, lass, instead of giving you a row,' he said to her. 'And it was you that raised the alarm. Why did you come down to the farm again? Did you know something was wrong?'

'Not exactly,' said Jenny. 'Jess came and fetched me. He must have smelled the smoke.'

Fraser smiled wearily. 'Jess again,' he said. 'I don't know what we'd do without that dog. Things could have been a lot worse if it hadn't been for him.'

'It's bad enough,' Matt said dismally. 'The stable is gutted. The upstairs of the house is in ruins – and we've lost the lambing barn.'

'Surely the insurance will pay for all the damage?' Mrs Grace said.

Fraser turned to her. His face was streaked with smoke and dirt and he looked utterly weary. 'Aye. They'll pay for the house and the stables,' he said. 'But not for the lambing barn.'

Jenny drew in her breath.

'I hadn't got round to increasing the insurance cover,' Fraser explained. 'I was going to go into Greybridge after the weekend to arrange that. I've had so much on my mind lately. All the profits from the last lambing went into the barn. I might just as well have set fire to the money.'

'You can't blame yourself, Dad,' Jenny protested. 'It isn't your fault. You were going to insure it. Anybody could have forgotten.'

'I shouldn't have forgotten, that's the point, Jenny,' her father said.

Jess rubbed his head against Jenny's legs and she bent to stroke him.

'It'll work out,' Jenny said desperately. 'We've been through bad times before. We've always managed.'

'We always had a place to live before,' Matt said.

'What do you mean?' asked Jenny.

Mrs Grace smiled gently. 'Look around you, Jenny,' she said. 'Windy Hill isn't fit to live in. We're homeless, lass.'

The fires were out now. There were no more flames or smoke, but Jenny could see that the whole place was glistening with the sheen of water. The smell of charred, wet wood filled the air. Mrs Grace was right; nobody would be living at Windy Hill for some time.

'We might have to find somewhere else to live for a while,' Jenny said. 'But we *will* come back to Windy Hill, won't we, Dad?'

Fraser Miles hung his head for a moment. Then he looked up. 'I hope so, Jenny,' he said. 'Right now it isn't looking too good – but I hope so.'

'What's going to happen to us?' Jenny asked.

Fraser Miles straightened up, his face grey with tiredness. 'I'm not quite sure,' he said. 'I'll have to find out what the damage is before we can make any decisions.'

Jenny felt a cold shiver run down her spine. If her dad didn't know what was going to happen to them then things must be bad. She looked across at the farmhouse. The officer in the white helmet was moving towards them. He was carrying a cardboard box.

'The house is safe now,' the chief fire officer said. 'And you should be able to use the stables once you clear them out. It looks as though the fire started in the front bedroom on the east side of the house. We can tell from the extent of the damage and the way a blaze radiates out from the source.'

Fraser looked at Jenny, surprised. 'That's your bedroom, Jenny,' he said.

Jenny frowned. 'I know,' she replied. 'When we first arrived there was smoke coming out of my bedroom window. But I don't remember leaving the window open.'

'I'm taking some materials away with me,' the fire officer told them. 'There was a melted candle and a few burnt out sparklers. Either of those could have started the fire.'

'But I blew my candle out,' Jenny insisted. 'You saw me, Dad.'

'I didn't actually see you blow it out,' Fraser Miles said. 'But I'm sure you did. It isn't like you to be careless.'

'What about the sparklers?' Matt asked.

'But I don't remember taking any sparklers up to my room,' Jenny said, puzzled.

'A fuse blew earlier on tonight,' Matt suggested. 'Could it have been that?'

The fire officer shook his head. 'The blaze started upstairs,' he said. 'The fuse box is downstairs.'

'The thing I want to know,' Ian said, 'is how did Jess get out?'

'What?' said Jenny.

'Look at the window!' Carrie pointed towards the house.

Jenny looked up. Her window gave onto a ledge that ran at an angle down to the porch over the front door. It was a narrow ledge but, if Jess had been desperate, he could have managed to inch his way along out of the window.

'I suppose he could,' Jenny said, puzzled. 'But I was sure I shut him in the kitchen — and, anyway, I *didn't* leave my window open!'

Matt sighed and shook his head. 'Just like you didn't leave a candle burning and you didn't light any sparklers,' he said.

Fraser Miles turned to him. 'That's enough, Matt,' he said. 'We're all upset. Now, leave it!'

Matt laid a hand on Jenny's arm. 'Sorry, Jen,' he said. 'I'm just trying to make sense of all this. *Something* must have happened to start the fire!'

Jenny watched miserably as Matt and Vicky got up and walked across the farmyard. Her father gave her a quick pat on the shoulder and followed them, the fire officer beside him.

Carrie looked across the yard. 'There's Mum. I'd better see what's happening.'

Ian gave Jenny a quick smile. 'You'll feel a lot better tomorrow,' he said as he too walked away.

Jenny watched him cross the yard. She felt as if everyone had abandoned her. Was everyone going to think that the fire had been her fault? A warm, wet tongue licked her hand. She knelt down and cuddled Jess to her.

'It *wasn't* my fault, Jess,' she said. 'You believe me, don't you?'

Jess looked up at her and nuzzled her cheek gently. Jess would always believe in her.

5

Jenny was still kneeling on the cobbles, her arms round Jess's neck, when she felt a hand on her shoulder. She turned to see Carrie standing beside her. Jenny looked up at her friend. 'Oh, Carrie, everyone will think I started the fire,' she said miserably.

Carrie knelt down beside her and gave her a hug. 'Don't worry about that now,' she said. 'Things will look better in the morning –

that's what Mum always says.'

Jenny shook her head. 'It isn't just the fire,' she explained, a tear sliding down her cheek. 'It's the insurance. Dad worked so hard to get the lambing barn and now it's gone and we can't afford to build a new one. Things were going so well, and now we're back where we started.'

Carrie put her hands on Jenny's shoulders. 'Look at me, Jenny,' she said firmly.

Jenny wiped a tear away and looked at her friend.

'Your dad has a lot of worries just now,' Carrie said seriously. 'If he sees that you're so upset he'll just worry even more. You've all got to pull together and try to make the best of things. Your dad isn't angry with you. He loves you, Jenny. Nothing can change that.'

Jenny nodded, unable to speak.

'The best thing we can do is try and sort out the mess. And that means a lot of hard work – starting tomorrow,' Carrie said briskly.

'Tomorrow,' Jenny repeated. 'But where are we going to go tonight?'

'You're coming home with us to Cliff House,' Carrie said. 'Mum's got it all arranged with Mrs

Grace. You're going to share with me. You don't mind, do you?'

Jenny shook her head. 'Jess too?' she asked.

'Especially Jess!' Carrie declared, helping Jenny to her feet.

Jenny gave her a watery smile. 'You're sure your mum won't mind having Jess around?' she asked.

Carrie snorted. 'Jess can't make as much of a mess as I do,' she assured Jenny.

Jenny gave a shaky laugh. 'Thanks, Carrie,' she said as she and Jess followed Carrie across the yard. 'Are we all going to Cliff House?'

Carrie smiled. 'Everybody!' she declared. 'We'll manage – for a while, at least. But we've got Australian relatives coming to stay for Christmas and New Year.'

'Oh, I'm sure everything will be sorted out long before they arrive,' Pam Turner said, bustling up to them.

Jenny looked gratefully at Mrs Turner's smiling face. Carrie's mum was always cheerful and positive.

'I hate the thought of being away from Windy Hill,' Jenny confessed.

'Of course you do,' Pam Turner replied. 'But

you won't be far, and you'll have plenty of opportunities to visit while the repairs are being done. After all, your dad will still have to come over to look after the sheep.' Mrs Turner scratched her shoulder as she thought. 'In fact,' she mused, 'we've got a caravan that Fraser can borrow if he'd rather base himself on site at Windy Hill.'

Carrie hooked her arm around Jenny's. 'Come on,' she said. 'Let's go.'

As they walked away, Jenny looked back one last time at her ruined home. Its walls were black with smoke and the cobbles in the yard were still wet from the fire hoses. The smell of charred wood was everywhere. The lambing barn lay in ruins and some of the upstairs windows of the house were broken. It looked derelict, but Jenny couldn't imagine anywhere else feeling like home for her.

Jenny opened her eyes on Sunday morning and took in unfamiliar white painted walls, blue curtains and the noise of the sea blowing in from the open window. She couldn't work out where she was.

She looked across the room, and there, fast asleep in a nearby bed was Carrie. And then Jenny remembered . . .

The shock and unhappiness of the night before came flooding back. Quietly Jenny got out of bed and went over to the window. She drew the curtains aside and pushed the window further open, leaning out to draw in the fresh sea air. The sea sparkled in the morning sun.

'It's a great view, isn't it?' Carrie said sleepily from the other side of the room.

Jenny turned and smiled at her friend. 'It's wonderful,' she replied.

Carrie sat up in bed, her hair tousled. She yawned. 'But so is the view from your bedroom at Windy Hill.'

Jenny didn't say anything.

Carrie jumped out of bed and came to stand beside Jenny. 'And you'll have that view again, Jenny. Really you will!' she said. 'Come on, let's get dressed and go downstairs.'

Jenny looked at Carrie in dismay. 'But I haven't got any clothes!' she replied. She had borrowed a nightie from Carrie. 'The things I was wearing last night are all in the wash – and

the rest were burned in the fire.'

Carrie darted over to her wardrobe and hauled the door open. 'Take whatever you want!' she said, as a pile of jumpers fell out from the top shelf. 'Oops!' she exclaimed. 'I told you my room was a tip.'

Jenny smiled in spite of herself and picked up a jumper. 'Thanks, Carrie,' she said.

Carrie dragged a pair of jeans off another shelf and handed them to Jenny. 'You'll have to roll the legs up. They'll be a bit big for you.'

Ten minutes later the girls had washed and made their way downstairs. Jess launched himself at Jenny as soon as she opened the kitchen door. He'd slept in the kitchen on a hastily made up bed. Jenny hugged him, feeling better already. 'Jess, you smell of smoke,' she said. 'I'm afraid that means a bath for you later!'

Mrs Grace was in the kitchen, bustling about, getting breakfast ready. She popped a couple of slices of bread in the toaster. 'I told your mother we would share the cooking, Carrie,' she said, smiling. 'I'll do breakfast and lunch and she'll do dinner. Your mum has just popped down to the

village and your dad went down to the harbour
to do some work on the boat.'

Carrie grinned. 'That's OK with me, Mrs
Grace,' she said. 'You're a great cook!'

'Is Dad up yet?' Jenny asked.

Mrs Grace nodded. 'He, Matt and Ian were
up early. They've taken Mr Turner's caravan up
to Windy Hill. They'll be back in an hour or so.'

'But I wanted to go with them,' Jenny
protested.

Mrs Grace shook her head. 'Your dad told me
to let you sleep while he gets the caravan sorted
out,' she explained. 'He reckons he'll be better
off staying at Windy Hill as much as he can. It'll
give us all more room here, as well as meaning
he can be on the spot to look after the sheep.'

Jenny nodded. 'Matt and Vicky have to go
back to college later today,' she said. 'At least
we'll have more room then.' She sighed. She
knew it was going to be hard on her father
without Matt's help.

Carrie took the toast as it popped up
and spread the slices thickly with butter and
marmalade, handing one to Jenny. 'How about
taking Jess for a walk on the beach?' she

suggested. 'He always likes that.'

Jenny looked doubtful. 'So long as we're back before Dad,' she said.

'We'll be back,' Carrie promised.

'A walk sounds a good idea,' Mrs Grace put in.

Jenny looked at Jess. The Border collie was already at the kitchen door, waiting. He had recognised the word 'walk'. 'All right,' she said. 'Jess *would* like that.'

'We'll easily be back in an hour,' Jenny promised Mrs Grace.

Ellen Grace nodded. 'You'll get a proper breakfast when you come back,' she said. Jess was out of the door as soon as it was open, speeding ahead.

The girls were heading down the high street in Cliffbay towards the harbour when Carrie pulled on Jenny's arm. 'That's Mr McLay's Land Rover,' she said.

Jenny turned as the Land Rover swept past them and drew up outside the newsagent's. Paul was in the back with Fiona and, as his father got out of the driver's door, the little boy scrambled out of the back and came running towards them with Toby at his heels.

Jenny watched Mr McLay walk into the newsagent's. He was a big man with short dark hair, like Fiona's.

'Jenny!' Paul cried as he reached them. Jess and Toby immediately started chasing each other. Paul seemed to hesitate, then he asked, 'Is Windy Hill going to be all right?'

Jenny smiled at him. 'We hope so, Paul,' she said. 'There's an awful lot of work to be done. We'll have to wait and see what repairs are needed.'

Suddenly the hackles rose on Jess's neck and he growled fiercely. Jenny looked at him in surprise. 'Jess, what on earth's the matter?' She'd never heard him growl quite so fiercely before. Jenny followed Jess's gaze and saw Fiona McLay walking towards them.

'More like rebuilding, I hear,' she said in a mocking voice. As she drew closer, Jess's growling grew louder. Looking at him, Fiona decided to take no chances and stayed a safe distance away. Her pale blue eyes flicked to Jenny, looking her up and down. 'Nice jeans,' she remarked. 'Hand-me-downs, are they? You can't have bought something so nice yourself.'

Jenny flushed. Fiona had always taunted her about not having expensive, fashionable clothes.

But Carrie leaped to Jenny's defence. 'Jenny lost everything in the fire,' she said. 'She borrowed a pair of my jeans. What's wrong with that?'

Fiona shrugged. 'Jenny never cared what she wore anyway so I don't suppose she minds cast-offs,' she sneered.

Jenny shook her hair back from her face. 'No, I don't,' she said to Fiona. 'It was good of Carrie to lend them to me. I didn't have anything else to wear.'

'You shouldn't have been so careless then, should you?' said Fiona.

Jenny gasped. 'What do you mean?' she asked.

Fiona shrugged. 'Everyone's talking about it,' she said. 'We all know how the fire started – that *you* burned down your precious Windy Hill.' Fiona's eyes narrowed. 'So how do you feel about that, Jenny Miles?' she challenged.

'But it's not true!' Jenny protested.

Carrie took a step towards Fiona but Jess was ahead of her. Placing himself between Jenny and

Fiona, he stood there stiffly, growling up at the other girl.

Fiona stepped back quickly as Jess gave a sharp bark and moved towards her. 'Call that dog off!' she cried in a rising voice. 'He's going to bite me!'

'Jess wouldn't bite anybody,' Jenny said.

Fiona looked at her, her face flushed. 'Yeah, and you don't start fires, do you?' she said, then she turned on her heel and marched off back to her father's Land Rover.

Jess stood there, still growling softly and Jenny bent to reassure him. She stroked him gently until he began to calm down. 'Well!' she said, turning to Carrie. 'What was *that* all about? I've never seen Jess behave like that before!'

Carrie shook her head. 'I don't know, but he certainly seems to have something against Fiona – though goodness knows what!'

Jenny looked up at her. 'Do you think what she said is true? Does everyone think it was my fault?'

Paul laid a hand on her arm. 'I don't, Jenny,' he said. 'I don't care what anybody says. I don't believe it.'

80

Jenny felt tears prick the back of her eyes. 'Thanks, Paul,' she said softly. But it was clear that the rumours were spreading already.

'Paul!' Mr McLay called as he came out of the newsagent's.

Jenny looked up.

Calum McLay took a few steps towards her. 'Oh, it's you,' he said to Jenny. 'I heard you lost your home,' he said shortly.

He led Paul away, back to the Land Rover. But before he got in he turned back to look at Jenny. 'You ought to be more careful, you know,' he said. 'Starting fires is a serious business.'

Jenny watched dumbly as the Land Rover started up and drove away. It was true then. The whole of Graston and Cliffbay thought the fire was her fault. She had been so sure she had put out that candle . . .

'Jenny,' Carrie said gently, 'let's take Jess down to the beach.'

Jenny swallowed hard and nodded.

6

Later that day, after the firemen had declared it safe, Jenny and her family returned to Windy Hill to help clear up and salvage what hadn't been ruined in the fire. It was like re-visiting a nightmare. Her bedroom was a charred shell. The bright yellow walls were now black and smeared with soot and water. The remains of the curtains hung like limp, black rags at the window. And everywhere there was the choking smell of burning.

Jenny recognised her bookcase amongst the debris and felt a lump in her throat as she looked at the sodden, burned remains of all her favourite books. She had kept all of the picture books that her mother had read to her when she was little and now they were gone. She remembered how she and her mother had painted the little bookcase together a few years ago.

As Jenny sifted through the remains, a subdued Jess staying close by her side, she remembered an even more precious, irreplaceable item, that had now been lost for ever: the photograph of her mother as the Graston Lass that she'd kept on her bedside table. Jenny's eyes filled with hot tears. So much of her life had gone up in flames.

She felt Jess lick her hand reassuringly and looked down at him. 'It's OK, boy,' she said. 'I know. We've still got the most important thing – each other.'

Jenny heard footsteps coming towards the bedroom. Carrie had turned up to help as well. Ian followed her into the room carrying a box of sodden blackened clothes and books. He dumped it down on the floor and looked around. 'Goodness, Jen,' he said. 'There isn't much left to salvage here, is there?' he said sympathetically.

Jenny shook her head and turned away.

Carrie came over and gave her a hug. 'I know it's terrible, Jenny, but we've got to look on the bright side. Just think! As soon as the insurance money has been paid out, we can go and choose you a whole new wardrobe. It'll be great fun!'

Jenny smiled. She could tell that Carrie was just as shocked by the charred, ruined room, but was trying hard to be cheerful for her sake.

Jenny pointed to her desk. It was blackened and scorched, the books and project work on top of it now a pile of ashes.

'Oh, the Geography project,' Carrie dismissed. 'Don't worry about that. You can share mine!'

'We could do a new one together if you like,' Ian offered. 'My bedroom escaped the fire but my project work got soaked. It's ruined. There's a lot of water damage from the fire hoses.'

Jenny nodded, then walked over to the charred bedroom doorway. 'Come on, let's go and see what's happening outside.'

With Jess running ahead, Jenny, Carrie and Ian went downstairs and out into the farmyard.

There was no shortage of helpers today, Jenny noticed. Many of the people who had been at the bonfire party had turned out to lend a hand with the salvage operation.

Gordon Turner was helping Fraser in the stables, clearing out the debris. The caravan Fraser planned to stay in was parked at the far end of the farmyard.

It would be strange to have her father living here amongst the ruins of Windy Hill while she was at Cliff House, Jenny thought. But she could see the sense in it. He would want to be on the spot, not just for the animals' sake, but to oversee the repairs to the buildings.

'Mercury should be OK in the less damaged end of the stables now,' Matt said, as he passed with a barrowload of blackened wood and tipped it on to the growing pile in the middle of the yard. Mercury had had to spend the previous night in an adjoining field. 'And once they've been cleaned out, we'll be able to use the other end to house some of the ewes, if need be.'

Jenny looked up at her bedroom window. She was still mystified as to how the fire could have started in there. She didn't hear her father approach.

'We'll be able to replace most of what you've lost in time, lass,' he said. 'Now, I'm going up to take a look at the breeding ewes. Mr Turner is finishing up in the stables and Mrs Grace is going through the kitchen, trying to salvage as much as she can. If anyone comes about the insurance I'll be back in an hour.'

Jenny nodded but as Fraser walked away, a tear slid down her cheek.

'What is it, Jenny?' Ian asked.

Jenny looked at him. 'What if I really didn't blow that candle out properly? What if it *was* my fault? I'm so confused now that I can't be sure any longer.'

'It must be so hard for you,' Carrie said sympathetically. 'But whatever happened, it was an accident. You can't blame yourself, Jenny.'

Jenny dashed away the tears, impatient with herself. 'It's just that there are some things that can never be replaced,' she answered. 'Like the photograph of Mum I kept on my bedside table – and Mrs Turner's sketch of Jess as a puppy.'

Ian put his hand on her arm. 'Come on,' he

said. 'There's a pile of stuff over here that escaped the fire. Let's go through it. You never know what you might find.'

'Jess has made a start on it already,' Carrie said. 'Look at him!'

Jess had scampered across to the pile of debris in the corner of the yard and was snuffling at it.

'OK,' said Jenny, forcing a smile. 'We might as well give him a hand.'

Jenny and Carrie followed Ian to the corner of the yard and began to sort through the pile. Jess was rooting around, sniffing furiously and dragging out bits and pieces for their inspection.

'Oh, look,' said Jenny, delighted. 'You've found your feeding bowl, Jess. Good boy!'

Jess wagged his tail hard and started rooting in the pile again. This time he came up with his old blue blanket and brought it proudly over to Jenny. Jenny took it from him gently. It was wet and dirty and smelled of smoke but to Jenny it looked beautiful. This was the blanket she had wrapped Jess in just after he was born. 'Oh, Jess,' she said softly. 'I'm so glad you found this. I'll wash it for you and it'll be as good as new. It'll make you feel at home

while we're living at Cliff House.'

Jess licked her cheek and Jenny smiled. Maybe they would find other treasures too.

An hour later Jenny stood up and stretched her arms above her head, loosening out her aching back. A small heap of objects lay to one side, the result of sifting through the salvage pile. There was a book that she'd left on an arm of the sofa downstairs, a bit smoky but still readable. And her new jacket that had been in the downstairs cloakroom.

There was also a pile of sports equipment – tennis racquet, roller skates and her hockey stick, which had been in the cupboard under the stairs.

'Well, at least you'll be able to play in the school hockey team,' Carrie grinned.

Jenny grinned back, feeling better. 'Just look at the state of us!' she said. They were grimy with soot.

'Looks like we've got a visitor,' Ian announced, turning round.

Jenny turned to see a car drawing into the farmyard. A youngish woman got out. Jenny looked at the woman with interest. She was wearing a smart bright blue suit and high-heeled shoes – not the sort of clothes people usually wore when they came to visit a farm.

'Who's that?' said Carrie, straightening up.

'Dad was expecting someone from the insurance company,' Jenny said. 'I suppose that's her.'

The woman looked around the yard and, as her eyes fell on Jenny, Carrie and Ian, she began to walk towards them.

'Hello, I'm Marion Stewart,' the woman said in a bright voice as she reached them. 'I'm from Capital Insurance and I arranged to meet Mr Fraser Miles here.'

Jenny wiped her right hand on her jeans and held it out. 'I'm Jenny Miles,' she said. 'Fraser Miles is my father. He should be back soon.'

Marion Stewart took a quick look at Jenny's grubby hand and pretended she hadn't noticed that Jenny had offered to shake hands. She took a step back. 'I hope he won't keep me waiting. It's inconvenient enough, being called out on a Sunday.'

Carrie and Ian looked at Jenny as the woman turned away towards her car, carefully picking her way through the charred rubble in the yard in her high heels.

'You'd think she'd have realised it would be messy up here, after a fire,' Ian said scornfully.

Carrie giggled. 'Look at Jess,' she said.

The Border collie had unearthed a smoke-blackened cushion from the pile of debris and had decided to present it to Marion Stewart. Jenny watched as Jess scampered in front of the woman and laid his present at her feet.

'Ugh!' said Marion Stewart as the filthy object landed on her highly polished shoes. 'Shoo! Go away, bad dog!'

Jess looked up at her appealingly and licked her hand. She snatched it away. 'Whose dog is this?' she demanded.

'Mine,' said Jenny, trying to keep a straight face. 'He's only trying to be friendly, Miss Stewart. He's brought you a present.'

'Well, I can do without presents like that,' Miss Stewart said sniffily.

Jenny called Jess back. The Border collie picked up his cushion and trotted back to the pile of debris with it. He began rooting around for something else.

Miss Stewart breathed a sigh of relief, then leaned into her car and took out a sheaf of papers from a folder on the passenger seat. 'I shall need a list of all the things you've lost. Do you think you could help with that?'

Jenny nodded. As she began to move towards Miss Stewart's car, Jess laid something at her feet. Jenny looked down, smiling. 'I like your presents, Jess, even if some people don't,' she said, bending to pick up the flat, blackened object. She rubbed a corner of it clean and gasped. It was a photo frame.

'Ian, Carrie!' she breathed. 'It's my photo of Mum. Oh, Jess, you clever thing. You've found the thing that mattered most.' She bent down to give the Border collie a hug. Jess wagged his tail delightedly at the happy tone in Jenny's voice and gave her a sooty lick on the cheek.

Carrie and Ian gathered round to admire Jess's find and Marion Stewart strode back towards them. 'What's that?' she asked. 'I have to make a list of anything you salvage from the fire.' She leaned over and looked down at the photo as Jenny scrubbed its glass front clean with her sleeve.

'It's a photo of my mother when she was the Graston Lass,' Jenny explained. Every year in Graston, a girl was chosen to be a sort of queen for the day when a spring celebration called the Riding of the Marches took place. The Graston Lass had to ride round the town at the head of a procession. It was a great honour and Jenny had been chosen as Graston Lass herself the previous spring. What was more, Mrs Grace had remembered that she had an old photograph of Sheena Miles as the Graston Lass. She'd hunted the photograph out and had given it to Jenny.

Jenny smiled down at the photograph of her mother. 'Mum died in a riding accident the summer before last,' Jenny said, still gazing at the picture.

Marion Stewart tutted. 'I'm sorry to hear that,' she said. Then she looked thoughtful. 'I didn't know your father was a widower. There's no mention of it on our paperwork.'

Jenny smiled bleakly and tucked her treasure safely into the pocket of her jacket. 'He doesn't talk about losing Mum much,' she said. Then she looked up as her father drove into the yard. 'Here he is now.'

Fraser Miles strode across the farmyard and held out his hand to Miss Stewart, his deep blue eyes looking tired, but relieved to see her.

Marion Stewart fixed her eyes on Fraser's face and held out her own hand. Jenny noticed that she didn't even look to see if Fraser's hand was clean.

'How do you do, Mr Miles,' she said. 'I'm Marion Stewart, from Capital Insurance.'

'Hello, Miss Stewart,' Fraser replied. 'I hope I haven't kept you waiting.'

Marion Stewart gave him a dazzling smile. 'Not at all,' she said. 'And please, call me Marion.'

'Do you know what I think?' Carrie said as Mr Miles and Marion Stewart walked off towards the caravan.

'What?' asked Jenny.

'I reckon Miss Stewart has taken a shine to your dad,' Carrie said.

Jenny whirled round. 'What?' she squeaked. 'But she can't have – he's Dad!'

Carrie grinned. 'OK, don't fly off the handle. But she looked very interested in him, to me.'

Jenny frowned as she remembered Marion's change of attitude the moment she met Fraser

Miles. Maybe Carrie was right. Maybe Marion Stewart *had* taken a shine to her father. Jenny wasn't at all sure how she felt about the idea.

'Did the insurance representative come yet?' Mrs Grace asked Jenny, as she came out of the house a while later with a box of soot-smeared crockery.

Ellen Grace's hair was coming down round her face and she had a black streak across one cheek. She was dressed in old jeans and a checked shirt, but it occurred to Jenny that given the choice between a dishevelled Ellen Grace and the smart Miss Stewart, she would rather have Mrs Grace any day.

Jenny nodded. 'They're going over some paperwork in the caravan,' she said. 'But I don't think Miss Stewart likes farms very much – at least she isn't very keen on animals, or mess!'

'Hmm,' Mrs Grace said thoughtfully. 'I hope that won't stop her from appreciating just what a disaster the fire at Windy Hill is for your father. Sheep farming is his whole life.'

Jenny stood up and tucked a hand through

Mrs Grace's arm. 'You understand though, don't you, Mrs Grace?' she said.

'Indeed I do, Jenny,' Ellen Grace replied. 'And I know how important it is to you and Matt too.'

Jenny squeezed Mrs Grace's arm affectionately. 'Jess found the photo of Mum you gave me,' she said. 'It wasn't burnt up in the fire.'

Ellen Grace's face lit up. 'Oh, I'm so glad for you, lass,' she said. 'I know you would have hated to lose that.'

'You're right,' Jenny smiled. 'You know us all so well, Mrs Grace,' she said. 'What would we do without you?'

7

Waking up in Carrie's bedroom wasn't such a shock the next morning, though Jenny resented having to go to school when there was still so much work to be done on the farm. But her father had insisted that her education came first, so, reluctantly, Jenny went off to school with Carrie and Ian.

She was hardly through the school gates before people started coming up to her to ask how she was. The classmates who had been at the bonfire knew about the disaster already, of course, and news had quickly spread throughout the school.

'People are being really kind,' Jenny said to Carrie, after Zoe Burns, one of her classmates, stopped to offer Jenny a personal stereo. 'I know you lost everything,' Zoe had said. 'I got a new one for my birthday so you can have this for as long as you want.'

The good wishes and offers of help flooded in.

'But not everyone is being kind,' Carrie pointed out disapprovingly. 'You should see the look Fiona McLay just gave you. I don't understand why she can't let up, after all you've gone through.'

Jenny looked around and caught Fiona's eye as she crossed the playground. Fiona tried to sidle past the group round Jenny but Amy Jarrow stopped her.

'Oh, Fiona, did you hear about the terrible fire at Windy Hill?' Amy asked.

Fiona stopped and looked challengingly at Jenny. 'You mean the one that Jenny started?' she said.

Amy gasped. 'That's a horrible thing to say,' she exclaimed.

Several of the others were surprised at Fiona's comment. 'You've got no right to go around making accusations like that,' said Mark Armstrong, a friend of Ian's.

Fiona shrugged. 'Believe what you want,' she said, flushing. 'Everyone seems to think that Jenny Miles is an angel – but she isn't. You'll see!' She walked on, then turned back again, a sneer on her lips. 'Anyway, the Mileses are always in trouble. Jenny should be used to it by now. All this fuss about her precious Windy Hill!' she scoffed. 'It's just a little farm.'

Jenny felt herself go pale as Fiona brushed past her. 'Windy Hill is the best sheep farm in the Borders!' she called after her.

'Well, of all the cheek,' Carrie said. 'What a pain in the neck she is! Don't listen to her, Jen.'

Jenny forced herself not to cry. The worst thing she could do was let Fiona see how hurt she was. She shrugged. 'Oh, who cares about Fiona?' she said, as lightly as she could. 'What harm can she do?'

★ ★ ★

Miss Kerr, who was also Jenny's form teacher, called her out before registration and spoke quietly to her.

'I'm all right, really,' Jenny told her. 'No one was hurt and the animals are safe. I suppose that's all that really matters.'

Miss Kerr looked at her sympathetically. 'Just try to concentrate on your work and don't worry too much, Jenny. I'm sure things will work out,' she said.

During their first lesson, Fiona leaned over towards Jenny's desk. 'Did you tell Miss Kerr that you started the fire, Jenny?' she taunted.

Jenny turned to Fiona. 'You seem to be really pleased that Windy Hill burned down, Fiona,' she said, shaking her head. 'Why?'

Carrie had heard Fiona's taunts too. 'Leave off, Fiona,' she hissed. 'If you can't say anything nice, you'd better keep your nasty mouth shut!'

Fiona flushed a deep red.

Catching the disapproving eye of their teacher, the girls turned back to their work.

But Jenny couldn't get over Fiona's apparent satisfaction at the Mileses' misfortune. She turned back to the other girl. 'How can you be like this?' she asked. 'Somebody could have been killed in that fire. There were animals there. Jess was in the house.' Jenny shook her head in disbelief, adding, 'No wonder nobody likes you.'

Fiona flinched and went white.

Jenny bit her lip. Fiona's unkind words had the effect of dragging her down to the same level. 'I'm sorry, Fiona,' she said. 'I shouldn't have said that.'

Fiona looked at her for a long moment. 'But everybody likes *you*, don't they? Little Miss Popular!'

Jenny was amazed to see that Fiona's eyes were shiny with tears. Blinking them away, Fiona turned back to her desk, her cheeks flaming.

Jenny sighed. She didn't think she would ever understand Fiona McLay, but right now she didn't even care to try. Fiona McLay was just plain nasty.

Jenny tried to avoid Fiona as much as possible but on Wednesday she found herself sharing a bench with her for a chemistry lesson. The class were gathered round Miss Eevers, the chemistry teacher, who was demonstrating an experiment.

Picking out a piece of sodium from the glass dish she was holding, the teacher dropped the grey substance into a bowl of water. The sodium began to whizz round the surface of the water, giving off flames.

Everyone craned forward to watch. Amy Jarrow leaned too far over and jogged Miss Eevers's arm. The glass dish in her hand tilted and the rest of the sodium slid into the bowl of water. At once, the flames ignited much higher. Everyone gasped and drew back.

Miss Eevers calmly reached for a fire blanket and dropped it quickly over the flames. Jenny shivered. The flames reminded her of the fire at Windy Hill. Then she heard Fiona's stool scrape back.

'Miss Eevers, can I go to the loo?' Fiona asked.

Miss Eevers nodded abstractedly as she lifted the fire blanket and checked the fire was out.

'What's up with Fiona?' Ian said. 'She looked white as a sheet.'

'Maybe she felt sick,' Carrie suggested. Then she frowned. 'But who cares about her anyway!'

Jenny didn't argue with that. She didn't have any sympathy to waste on Fiona.

★ ★ ★

Fiona didn't return to the chemistry class and she wasn't at school the next day either. Jenny decided she must have been taken ill.

'Has anyone been in touch with Fiona McLay?' Miss Kerr asked, when Fiona had still not returned by the end of the week. 'I was wondering how she was.'

There was silence in the class.

'I see her little brother sometimes,' Jenny offered, eventually. 'I could ask him about her.'

'That would be good of you, Jenny,' Miss Kerr replied.

'Why did you offer to find out how Fiona is?' Carrie asked, as they came out of class. 'She wouldn't do the same for you.'

Jenny shrugged. 'Paul is coming over after school anyway. I'm not going to any trouble.'

Paul, Jenny and Carrie often walked the dogs on the beach at Cliffbay. It was one of Jess's favourite places, and anywhere Jess was, Toby was happy to be there too. Paul's little terrier adored Jess.

'Is Fiona any better?' Jenny asked Paul later that afternoon, as they walked along the beach, throwing sticks for Toby and Jess. The wind blew cold, whipping the waves into white caps. Jenny shivered despite her warm jacket and woolly hat.

'I don't think so,' Paul replied, vaguely.

'What do you mean?' Carrie asked, looking puzzled. 'Can't you tell if she's getting better?'

Paul stopped to pick up the stick Toby had dropped at his feet. 'Well, the thing is, I don't really know what's wrong with her,' he admitted. 'I mean, she hasn't got the measles or anything, I know that. But last night she woke us all up, crying really loudly. It was terrible!' He watched the dogs racing around for a while, then continued. 'She was really upset and wouldn't go back to bed. Mum sat up with her in the living room. She says she keeps having bad dreams.'

'No wonder,' Carrie muttered under her breath. 'Fiona's mind is so nasty, I can't imagine her dreams are any better.' She threw the stick wildly and it landed at the water's edge. A wave rolled in and drew it out into deeper water.

Jenny looked out to sea. Dark clouds were gathering. It looked as if it would be a stormy night. Toby and Jess didn't seem to mind. They were having a wonderful romp along the beach. Jess plunged into the water to retrieve the stick Carrie had thrown, getting to it just before Toby did. The dogs raced back, shaking themselves dry and spattering droplets of freezing cold water all over the place.

'Do you know what the dreams are about?' Jenny asked Paul, as she took a turn to throw the stick.

Paul shrugged. 'She won't tell us. Mum is really worried about her.' He looked up at Jenny. 'It's no fun at home just now,' he said. 'I much prefer being here with you and Jess.'

Jenny grinned at him. It couldn't be easy for Paul, having a sister like Fiona.

'Well, you and Toby can come over to Cliff House whenever you want,' Carrie said. 'Mum won't mind, even if it is a bit crowded at the moment.'

Marion Stewart turned up at Windy Hill that weekend. Jenny, Mrs Grace, Ian and Carrie were in the house, getting stuck into cleaning up the downstairs' walls before they could be redecorated. Though the ground floor rooms hadn't been burned, they'd been ruined by smoke and water damage.

Fraser and Matt were loading sacks of feed into the back of the jeep in the yard when the insurance representative's car turned in at the gate. Fraser went to meet her while Matt heaved another sack into the jeep, ready to transport to the feeding troughs in the fields.

'What does she want now?' Matt said to Jenny, who had taken mugs of tea out to them. 'Dad says she's been to see him twice already this week.'

'There certainly *does* seem to be a lot of paperwork,' Mrs Grace said, as she and Carrie came out into the yard too. She frowned. 'I hope this doesn't mean another hold-up.'

Jenny and Carrie looked at each other. 'I think she just likes coming to see Mr Miles,' Carrie muttered.

Jenny was beginning to think that Carrie was right. Maybe Marion Stewart really *was* making excuses to come and see her father.

But perhaps that wasn't the case at all. When Fraser Miles had finished talking to Miss Stewart and seen her off, he came over to them, looking worried.

'What is it, Dad?' Jenny asked, as her father started loading sacks into the jeep.

'Marion says she'll need to make a few more visits before she can put in her report,' Fraser Miles replied. 'Her boss is being a bit sticky about the claim. I'll try and get in to see him myself on Monday.' He stopped and rubbed his eyes wearily. 'I had hoped the repairs would be under way by now.'

Jenny looked at her father. He looked tired. It wasn't easy clearing up the aftermath of the fire and looking after the flock at the same time. He swung another sack into the back of the jeep and climbed into the driver's seat. 'Ready, Matt?' he asked.

Matt got in and they drove away.

'It'll work out,' Carrie said, putting her arm round Jenny's shoulder.

Jenny looked at her. 'But when?' she asked. 'We can't stay with you at Cliff House forever.'

The subject came up again the following evening, when they were all sitting round the

110

big kitchen table at Cliff House. Outside, the wind was howling and the moon shone brightly on the storm-tossed sea.

Matt had gone back to college, promising to return the following weekend. On the two nights he was home he would share the caravan with his father. Cliff House was big enough to accommodate Jenny, Ian and Mrs Grace, but putting Matt up too would stretch things to the limit.

'I'd thought we'd be well on the way towards making Windy Hill habitable by now,' Fraser said. 'But while the insurance company delays paying out for the work that needs to be done, we're not getting anywhere.'

'When will Marion be able to give permission for the repairs to get started?' Mrs Grace asked. 'We can't stay here indefinitely – no matter how welcome we are.'

Pam Turner smiled. 'I'm afraid that's true,' she said. 'We've got our Australian relatives coming at the beginning of next month and I've promised to put them up.'

Jenny looked closely at her father. He still looked exhausted. Deep lines were etched around his mouth. He had to work all the daylight hours just to keep things ticking over at Windy Hill.

'I've been in touch with the builders,' Fraser replied. 'They'll be ready to start just as soon as they get the go-ahead from Marion. Let's hope that doesn't take too much longer.'

But by the following weekend the insurance company still hadn't paid up. Fraser was beside himself with frustration and worry. And the weather had taken a turn for the worse. It had been a stormy week and there was a stiff breeze coming off the sea.

Jenny, Ian and Carrie were helping Matt to fix pens in the stables so that Fraser could winter the weaker ewes under shelter. At least with the stables and the shearing shed still in use, Windy Hill would be all right as far as the sheep were concerned.

Jenny went to the door of the stables and looked at the clouds massing on the horizon. 'Do those look like rain clouds to you?' she asked Carrie.

Carrie pulled her woolly hat further

down over her ears and shivered. 'Dad said this morning that he thought it would snow before long,' she said.

'Let's hope your dad can get the work on the house started before winter really sets in,' Ian put in. 'If we get a really bad winter it could be spring before the repairs get underway.'

Jenny sighed. *And where would we live until then?* she thought worriedly.

Just then, Fraser Miles called a halt for lunch. They were tucking into sandwiches and bowls of soup that Mrs Grace had heated on the caravan's gas cooker when Marion Stewart arrived again.

'Let's hope there's some good news for a change,' Fraser said, as he went to meet her car.

He brought the insurance representative into the crowded little caravan, saying, 'Surely you can authorise the repairs now? If we don't get started on the repair work before the winter sets in, we'll be stranded! Surely Bob Elliot must realise that.'

Jenny had heard Bob Elliot's name mentioned before. He was Marion Stewart's boss at the insurance company.

Miss Stewart looked sympathetic. 'I'm sorry, Fraser,' she apologised. 'I'm doing my best but Bob is dragging his heels. I'm not sure why. I submitted my damage report almost two weeks ago, as you know. But when I chased him about it again this morning, he made some excuse about needing to check some details – and that was the last I heard of it. Then he rushed out to lunch with that neighbour of yours.'

Fraser looked at her narrowly. 'Neighbour?' he repeated.

Marion Stewart nodded. 'Someone called Calum McLay,' she said. 'I know, because Mr McLay left a message with me confirming that he could make their lunch date.'

At the mention of Calum McLay's name Fraser turned white. 'What details need to be checked?' he asked, tightly. Jenny could see that her father was having a hard time keeping his temper.

Marion shrugged. 'I really couldn't say,' she replied. 'We know that the fire started in Jenny's bedroom,' she said, giving Jenny a look. 'And that it was probably caused by a lighted candle falling over, which makes it an accident.' Jenny felt herself flushing as the woman went on talking. 'So, as I've reported on the cause and the damage, I really don't understand this delay.' She shook her head. 'I've never known Bob to be this slow about a claim.'

Jenny looked at her father again. 'I don't think it's a coincidence that Bob Elliot is having lunch with Calum McLay today,' Fraser said seriously. 'Thank you, Marion. I think I know what's going on here now.'

Marion looked puzzled but Fraser wouldn't say any more about it. Jenny decided to ask her father what he meant after Marion had gone.

'Do you think Mr McLay has got something to do with the delay?' she asked, as soon as Marion's car disappeared down the track.

Fraser nodded. 'Yes, I do.'

'But why would he want to interfere?' Jenny asked.

Her father shrugged. 'Maybe he thinks that if I have to wait long enough for the insurance money, I won't be able to keep Windy Hill running. Maybe he's still hoping to force me to sell up to him.'

'It could be even worse, Dad,' Matt said

worriedly. 'If Mr McLay really wants to cause trouble, he might try to persuade the insurance company that the fire was our fault . . .' Jenny caught him looking at her, and he looked away again, embarrassed. 'Then they might not pay out at all,' he finished.

Jenny's heart sank. She had always thought that losing Windy Hill would be the worst thing in the world. But if everyone thought that she was to blame, that would be even worse.

'Dad,' she said. 'I know they say the fire started in my room but, honestly, I blew that candle out – I'm sure I did.'

Fraser shook his head. 'Whatever happened with the candle can't be changed, lass,' he said sadly. 'The important thing now is to get the repairs started.'

'Maybe it was a spark from the bonfire,' Jenny said desperately.

'Look, let's stop pretending, Jenny,' Matt said impatiently. 'You know it wasn't.' He stopped when he saw Jenny's stricken face, then said more softly, 'Dad's right. What's done is done.'

'So you both think it was my candle?' Jenny said hoarsely.

'There seems to be no other reasonable explanation, lass,' her father said gently.

Jenny looked at him. He was looking at her so sadly that it made her want to cry. He wasn't blaming her. He wasn't angry with her. He simply didn't believe her – and who could blame him? As he had said, what other explanation was there? Marion Stewart obviously thought it was Jenny's fault too . . .

Jenny didn't know what to think any more. Maybe everyone else was right! Maybe she *had* caused the fire that had destroyed Windy Hill. She couldn't bear it!

Jenny looked at the sky. There were heavy dark clouds and there was a cold edge to the wind, but they weren't snow clouds – yet. She shivered. It wouldn't be long until the snow clouds *did* appear – and then the snow. Time was running out for them all.

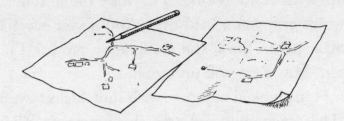

8

Fiona returned to school the following Monday. She looked so white and strained that, despite herself, Jenny felt a rush of sympathy for her. Fiona must have been very ill.

'Fiona,' she said, stopping the other girl in the corridor. 'Are you all right now?'

'What do *you* care?' Fiona replied, turning away.

Jenny reached out a hand and touched Fiona's

arm. 'It's just that you look so ill and worried,' she persisted. 'Are you concerned about catching up with schoolwork? I'm sure the teachers won't give you a hard time. And if you haven't managed to finish the Geography project, I'm sure Miss Kerr will understand.'

Fiona looked at Jenny with dull, lifeless eyes. 'The Geography project?' she repeated. 'Why are you talking about that?'

'They're due in today,' Jenny reminded her. 'I lost mine in the fire — and so did Ian, so we joined up with Carrie to do a joint one.'

Fiona took a step back, her eyes fixed on Jenny. Jenny noticed that her lips were dry and cracked and her hand trembled as she pushed a strand of hair behind her ear. But suddenly, she came to life.

'Mind your own business,' she snapped as she pushed past.

Later, in Geography, Jenny was miles away, thinking about Windy Hill.

'Hey! Wake up,' Carrie said, giving her a dig in the ribs. 'You're getting as bad as Fiona.'

'What do you mean?' said Jenny.

'Haven't you noticed?' Carrie said. 'She's acting really strangely today. She jumps every time anyone speaks to her.'

Jenny frowned. 'Well, I tried talking to her this morning and it was like talking to a zombie. Then I mentioned our Geography project and she just bit my head off and walked away.'

'Maybe it's because she knows our project is going to be the best in the class,' Carrie announced confidently.

'There's nothing like modesty!' Ian joked from the desk behind.

Jenny laughed. Carrie was always so positive. 'I hope Miss Kerr likes it.'

Part of the project had been to make a map of the Greybridge area, and then mark in the routes they all took to school, to friends' houses, to the shops and to other villages. Now Miss Kerr got the class to help her push several tables together so that they could lay out all the maps.

'That's amazing,' Ian said, pointing to the criss-crossing routes marked on the maps. 'We've managed to cover the whole area. Look at all the tracks we've got.'

The collection of maps was certainly

JESS THE BORDER COLLIE

impressive. Between them the class had mapped
out a complete circular area around the school.

'You should be able to see how many new
routes you take and the new friends you've made
since you came to Greybridge,' Miss Kerr said.

'Look!' Amy Jarrow said. 'There aren't any
paths to this house.' Amy bent over the map.
'Dunraven,' she said. 'Who lives there?'

Fiona coughed and everyone looked at her.
'Me,' she said in a strained voice.

'You were supposed to put in the routes you
take to your friends' houses,' Amy said helpfully.
Then she frowned. 'Hey, nobody's put in any
routes on their maps to your house, either . . .'

'That can't be right,' Miss Kerr said, smiling.
'Look again, Amy.'

Fiona made a strangled sound and rushed
from the room. Amy looked aghast.

Miss Kerr looked around the class. 'Would
someone go after her and see that she's all right?
Are any of you friends with Fiona?'

There were long moments of silence as everyone looked at one another. Nobody offered.

'I thought she had just forgotten to put in her
routes,' Amy said quietly. 'But it's true, isn't it?

Fiona *doesn't* have any friends.'

'Jenny?' Miss Kerr said. 'How about you? You volunteered to ask after Fiona when she was ill.'

Jenny knew she had to say yes. She nodded stiffly, then stood up. Carrie threw her a look of sympathy.

'Thank you, Jenny,' Miss Kerr said. 'Just see that she's OK. She doesn't need to come back to class until she feels better.'

Jenny closed the classroom door behind her and went in search of Fiona. It was the last thing she wanted to do at the moment.

She tried the girls' toilets first but there was no sign of her there. Then she thought of the cloakroom. Sure enough, Jenny found Fiona there, huddled in a corner.

'Fiona,' she said. 'Are you all right? Do you want to talk?'

Fiona turned to her, her face streaked with tears. 'What are *you* doing here?' she said, her voice catching.

'Miss Kerr asked me to come and see that you were all right,' Jenny replied.

Fiona's face twisted. 'I don't have any friends, do I? Everybody can see that now.'

Jenny didn't say anything for a while. 'People are worried about you,' she said at last. She hesitated. 'Especially Paul,' she continued. 'He says you've been having nightmares . . .'

Fiona whirled round. 'You've no right to go talking about me behind my back!' she said. 'Just leave me alone, do you hear me? Leave me alone!' And, with that, she rushed from the cloakroom.

Jenny stood for a moment, uncertain what to do. Well, Fiona certainly didn't want to discuss her problems. She sighed and trudged back to the classroom to report to Miss Kerr.

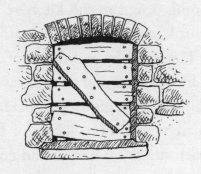

9

Fiona didn't appear at school the next day and, at the end of the week, Miss Kerr announced that Fiona would be off school until further notice.

Jenny and Ian went up to Windy Hill on Saturday morning to help Fraser and Matt move some ewes out of the fields and into the stables for shelter. The weather had turned so wet that the lower field was getting waterlogged.

Ellen Grace had accompanied them to do some more cleaning down in the kitchen.

Jenny looked around the ruined farm buildings. The upstairs windows of the house were now boarded up and the paintwork on the sills and frames was beginning to peel away from the damaged wood. The debris of the ruined lambing barn still lay where it had collapsed, its blackened timbers mingling with a heap of roof tiles that had been removed from the house roof for safety. It looked so desolate, it made Jenny want to cry. She hated to see Windy Hill in this state.

She was also finding it difficult to talk to Matt. He still seemed to blame her for the fire. They had always been the best of friends but now there seemed to be a shadow between them.

'When are the repairs going to start, Dad?' she asked, as her father called Jake and Nell to heel. Jess came bounding over with them.

'Well, Bob Elliott now wants an independent report,' Fraser Miles said in disgust.

'But what for?' Jenny asked. 'The weather is getting worse all the time and December is less than a week away. We'll have to leave Cliff House then! Where are we going to live while the repairs are being done?'

'I've been asking around,' her father said. 'There's a cottage on the other side of Graston that we could take, but the rent is high and it's too far away from Windy Hill for my liking. Still, we might have to go for that. Christmas is a bad time of year to be looking for a place to stay – especially since we only want a short-term let.'

'And it'll mean spending more money,' Matt put in. 'If things go on like this there's no way we'll get the insurance sorted out before Christmas. This is just what we need!'

Jenny flushed as her brother couldn't stop himself from giving her an accusing look. 'Matt . . .' she began pleadingly, but he turned away from her as a car drew into the farmyard. Jess sprang up and ran to meet it.

'That's Mrs McLay,' Ian said, surprised. 'Fiona is with her.'

'Fiona?' said Jenny. 'What on earth is *she* doing here?'

Jess ran up to Mrs McLay as she opened the car door, then backed away and growled as Fiona got out of the passenger seat. Hanging on to her mother's arm, Fiona followed Anna McLay over. She looked terribly pale and drawn, even worse then she had at school.

'Here, Jess,' Jenny called.

Jess came to her side slowly and sat in front of her, placing himself between her and Fiona, his eyes never leaving Fiona's face.

'I think Jess feels the same way about Fiona as we do,' Ian whispered as Jess gave another soft growl.

As the two visitors came close, Anna McLay bent and stroked Jess's muzzle. Jess wagged his tail and licked Mrs McLay's hand, but kept a wary eye on Fiona.

Then Mrs McLay looked up at the others. Her eyes resting on Fraser, she flushed bright red and shook her head. 'Oh, Fraser . . .' she started, haltingly. 'I found something out last night . . . something you need to know . . . But I honestly don't know where to start,' she said. 'I feel so mortified . . .' She drew Fiona forward and swallowed hard. 'Fiona has something to tell you.'

Jenny looked at Fiona in puzzlement. The girl

was looking at the house — at the smoke-blackened walls, the tiles missing from the roof, the boarded-up windows. Then she looked towards the pile of debris where the lambing barn had once stood and her face grew even paler.

'I didn't know it was as bad as this,' she said in a low voice. 'I haven't been here since the night of the bonfire.'

Jenny frowned. 'But you weren't here on Bonfire Night,' she said. 'You didn't come to the party.'

Fiona swallowed hard and clasped her hands together. 'Yes, I did,' she said. 'I came down to see what was happening.'

'We didn't see you,' Ian said, looking puzzled.

Fiona shook her head. She was clearly finding it difficult to speak. 'I didn't come up to the bonfire,' she went on at last. 'I just came to the house.'

'What?' said Jenny.

Fiona's head drooped. Her voice was so low they could hardly hear her. 'I wanted to watch,' she said. Silent tears began to course down her face. She wiped them away then took a long

JESS THE BORDER COLLIE

shuddering breath. 'I started the fire at Windy Hill,' she said brokenly.

Jenny gasped. *Fiona*! She couldn't believe what she had just heard.

'I think you'd better tell us everything, Fiona,' Fraser Miles said quietly.

Fiona began to sob. 'I felt really jealous of everybody else having fun at the bonfire,' she said, in a strangled voice. 'I thought about how much everyone would be enjoying themselves.'

'But I asked you to come,' Jenny protested.

Fiona shook her head. 'Only because you felt sorry for me,' she said.

'That isn't true, Fiona,' Jenny insisted.

Fiona shook her head again, as if she didn't believe Jenny. 'I sneaked over to Windy Hill to watch,' she went on. 'But that made me feel even more lonely and left out of things. I had some sparklers and matches with me and I lit some of the sparklers, then I crept into the house to have a look around. I went upstairs to Jenny's bedroom. I took the sparklers and the matches with me.'

Jenny remembered the sparklers the fire

officer had found in her bedroom. So they had been Fiona's.

'And you just set fire to the bedroom?' Matt asked, his face red with anger.

Fiona shook her head. 'No! It wasn't like that at all! I didn't mean to,' she said. 'I opened the window to see the fireworks better. I lit another sparkler. Then I saw your Geography project work on your desk, Jenny. It made me angry and jealous. There wasn't a single track to Dunraven on your map but there were lots of tracks between Windy Hill and loads of other houses and farms around. The sparkler went out but I didn't want to put on the light in case anyone saw me so I lit a candle to see the map better. The candle flame caught on the papers . . .' Fiona looked at her mother.

Anna McLay nodded support and Fiona continued.

'I . . . just watched it . . . all your project stuff burning up. But the fire seemed to spread so fast and I got frightened. Then I started to choke on the smoke. I panicked. Jess was barking. He must have heard me. I ran out of the door and down the stairs and right out of the house. Jess was barking all the time. He knew what I had done.'

'So that's why Jess has been acting strangely around you,' Jenny said. 'He knew you had started the fire.'

Fiona looked at Jenny, her eyes huge and dark in her gaunt, tormented face. 'I'm so, so sorry,' she said, her voice breaking again.

'I think we know the rest,' Anna McLay said, wearily. 'The fire took hold and by the time Jess alerted Jenny it was too late to save the house.'

'Or the lambing barn,' Fraser Miles said softly.

Fiona was sobbing again now, but Jenny barely noticed. She felt a great rush of anger. 'You let everybody think it was my fault!' she cried. 'You even accused me yourself. How could you do that, Fiona? What have I ever done to make you hate me so much?'

Fiona couldn't answer. She simply turned away, burying her face in her mother's shoulder.

Fraser Miles laid a hand on Jenny's arm and Jenny looked at him. The anger left her as soon as it had arrived. One thought filled her mind. *It hadn't been her fault. She hadn't been responsible for the fire.* All the guilt she had been feeling was gone. Yes, Windy Hill still lay in ruins about them

. . . but *she* hadn't destroyed it – and Jess had known that. He had tried to tell her who had been the guilty one.

But now, as Anna McLay led the still-sobbing Fiona to the car and settled her in the passenger seat, Jess remained silent. He seemed to understand that Fiona no longer posed a threat. Anna McLay walked back across the farmyard towards them. 'Fiona needed to confess,' she said, quietly. 'But I think she's had enough for one day.'

Mrs McLay drew herself up and looked directly at Fraser, her eyes pleading. 'Calum and I will, of course, take full financial responsibility for all the damage,' she went on, 'including the lambing barn. I know it wasn't insured, Fraser, but it will be rebuilt at our expense. If you want to prosecute . . .' Here, Anna McLay's voice broke. 'I know how it looks, Fraser,' she said falteringly. 'But you must believe me. It wasn't arson. Fiona didn't set fire to the house deliberately. You've seen how ill she's made herself worrying about what she did. I think she is truly sorry.' Anna McLay's voice broke off altogether.

Fraser returned her gaze. 'There's one thing I want to make clear,' he said. 'I don't want any more delays on the insurance settlement. I can't prove anything but I'm pretty sure Calum has been holding things up in the hope that I'll sell out to him. You can tell him from me, Anna, that it won't work. If I don't get that insurance claim tied up and settled tomorrow then I'm going to make things very sticky for him.'

Anna McLay flushed a deep red. 'I didn't know he'd been holding things up, Fraser,' she said. 'But he has been seeing a lot of Bob Elliot recently . . .' She frowned. 'Don't worry. He'll stop interfering now – and he'll build you the best lambing barn in the Borders. I'll see to that.'

'And what about Fiona?' Jenny asked quietly. 'What's going to happen to her?'

Anna McLay shook her head, the tears finally spilling over. 'I don't know, Jenny,' she said. 'That depends on you and your family. I hope that when you've had time to consider, you will agree that she's punished herself enough, without taking matters further. She was very wrong to put the blame on you – and she knows that. It took so much for her to come here today. I hope some day you'll be able to forgive her.'

Jenny didn't say anything. At that moment, she could never imagine forgiving Fiona.

'That's a lot to ask,' Fraser Miles said, putting his arm round Jenny's shoulder.

'I know it is,' Mrs McLay said. 'It's just that Fiona is a very sick girl and I'm worried about her.'

Fraser Miles nodded. 'Of course you are, Anna,' he said. After a pause, he said, 'I won't prosecute. Fiona is only a child and an unhappy one at that. But I won't stand any more nonsense from Calum.'

Anna McLay looked at him. 'Calum will behave himself,' she said firmly. 'Fiona nearly ruined you, Fraser. She made all of you homeless and caused Jenny terrible distress . . . But I'm going to do everything in my power to make it up to you all. I promise you that.'

Matt ran a hand through his hair. 'One problem that isn't solved is where we're going to live while the repairs are carried out. The Turners have guests coming for Christmas and New Year so we can't stay on at Cliff House.

And Dad needs to be near the farm to look after the sheep.'

'But you *can* be near Windy Hill, Fraser,' Anna McLay said. 'That was the other thing I came to tell you. We can offer you a home while Windy Hill is repaired.'

'At Dunraven?' Jenny said, unable to hide her horror.

Anna McLay coloured. 'Not exactly,' she said. 'No, I was talking about Thistle Cottage, the one Mrs Grace used to rent.'

Anna looked at Ellen Grace, who'd come out to see what was happening, and flushed again. Everyone knew that Calum McLay had refused to renew the lease on Thistle Cottage for Mrs Grace out of pure spite – because she'd gone to work for the Mileses. It had lain empty ever since, but things had worked out for the best despite Calum, because Ellen Grace had found a better home at Windy Hill.

Ellen Grace nodded encouragingly, and Mrs McLay went on. 'As you know, the cottage is quite near the boundary between Dunraven and Windy Hill and all it needs is a good airing and it'll be fit for you to live in.' She looked at Fraser.

'I know it isn't ideal, Fraser, but it was all I could think of. Calum will ensure that repairs to Windy Hill are done in double-quick time, and then you'll all be able to move back home.'

'That's very kind of you, Anna,' Mrs Grace said gently. 'But there really won't be enough room for us all at Thistle Cottage. There are four of us – five if you count Matt. He comes home at weekends.'

'You don't have to count me,' Ian reminded her. 'I'm going to Canada for Christmas and New Year to see Mum and Dad.'

Mrs Grace nodded. 'That's true,' she said. 'That'll help.'

'Well, perhaps, Ellen, you wouldn't mind a bed at Dunraven . . .?' Anna McLay suggested hesitantly. 'It's only a few minutes' walk from the cottage.'

Mrs Grace smiled and nodded. 'Thank you, Anna. That would be fine by me.' She looked at Fraser Miles. He nodded acceptance too.

Breathing a sigh of relief, Anna McLay continued. 'Well, that's sorted, then.' She looked round. 'I'd better get Fiona home now. And then Calum and I will get started on putting things right.' She walked over to her car, saying, 'Goodbye – and thank you. I'll be in touch shortly.'

'Taking Thistle Cottage means we'll all be separated,' Jenny said quietly, as Anna McLay drove off.

Fraser Miles put a hand on Jenny's shoulder. 'It looks like we'll just have to put up with it, lass. It's a roof over our heads. I'll get on to Marion Stewart first thing Monday morning and get things moving.'

Jenny nodded and put a hand on Jess's head. She wished that Mrs Grace didn't have to sleep at Dunraven, especially as Ian was going to be away in Canada. Still, she had Jess. At least she wouldn't be separated from him.

She looked at her father. He seemed to be waiting for her approval. Jess pushed his nose into Jenny's hand and she bent down to him, stroking his ears. 'What do you think, Jess?' she asked. Jess licked her hand, as if in encouragement. Jenny laughed. Her head came up. 'Let's do it,' she said. 'The sooner we get started, the sooner we can move back home.' For the first time, she felt confident that Windy

Hill would rise from the ashes.

'Too right,' said Matt. 'And not only will the insurance pay for the house and stables to be made as good as new, Calum McLay will build us a new lambing barn.'

'And, best of all,' Jenny added quietly, 'you know now that the fire wasn't my fault.'

Matt turned to Jenny. 'Jen,' he said. 'I'm so sorry I doubted you.'

Ian nodded sheepishly.

'We're all sorry,' Fraser Miles said.

'Do you forgive us?' Matt asked.

Jenny gave him a hug. 'Of course I do,' she assured him.

Ellen Grace put an arm round Jenny's shoulders. 'Well, thank goodness for that,' she said. 'You've got quite a girl here, Fraser,' she said, looking at Mr Miles.

'I know that, Ellen,' he replied gruffly.

Jenny grinned and laid her hand on Jess's head. 'And Jess is quite a dog! He was trying to tell us all the time who had started the fire.'

'Trust Jess,' said her father. 'Sometimes I think he's the best thing that's happened to Windy Hill.'

'Oh, he is,' Jenny declared. 'Aren't you, boy? The very best!'

Jenny looked around the farm – her home – and raised her face to the wind. Her voice floated over the ruined buildings and on up into the air. 'We'll be back soon,' she said. 'I promise – we'll be back!'

THE
SACRIFICE

The Sacrifice

Special thanks to Helen Magee

Text copyright © 1999 Working Partners Ltd
Series created by Ben M. Baglio, London W6 OQT
Illustrations copyright © 1999 Sheila Ratcliffe

First published as a single volume in Great Britain in 1999
by Hodder Children's Books

1

'So *that's* Thistle Cottage,' said Jenny Miles. She looked doubtfully at the little whitewashed house at the end of the muddy track, then at her father, Fraser Miles. 'It isn't very big, is it?'

It was Jenny's first look at the cottage that was to be their home for the next few weeks. Jess, Jenny's black-and-white Border collie, ran ahead and scrabbled at the cottage door.

'Jess looks as if he wants to explore,' Ellen

Grace said, encouragingly.

'Why don't you catch him up?' Fraser said, reaching in his pocket and giving Jenny the key.

Jenny ran after Jess. The wind blew her shoulder-length fair hair across her face. It was the beginning of December and the track beneath her feet was already rutted with frozen mud. She opened the door of the cottage and Jess disappeared at once, racing through the rooms.

'There are only two bedrooms,' Fraser said, as he reached the door. 'It'll be a bit of a squeeze when you're back from college, Matt.'

'Oh, I'll be all right sleeping on the sofa,' Jenny's brother Matt said, poking his head round the door.

Thistle Cottage belonged to the McLays. They had offered it to the Mileses to help make amends while their farmhouse, Windy Hill, was being repaired. It had been severely damaged by a fire, accidentally started by Fiona, Anna and Calum McLay's daughter.

Jenny followed her father into the kitchen. 'It must be funny coming back here, Mrs Grace,' Jenny said, as she looked round the tiny room. Ellen Grace had once rented Thistle Cottage from Calum McLay but because of a long-standing grudge against Fraser, he had evicted her out of spite when she came to work for the Mileses. It seemed very bare and basic compared to the big cluttered kitchen at Windy Hill. There was an ordinary cooker instead of the Aga Jenny was used to and the kitchen table was a small plastic-topped one, not at all like the huge wooden table in the farmhouse kitchen. But the walls were painted bright sunshine yellow and they looked cheerful even on a dull December day.

'It's a nice little cottage,' Ellen Grace said. 'I decorated it only last year. I hope you like the colours.'

'It's very cheerful,' Jenny said, smiling at Mrs Grace.

'It's just as well you'll be away at college during the week, Matt,' Fraser Miles said to him, peering into the sitting-room. 'But if you find it too uncomfortable, I can manage on my own most weekends.'

'No way,' said Matt firmly. 'You know I love helping out with the sheep, Dad, and you're going to have to start scanning the ewes soon to see how many are pregnant. You can't manage that on your own.'

Matt was nineteen and away at college, studying agriculture. He came home as often as he could to help with the work at the Mileses' sheep farm.

Jenny's father kept a thousand Scottish Blackface sheep with the help of only a couple of farmhands.

'OK,' Fraser gave in. 'If you're offering to help, I'm not going to refuse!'

'Good!' Matt said with a grin.

'What do you think of Thistle Cottage, Jess?' Jenny said as the Border collie came running into the kitchen. She bent down and gave him a cuddle. Jess wagged his tail and looked up at her, his head tilted to one side. 'There isn't very much to explore, is there?' she said, smiling.

The sheepdog sat down at Jenny's feet and gazed at her adoringly. He'd been born with a badly twisted leg which meant he would never make a working dog. Jenny had persuaded her father to let her keep the little puppy as a pet and to have his leg operated on. Now Jess was as good as new and the two of them were inseparable. No matter what happened to Jenny, as long as she had Jess by her side she was happy!

'He'd be quite content to live anywhere so long as you were there, Jenny.' Mrs Grace laughed, her warm blue eyes smiling at Jenny. 'Come on, I'll show you the other rooms.'

Ellen Grace had come to Windy Hill as

housekeeper some months after Jenny's mother had been killed in a riding accident. At first, Jenny had been wary of having someone take her mother's place but Mrs Grace had never tried to do that and now Jenny thought of her as one of the family.

Besides the kitchen, there was a small sitting-room, a bathroom and two tiny bedrooms. The sitting-room had a sofa and two armchairs, a drop-leaf table and a sideboard against the wall.

'Oh, this looks cosy!' Jenny exclaimed, as she took in the fresh white walls and rose-coloured curtains. She was even more delighted with her little bedroom. It had blue-patterned wallpaper and white paintwork and there was a striped blue and white blind at the window.

She turned to the housekeeper. 'I think you're a great interior decorator,' she said.

Mrs Grace laughed. 'I don't know about that,' she said. 'It's all very simple.'

'It's lovely,' Jenny insisted. 'It's just a pity you can't be here with us.'

Mrs Grace nodded. 'I know,' she said. 'But I'll come over every morning and evening to see to the cooking and housework.' As there wasn't enough room for the Mileses *and* Ellen Grace all to stay at Thistle Cottage, the housekeeper was going to help out Anna McLay and sleep at Dunraven until the repairs to Windy Hill were complete.

'What about Jess?' Jenny said.

'I thought I'd take him with me to Dunraven,' Mrs Grace replied. 'Rather than leaving him on his own while you're at school.'

'That's a good idea, isn't it, Jess? You'll have Toby to play with,' Jenny said, rubbing Jess's ears. 'You and Toby are great friends.' Toby was a Border terrier. He belonged to young Paul McLay, the McLays' eight-year-old son.

'OK,' said Fraser Miles, putting his head round the bedroom door. 'Let's get moving. I want to look in on Windy Hill. The builder should have arrived by now to start the repairs.'

Jenny's heart sank as her father turned his jeep into the farmyard at Windy Hill. She still hadn't got used to the state their home was in, although it was more than a month now since the fire. The old stone farmhouse stood desolate and empty, its red roof scorched and sagging in places. The entire upstairs floor was badly water-damaged and Jenny's bedroom – which had been gutted by the fire – had boarded-up windows. The paintwork was peeling where it had been burned and the walls were blackened by smoke. It was such a sorry sight it made Jenny want to cry. The stables had survived and Fraser Miles was still able to use them but the new lambing barn that he had built with the profits of the previous year's lambing had been burned to the ground. The builders had cleared away the remains but Jenny felt a lump in her throat as she remembered how proud her father had been of his new barn.

There was a white van already parked in the yard and a grey-haired man in a waxed jacket was standing with a clipboard in his hand, looking up at the gable wall of the farmhouse. He turned as Mr Miles drew to a halt and began to walk towards them.

'That's Joe Thorburn, the builder,' Matt said, as Fraser leaped out of the driver's seat and went to meet him.

Jenny, Matt and Mrs Grace followed.

'I've got a fair idea of the repairs that need to be done,' Mr Thorburn said, as he and Fraser shook hands. 'We'll start on the house this afternoon. I guess that's the most important thing. We'll do the roof first, then I'll get some of the men working on the new barn and the rest can concentrate on the inside of the house.'

Fraser Miles nodded. 'The sooner we can move back in the better,' he said. 'How long do you think it'll take?'

Joe Thorburn looked at the sky. 'That depends on the weather,' he said. 'Let's see. If we can work right through then we should get finished by the end of January, but if we get really heavy snow that's going to hold things up. We could be talking well into February.'

'February!' Jenny protested. 'But that's *ages* away.'

Joe shook his head. 'You can't argue with the weather, lass,' he said. 'Let's just hope the snow holds off until we get the outside work done. If things get really bad it could be March before we get the house habitable. But I promise you we'll work as quickly as we can.'

Jenny looked up. The sky was heavy with clouds but they weren't snow clouds – not yet. Windy Hill was on the border between Scotland and England, its fields to the east stretching to the cliffs that ran along the coast. She shivered as a sudden wind blew a chill off the sea. Winters in the Borders could be harsh.

'Just do the best you can, Joe,' Fraser said, his eyes

serious. He turned as a car drew into the farmyard.

'There's Miss Stewart,' Ellen Grace said, as a woman with short dark hair got out of a car that had just pulled into the yard.

Marion Stewart was the insurance representative from the company that had insured Windy Hill. According to Carrie Turner, Jenny's best friend, Miss Stewart had taken a shine to Fraser Miles – and Jenny wasn't at all sure she liked that idea.

Marion Stewart walked across the yard, her eyes on Fraser. She smiled as she approached and laid her hand on his arm. 'I hoped I'd find you here, Fraser,' she said. 'I take it everything is going smoothly?'

Mr Miles ran a hand through his hair. 'It's a bit early to say, Marion,' he told her. Then he added, 'I hope you haven't brought any bad news.'

Marion shook her head. 'Not at all,' she assured him. 'I came to agree some estimates with Joe.'

'That's all right then,' Fraser said. 'I'll leave you to it. We've got to move house this afternoon.'

Marion swung round as Fraser and the others made to leave. 'I'd be delighted to help you,' she offered.

Fraser smiled as he looked at Marion Stewart's smart blue suit, then shifted his gaze to Matt, Jenny and Ellen. They were all wearing jeans. 'Thanks for the offer,' he said, 'but you'd probably spoil your clothes.'

Jenny cast a look behind her as they went. Marion Stewart was watching them go. She looked disappointed. Jenny began to think that perhaps Carrie was right about Miss Stewart.

Carrie rushed out of the house to meet them as they drove into Cliffbay, the nearby fishing village where the Turners lived. The Mileses had been staying with them since the fire. Cliff House was down by the harbour, a big stone house facing the sea. Carrie's mother, Pam, was an artist and Gordon, her father, ran boat trips to Puffin Island, a nature reserve just off the coast.

'What's the cottage like?' Carrie asked breathlessly, her bright red hair streaming out behind her as she ran towards them.

'Small,' said Jenny. 'But Mrs Grace has done it up really nicely.'

Carrie bent to pat Jess. The Border collie leaped up, enjoying the fuss Carrie made of him. 'What about your room?'

'For goodness sake, Carrie, let them get inside

before you bombard them with questions,' her mother said, laughing, as she too came to greet them. Pam Turner, like Carrie, had red hair, but hers was cut short. 'Come and have some lunch before you pack up.'

Jenny and the others followed Mrs Turner into Cliff House while Carrie continued her barrage of questions.

'I knew it,' she said, grinning, when Jenny told her about Marion Stewart. 'I reckon she's after your dad.'

Jenny looked at her father as he sat down at the big kitchen table. 'I think Dad's got too much on his mind to be bothered with Miss Stewart,' she said, looking at her father's face. He was smiling and chatting but Jenny could see the shadow of worry behind his eyes.

'I'm starving,' Matt said as he sat down.

'So what else is new?' Mrs Grace joked and everyone laughed.

'I wish our relatives from Australia weren't coming so soon and that you could stay on at Cliff House,' Carrie confessed to Jenny.

'You can come and visit at Thistle Cottage,' Jenny said. 'And we'll see each other all the time at school.'

'Only two weeks till the Christmas holidays,'

Carrie said. 'I wonder how Ian will enjoy Christmas in Canada. He was so lucky getting off school early.' Ian Amery was Mrs Grace's nephew. He had chosen to live in Scotland with Mrs Grace, but had gone to Canada to spend the Christmas holiday with his parents.

'He says he's going to learn to ski and then teach us when he gets back — if there's any snow,' Jenny told Carrie.

Carrie snorted. 'Of course there'll be snow!' she said. 'That would be great fun.'

But Jenny wasn't so sure about how great a long, hard winter would be. Snow wouldn't be good for the sheep *or* the building work at Windy Hill.

'That's the last of the boxes,' Carrie said, as she heaved a carton into the back of the jeep. She looked at what was left of the Mileses possessions. 'There isn't much, is there? Honestly, Jenny, don't you feel really angry with Fiona?'

Jenny sighed. Fiona McLay had accidentally started the fire in Jenny's bedroom on Bonfire Night when she had been snooping around Windy Hill. Very little belonging to Jenny had survived the fire. Luckily the possession that Jenny valued the most

had been salvaged – a photograph of her mother.

'Of course I'm angry,' she said to Carrie. 'But Fiona made herself really ill with worry about what she did.'

Carrie shook her hair back from her face. 'That doesn't make it all right,' she said fiercely. 'Fiona has always hated you. I bet she hasn't changed.'

Carrie was right. Fiona McLay had always picked on Jenny, laughing at her for not being interested in fashionable clothes. She had called Jess names too, saying he was Jenny's 'lame dog'. And her father, Calum McLay, was just as bad. He had been trying for years to make Fraser Miles sell Windy Hill to him because he wanted to plant trees on the land.

'Time to go home, Jenny,' Mrs Grace said, as she came out of the house.

Jenny looked at her, suddenly miserable. 'Thistle Cottage isn't home,' she said. 'Only one place is home – Windy Hill.'

Ellen Grace laid a hand on her arm. 'We'll all live there again, Jenny,' she said. 'You'll see.'

Jenny reached her hand into the box Carrie had just loaded. She lifted the framed photograph of her mother out and gazed at it. The photograph had been taken when her mother had been eleven years old and Jenny was always amazed at how like her mother she looked.

Jenny sighed and a warm tongue licked her hand. She looked down as Jess put his head on one side and looked up at her appealingly.

'Oh, I miss Windy Hill so much, Jess,' she said. 'When are we going to be able to go back there?'

Jess licked her hand again and made a soft snuffling sound in his throat. Jenny smiled and bent to give him a hug. 'No matter what happens, I'll always have you,' she whispered. 'No one will ever take you away from me.'

2

It seemed strange to Jenny to return to Thistle
Cottage the next day after school instead of going
home with Carrie. The school bus dropped her off
at Dunraven and Jenny hurried down the track to
the little cottage, eager to see Jess.

Jess hurled himself at Jenny, almost knocking her
over. He was nearly a year old now, no longer a
puppy, but with his four white socks and white chest
he still looked adorable.

'How did Jess get on at Dunraven, Mrs Grace?' she asked, as she dumped her schoolbag on the kitchen floor.

'He and Toby had a great time together,' Mrs Grace assured her, as Jenny hugged Jess.

'Is Fiona all right with him?' Jenny persisted. 'She's never liked him. She even threw a stick at him once.'

'Oh, Fiona didn't take any notice of him,' Mrs Grace replied, frowning. 'In fact she hardly came out of her room all day. She's very ill and depressed, Jenny. Anna McLay is afraid she's heading for a nervous breakdown.'

'She must feel so guilty about what she did,' Jenny said seriously. Then she smiled as Jess butted her. 'I'm glad you had a good time with Toby, Jess,' she said.

Mrs Grace was stirring a dark mixture in a big bowl. Jenny dipped a finger in the bowl and tasted the mixture. 'Christmas pudding,' she said. 'It tastes great.'

'It'll taste even better when it's cooked,' Mrs Grace laughed. She handed Jenny a wooden spoon. 'Here, make a wish.'

Jenny stirred the mixture in the bowl and closed her eyes. She had only one wish – to get back to

Windy Hill as soon as possible.

'Your turn,' Jenny said, giving the spoon back.

The housekeeper opened her eyes. 'I've wished,' she said.

'What did you wish for?' Jenny said when she noticed how worried Mrs Grace looked.

Mrs Grace sighed. 'For Fiona to get better,' she said. 'Her mum says she hardly ever speaks to anybody and she bursts into tears if Anna mentions inviting somebody to visit.'

Jenny hated to see Mrs Grace worried. She was usually so cheerful. 'Is there anything I can do?' she asked.

Mrs Grace shook her head. 'I don't think there's anything anyone can do, Jenny,' she said. 'All I know is that Anna is at her wits' end.' The housekeeper looked at Jenny and Jess and her frown softened. 'Anyway, it's good to see you two so happy,' she said. 'Dunraven is such an unhappy house at the moment.'

Jenny gave Jess another cuddle. Thistle Cottage wasn't ideal but at least she had Jess. 'Jess always helps me when I feel sad,' she said.

'You're lucky,' Mrs Grace replied. 'I don't think anyone can help Fiona at the moment.'

★ ★ ★

However, a few days later Mrs Grace told Jenny that Fiona seemed to be making some progress.

'At first she wouldn't come out of her room at all when I was there,' the housekeeper said on Wednesday. 'But today she was sitting in the living-room when I arrived and instead of rushing off to her room, she stayed for a little while. She seemed to be watching Jess.'

Jenny felt an immediate alarm. 'She didn't do anything to him, did she?'

Ellen Grace looked shocked. 'No, Jenny, she just watched him. It's odd. She doesn't bother with Toby but she seems to like Jess.'

Jenny didn't say anything. She couldn't believe that Fiona could have changed her attitude towards Jess.

When she told Carrie what Mrs Grace had said, Carrie agreed. 'Huh!' she scoffed next day at school. 'Fiona will never change. She's always made fun of Jess. Just you tell Mrs Grace to watch out for her. I wouldn't trust Fiona McLay with *my* dog.'

Jenny sighed. 'Maybe we should feel sorry for her,' she said. 'After all, she must be lonely up at Dunraven with no one her own age to talk to.'

Carrie looked at Jenny in amazement. 'How can you even *think* of feeling sorry for her after what she did to you?' she asked. 'Fiona was perfectly happy to let you take the blame for the fire at Windy Hill.'

Jenny sighed again. What Carrie said was true. Fiona *had* let everyone believe that Jenny had caused the fire by leaving a candle lit in her bedroom. She'd even spread rumours at school that the fire was Jenny's fault.

'Forget Fiona,' Carrie advised. 'It'll be Christmas soon and there's lots of things to look forward to.'

On the last day of term, Jenny rushed in from school full of news about the class Christmas party.

'We had mince pies and cake and a disco in the school hall,' she told Mrs Grace, as Jess launched himself at her in welcome. She plonked herself down at the little kitchen table and Jess put his head in her lap. 'Thank goodness it's the school holidays. Now I can have you with me all the time,' she said, looking down at the Border collie. Jess's tail thumped happily on the floor.

'How's Fiona?' Jenny asked.

Mrs Grace smiled. 'A little better, I think,' she

replied. 'You know, I'm certain she looks forward to seeing Jess every day. She certainly seems to perk up when he arrives.'

'That's good,' Jenny agreed.

Then Jenny noticed that Mrs Grace was frowning. 'What's wrong?' she asked. 'If Jess is helping Fiona you should be glad.'

'Of course I am, Jenny,' Mrs Grace assured her. 'That isn't what I'm worried about.'

'What then?' asked Jenny.

Mrs Grace shrugged. 'I'm just wondering how Fiona will get on without Jess,' she said. 'As you said, Jenny, now that you're on holiday Jess won't be going to Dunraven for a while. I think Fiona will really miss him.'

Jenny frowned. She was pleased that Jess was being a help, but a part of her resented the time Fiona spent with Jess – and she was still a little suspicious of Fiona's new attitude to him. She couldn't help feeling that Fiona was up to something.

Mrs Grace didn't mention the subject of Fiona and Jess again until a few days later. It was three days before Christmas. As Jenny was going to spend the morning at Windy Hill with her father and Matt, who was home for the Christmas holidays, Mrs Grace asked if she could take Jess to Dunraven with her. Reluctantly, Jenny agreed.

'Thank you, Jenny. I think Fiona will be very glad to see him,' Mrs Grace said as she left. 'We'll be back just after lunch. See you then.'

Jenny waved goodbye as Mrs Grace and Jess set off up the track to Dunraven; then her father called her and she swung round. She was really looking forward to seeing how the work was going on – and she was going to help scan the pregnant ewes!

Jenny looked anxiously at the farmhouse as they turned into the yard; it was a hive of activity and noise. There were ladders propped against the walls and a pile of wooden beams stacked in a corner under a tarpaulin cover. A lorry stood at the far end of the farmyard and two men were unloading bags of cement from it. Two others were operating a cement mixer. The builders had done some work to the stables so that Fraser could use them for penning ewes but it was the work on the house that most interested Jenny.

'It looks so strange,' she said to Matt, gazing up at the roof of the farmhouse. The roof was stripped down to the beams. It no longer looked like their old house.

'They're having to replace some of the rafters before tiling it,' Matt told Jenny.

The downstairs windows still had glass in them but most of the upstairs ones were boarded up and there was a growing pile of rubble in the yard in front of the house.

'How does Joe think it's going, Dad?' Matt asked.

'Pretty well,' said Fraser. 'The weather has been good so far and, once they get the roof done, they can start on the inside. Joe intends to drop by later. But meantime, we have the ewes to scan.' He turned as a van drew into the yard. 'Here's Tim Dobson now.'

Fraser Miles had hired Mr Dobson to come to the farm and scan the pregnant ewes to see how many lambs they could expect. He was a young man, only a few years out of agricultural college, with fair hair. Matt and Jenny helped to herd the ewes from the lower field into the holding pens in the farmyard while Tim and Fraser set up the equipment. Jake and Nell, Fraser Miles's two working sheepdogs, wove in and out of the flock, guiding them towards the pens. There were more pens set up in the stables so that the ewes could be divided after scanning. The dogs were used to this work but Jenny always admired how quickly they could separate the ewes, herding them into pens at Matt's command.

'Jess would be good at this,' Jenny said, as she closed the door of the last pen and bent to give Jake's ears a rub. Jake and Nell were Jess's parents.

Jenny watched as Mr Dobson and her father checked the scanning machine in the stables. There was a box with a waterproof cover and inside it was a monitor with several control knobs below it.

'You'll be able to see the unborn lambs on the screen, Jenny,' Fraser Miles said. He turned to Matt. 'Let's get going then, son.'

Jenny stood beside Tim as he plugged in the probe that would scan the ewes. It fitted into the front of the monitor. He twiddled a knob, and nodded at Fraser. 'Ready.'

Fraser and Matt brought out the first ewe, turning her on her back while Mr Dobson passed the probe over the animal's belly. 'Look at the screen,' he said to Jenny.

Jenny looked. 'I can't see anything,' she said,

frowning. 'Just fuzzy lines.'

Tim Dobson reached across and pointed with his free hand. 'There,' he said. 'Look! Can't you see something moving?' His finger traced the outline of the image on the screen. Jenny looked closely at the monitor and suddenly the picture began to make sense. 'Is that a lamb?' she breathed, leaning even closer. 'Oh, look, Dad, you can see it moving.'

Fraser Miles smiled. 'Only one lamb there,' he said. 'You can put this ewe in the far pen, Jenny. We'll put the ewes with two or more in the nearer pen, they'll need more feeding.'

Jenny jumped up as her father let the ewe go. 'Come on, Nell, We've got work to do,' she called.

Jenny worked alongside her father and Matt all morning while the sounds of the repairs continued outside. When they stopped for lunch Jenny went out to have another look at how the work was going. The builders had stopped for lunch too but standing in the yard was a stack of roof tiles that hadn't been there before.

'Oh good, they're red,' Jenny remarked. 'Just like the old ones.'

'You wait,' said her father. 'It's going to look just like the old Windy Hill when it's finished.'

Jenny smiled. She couldn't think of anything she wanted more!

Joe Thorburn arrived as they were finishing their sandwiches and he and Fraser had a long conversation about the progress of the repairs.

'I dropped some paperwork off at Thistle Cottage on my way past,' Mr Thorburn said to Fraser. Then he looked at Jenny. 'Anna McLay is there with Mrs Grace. She said she's hoping to have a word with you, Jenny.'

'With me?' Jenny said, puzzled.

Fraser Miles looked at his watch. 'I could take Jenny back,' he said. 'But if you're passing that way, you could drop her off, Joe.'

'But I want to carry on helping,' Jenny protested.

Matt grinned. 'You *have* helped, Jenny,' he said. 'And if Ellen is there, Jess will be there too. He'll be looking for you.'

'OK,' Jenny said. 'But I can come again tomorrow and help with the scanning, can't I?'

'Of course you can,' her father assured her. 'Now go and see what Anna McLay has to say to you.'

Jenny gave Jake and Nell a hug, then got into the passenger seat of Mr Thorburn's van. What on earth could Fiona's mother want to talk to her about?

★ ★ ★

Jess shot out of the front door of Thistle Cottage as Jenny waved goodbye to Mr Thorburn.

'Hello, boy!' Jenny exclaimed as the Border collie jumped up at her. She buried her face in his soft fur and looked over his head at Mrs Grace. The housekeeper was standing in the doorway, looking serious.

'Is anything the matter?' Jenny asked.

Ellen Grace stood aside as Jenny and Jess came in. 'Mrs McLay has something she wants to ask you, Jenny,' she said, leading the way into the living-room. 'But I thought your father was bringing you home and that she would be able to speak to him about it first.'

'Mr Thorburn gave me a lift,' Jenny said. 'What is it?'

Ellen Grace hesitated then she seemed to make up her mind. 'I don't suppose your dad would mind her speaking to you . . .' she said. 'You don't have to agree but Mrs McLay is at the end of her tether. So hear her out, won't you?'

Jenny frowned, but she was already in the living-room and Anna McLay had got up from the sofa and now stood facing her. She looked

172

drawn and very serious.

'What is it, Mrs McLay?' Jenny asked.

Anna McLay took a deep breath. 'It's about Fiona, Jenny,' she said. She looked at Mrs Grace and the housekeeper nodded.

'Go on, Anna,' she said.

Jenny felt a shiver of apprehension. She reached a hand down and Jess licked her fingers. 'How is Fiona?' she asked.

Mrs McLay shook her head. 'She isn't very well at all, Jenny,' she said gently. 'In fact she's been going steadily downhill ever since Jess stopped coming up to Dunraven.'

Ellen Grace looked at Jenny kindly. 'Anna had a word with the doctor,' she put in. 'He said that Jess seemed to have reached Fiona. Somehow, having him at Dunraven seems to help her.'

'What do you mean?' Jenny asked quietly. Her sense of foreboding was beginning to grow.

Anna McLay shook her head. 'I'm not quite sure exactly *how* Jess is helping,' she said. 'Fiona still can't talk about the fire to anyone. In fact she hardly talks at all. She just broods on what she's done. The only time she's been relaxed was when Jess was there. When he stopped coming to Dunraven every day,

Fiona got a lot worse. Dr Scott thinks that her relapse is due to her missing Jess. And seeing Fiona's improvement at having Jess around this morning, I have to agree. She plays with him and it takes her mind off her guilty feelings. Dr Scott thinks that if Fiona can have Jess with her all the time she'll be able to start talking about the fire. If she doesn't do that soon, he says she really will have a serious breakdown.' Mrs McLay paused.

Jenny's heart began to beat very fast. 'All the time . . .' she repeated, putting her hand protectively on Jess's neck. 'What do you want me to do, Mrs McLay?' she asked.

Anna McLay looked pleadingly at Jenny. 'I want to know if you would let Jess come and stay at Dunraven with Fiona until she's better,' she said quietly. 'The doctor is convinced that Jess can help her to come out of her shell. If Fiona goes on the way she's going, she'll have to go into hospital. Jess is Fiona's last chance of getting well at home.'

Jenny drew in her breath sharply and her fingers twisted in the fur at Jess's neck. 'No!' she gasped.

'I know it's a big sacrifice, Jenny,' Mrs McLay went on. 'But won't you think about it?'

Jenny stood up, shoving back her chair. Jess was

at her side, close to her, sensing her distress. 'No!' she said again. 'Jess is *my* dog – not Fiona's. Fiona has never liked him. She made fun of his twisted leg. She called me names. She set fire to Windy Hill. And now she wants to take Jess away from me. It's just another one of her schemes. Don't you see? She only wants Jess because he's mine. Well, she isn't going to get him. He's mine. Do you understand? Mine!'

There was silence. Anna McLay bowed her head. 'Of course I understand, Jenny,' she said, her voice

wavering. 'But I had to try for the sake of my daughter.'

Tears stood in Jenny's eyes and she dashed them away. Then she rushed from the room. 'Come, Jess,' she called. 'Come on, boy!' Good, faithful Jess was at her heels as she ran out of the front door.

She heard Mrs Grace's voice behind her. 'Jenny! Where are you going?'

Jenny ignored her. She was going to the place she always went when she was upset – to Darktarn Keep – and Jess was coming with her. She would *never* be parted from Jess – no matter what anybody said!

3

The wind blew chill as Jenny and Jess made their way across the fields towards Darktarn Keep. Jenny's breath came in great gasps as she hurried towards her refuge. She had always loved Darktarn. Her mother, Sheena Miles, had taken her there often when she was a little girl and had told her stories of the old Border reivers, the sheep rustlers who had raided back and forth across the Scottish–English border, stealing each other's sheep. Jenny had called Jess after one of the most famous reivers – Jess of Beacon Brae. Now, as she stumbled towards Darktarn, Jenny remembered her mother and the tears slid down her cheeks.

'Mum would never have let them take you away from me, Jess,' she cried, as she laid a hand to steady herself on the drystone wall that stood below the keep.

Jess jumped up on the wall and put his head on Jenny's shoulder. She cuddled him to her as she looked up at the keep. Darktarn was a ruin now but hundreds of years ago it had been a tower stronghold, a place where people went to be safe from their enemies. Just at this moment Jenny felt that she too needed a place to be safe – *and* to keep Jess safe.

The tower's broken, jagged walls stood up black against the sky behind. It looked forbidding in the light of the winter afternoon and the tarn – the little lake below it, looked dark and dangerous. This was where Jenny's mother had died. There had been a storm. Her horse had bolted and Sheena Miles had fallen. But Jenny still loved the place. She always came here when she was upset or worried. Jenny pushed the hair out of her eyes and scrambled over the wall after Jess.

'Come on, boy,' she urged him.

Jenny made for a corner of the wall, which gave protection from the wind. As she huddled there with Jess beside her, Jenny fought against her tears. How could Mrs McLay ask this of her? Didn't she know how important Jess was to her? Jenny wiped a hand across her eyes. And how could Mrs Grace, of all people, expect her to give Jess up to Fiona?

Jess licked Jenny's tears away.

'I'll never let you go, Jess,' Jenny promised. 'Fiona can't really like you. Not after what she's done. Not after all the nasty things she's said about you. She just wants to take you away from me.'

A while later, Jenny looked up at the sky. It would soon be dark and Mrs Grace would be worried about her. 'We'd better go home, Jess,' she said. The word stuck in her throat. Home was Windy Hill, not the tiny cottage that Calum McLay owned.

Jenny decided to go back to Thistle Cottage by the track instead of crossing the fields in the gathering dark. The track led past Dunraven and as Jenny approached the farmhouse she increased her pace. As they passed the gate to the farmhouse Jess suddenly gave a loud bark and scampered under the gate.

'Jess!' Jenny called, but Jess ran on towards the door of the farmhouse.

Jenny put her hand on the gate, then stopped as the door opened and a figure came out into the yard. Jenny hadn't seen Fiona since the day she had confessed to starting the fire. Now she hardly recognised her. At first she thought Fiona had grown taller, then she realised that she only *looked* taller because she was so thin. Jenny's breath stopped in her throat as she took in the girl's changed appearance. Fiona was gaunt, her clothes hanging loosely on her, and her hair looked lank and uncared for. But it was her face that shocked Jenny the most. Fiona's eyes seemed to be huge. There were dark circles under them and her skin was white and drawn. Jenny had never seen anyone look so ill – or so unhappy.

Then Fiona saw Jess and bent down, holding out her arms. At once her face changed, her eyes lit up and she smiled and called out. 'Jess,' she cried. 'Oh, Jess, you've come back to me.'

Jess ran up to her, wagging his tail, licking her face, and Fiona laughed and put her arms round him.

Jenny stood, frozen to the spot, unable to speak.

In a blinding moment, she realised she had been wrong. Fiona *did* love Jess. There was no mistaking her welcome for him. Jenny pushed the gate and Fiona looked up. At once all the pleasure left her face and was replaced by distress. 'Jenny...' she faltered, stumbling to her feet. Then she gave a little moan and rushed back into the house, slamming the door behind her.

Jenny stood for a moment, unsure what to do. Fiona clearly didn't want to speak to her. Jess scampered back over to her and butted the side of her leg. Jenny stretched her hand out to him and he gazed up at her. 'Oh, Jess,' she said. 'What are we going to do?'

Although Dunraven was only ten minutes' walk away, it was growing dark by the time Jenny got back to Thistle Cottage. The jeep was parked at the end of the track. Her father and Matt were home. Jenny took a moment to go round to the shed at the side of the cottage where Jake and Nell had their beds. The dogs greeted her affectionately and Jenny patted them.

'Good dogs,' she said, as Jess licked Nell on the nose. Then she turned towards the cottage. She had a big decision to make.

Light spilled out of the front door as she and Jess made their way up the path. Jenny looked at the figures framed in the doorway. Her father was looking anxious and Mrs Grace's eyes were filled with concern. Matt stood behind them, looking serious. Mrs McLay had gone.

'I'm sorry I ran off like that, Mrs Grace,' Jenny apologised.

At once Mrs Grace's face broke into a smile. 'No Jenny, I'm sorry Anna and I upset you so much. I've told your father and Matt what happened.'

'Come in out of the cold and we'll say no more about it,' Fraser Miles said.

Mrs Grace gave Jenny a quick hug and Matt ruffled her hair. 'Don't you worry, Jen,' he said. 'Jess isn't going anywhere.'

Fraser Miles put his arm round Jenny's shoulders as they walked into the cottage. 'How would you like to lend a hand with the scanning again tomorrow?' he asked.

'I'd love to,' Jenny replied. She looked up at her father. 'Will you get all the ewes scanned before the weather turns too bad?'

Fraser Miles nodded. 'Yes, we should finish up tomorrow.' He looked at her seriously. 'Are you sure you're all right?' he asked.

Jenny swallowed hard. She knew what she had to do.

'About Fiona . . .' she began.

Fraser looked down at her. 'We'll say no more about that,' he said gently. 'Anna McLay didn't mean to upset you. It's just that she's beside herself with worry and she's convinced herself that Jess is Fiona's only hope. It's only natural. Your mum would have been just as worried about you. She would have tried anything to make you happy again.'

Jenny took a deep breath, thinking about her mother. Sheena Miles had been the kindest person in the world. She had always thought of everyone else before herself. She would never have refused to help Fiona. Jenny realised that, ever since she had seen Fiona and Jess together she had been working her way towards her decision. 'I was thinking, Dad,' she said. 'If Jess *is* able to help Fiona, I shouldn't stop him. It wouldn't be right. I passed Dunraven on the way back. Fiona came out when she heard Jess barking. I think Mrs McLay is right. I think Fiona really does need Jess.'

Fraser Miles looked seriously at his daughter. 'You mean you're willing to let him go?' he asked.

Jenny nodded. 'But only on condition that if he shows signs of wanting to come home then he should be allowed to.'

Fraser Miles was silent for a long moment, and then he put an arm round Jenny's shoulders. 'I know how hard this is for you, lass,' he said. 'And I'm proud of you. Your mum would be too.'

Jenny swallowed hard. 'It was thinking about Mum that finally made up my mind,' she said. 'And Jess seemed to know Fiona would want to see him. He ran into the yard at Dunraven.'

Fraser Miles shook his head. 'Nothing would surprise me about Jess,' he said, 'He's a very clever dog.'

Jenny nodded. Jess *was* clever. He was also loyal and brave. And Jenny would have to be even braver while Jess was at Dunraven. She was going to be very, very lonely without him, especially with Christmas just around the corner . . .

4

The next day was the day before Christmas Eve —
the day Jess was to go to Dunraven. Matt and Fraser
Miles had breakfasted before Mrs Grace arrived at
Thistle Cottage and had already left for Windy Hill.
Another batch of ewes needed to be brought in
from the fields for scanning.

Jenny heard the front door open as she popped
two slices of bread in the toaster. Mrs Grace came
into the kitchen, her cheeks flushed from the brisk

half-mile walk from Dunraven. Jess ran to meet her, his tail wagging.

'Dad and Matt have already gone,' Jenny told her. 'Matt promised to pop down and collect me later so that I can help with the sheep. They're hoping to finish today.'

Ellen Grace took off her thick jacket and sat down at the kitchen table while Jenny ate her toast and told her about the building progress at Windy Hill.

'It all sounds like it's coming along nicely,' Mrs Grace said, smiling. She put her hand on Jenny's arm. 'I'll take Jess up to Dunraven with me before lunch, Jenny, if that's OK,' she said.

Jenny nodded. 'I'll get his things ready. He'll feel better having his own basket and feeding bowl with him – and his blanket.'

Mrs Grace looked at her sympathetically. 'Are you sure about this, Jenny?'

Jenny nodded. 'If Jess can help Fiona it would be mean of me not to let him try.'

'You've got a good heart, just like your mother,' Ellen Grace told her. 'I'll bring you lots of news of him,' she added.

Jenny tried to smile but it wasn't a very successful

attempt. Jess trotted up to her and butted her knees with his nose.

'Have I got time to take him for one last walk?' Jenny asked.

Ellen Grace nodded. 'I want to ice the Christmas cake and make up a packed lunch for your father and Matt. You can take it up to Windy Hill when Matt comes to collect you. Give me an hour.'

Jenny watched as Mrs Grace unwrapped the Christmas cake from its tinfoil covering. 'This one won't be up to my usual standard,' she said. 'And I've been so busy, I forgot to get new decorations for it.'

Mrs Grace always made a Christmas cake at the beginning of November but this year it had been destroyed in the fire.

'It'll be yummy,' Jenny assured her. 'Carrie's mum is taking us into Greybridge tomorrow to do some last minute shopping, so I can get some new Christmas cake decorations.'

'That would be marvellous,' Mrs Grace smiled. 'Now, off you go. You and Jess don't have much time left together.'

Jenny nodded. An hour! That was all the time she had left with Jess.

'Come on, boy,' she called to him as she fastened her jacket and pulled on thick woollen gloves. 'Walk time!'

Jess barked excitedly and rushed out of the kitchen door as soon as Jenny opened it. She took a deep breath of the sharp, clean air. There was a stiff breeze blowing off the sea, driving scattered white clouds across the clear blue sky. Jenny looked farther across the water, to beyond Puffin Island. There were darker clouds massed out there. It looked as if there was snow to come.

Jess barked and Jenny whirled round. 'OK, I'm coming, Jess,' Jenny called.

The Border collie loped away from her, turning now and again to see if she was following. Jenny raced after him, taking in great lungfuls of the frosty air. Jess leaped and bounded beside her. In the distance, the sea sparkled in the sun. Jenny laughed as Jess launched himself at her, knocking her over. He licked her face, his tongue warm and rough on her cold cheeks.

'Oh, Jess,' Jenny said, putting her arms round him. 'I'm going to miss you so much.'

Jess darted off, barking at her to follow and Jenny shot to her feet. 'All right, Jess,' she called. 'We might

as well enjoy ourselves. It could be a while before we get to do this again.'

Jenny was so engrossed with Jess that she was late getting back to Thistle Cottage.

'Sorry, Mrs Grace,' she apologised, as she and Jess burst into the kitchen. 'Jess and I were having such a good time I forgot to look at my watch.'

Mrs Grace looked at Jenny's rosy cheeks and bright eyes. 'You two always have a good time together,' she said. 'I'm glad you had a nice walk.'

'It might be the last one for a while,' Jenny said, her eyes losing some of their brightness.

'I know,' Mrs Grace sympathised. 'I know...'

'It must be time to go,' Jenny said firmly, guessing what Mrs Grace was going to say next. She had made her decision and there was no turning back. 'I'll get Jess's things.'

Ellen Grace was late and in a hurry, which made packing up Jess's belongings easier for Jenny as she didn't have much time. The hardest part was folding up Jess's old blue blanket and tucking it into his basket. This was the blanket Jenny had wrapped the tiny puppy in when she had brought him into the kitchen at Windy Hill to get warm after his mother rejected him. At that time Jenny had still thought her father meant to put him down because he was small and deformed and wouldn't make a working dog. She had taken Jess up to Darktarn, still wrapped in this blanket. Jenny held it to her cheek for a moment, feeling its familiar softness before she put it into the basket and walked out of the cottage.

'I'll take the car for a change,' Mrs Grace said. 'It'll be easier than carrying all of Jess's stuff.'

Jenny put Jess's basket, packed with everything he would need, in the boot of Mrs Grace's car. Jess trotted behind her, anxious to see where all his things were going. He knew that his basket, blanket and bowl belonged in the kitchen at Thistle Cottage.

'It's all right, Jess,' Jenny said. 'You'll have them back when you get to Dunraven.'

Jess whined and put a paw on her knee. Jenny ruffled the fur at his neck. Then she opened the rear door of the car. 'Up, Jess,' she said. 'In you get.' Jess looked at her, puzzled. 'Up, Jess!' Jenny said again, her voice breaking a little.

Jess heard the note of distress in her voice and stood his ground, refusing to get into the car. Instead, he moved slowly towards her and laid his head against her leg. Jenny bent down and put her arms round his neck. 'You've got to go, Jess,' she whispered. 'I'll miss you and I know you'll miss me, but Fiona needs you.'

Jess licked her cheek and allowed himself to be led towards the car door. Jenny gave him a gentle push and he hopped up on the back seat.

'That was very bravely done, Jenny,' Mrs Grace said as she settled herself behind the wheel of the car.

Jenny smiled a little mistily. 'I don't feel very brave,' she confessed.

Mrs Grace gave her a reassuring smile. 'Don't worry about Jess,' she said. 'He'll be well looked after, I'll make sure of that.'

Jenny nodded. 'I'm not worried about that,' she said. 'It's just that this is the first time we've ever been separated.'

Mrs Grace smiled sympathetically. 'You're making a big sacrifice. I'm sure Anna McLay will hugely appreciate your help, and Jess will get extra-special care,' she said softly.

Jenny gave Jess a final kiss on the nose, then she closed the car door and stepped back. Jess jumped up and looked out of the back window as the car pulled out of the yard. Jenny stood there for a long time, looking at the empty track.

Eventually, she turned and went back into the cottage. There was nothing there for her now – no furry companion waiting to play or needing to be fed or walked. Now that Jess had gone, the cottage had lost its last bit of homeliness. It felt strange and empty without him.

Jenny spent the rest of the morning wrapping her Christmas presents. She had bought a thick woolly scarf for her father. Matt was getting a set of colourful cardboard folders to keep his college course notes in and she had bought Matt's girlfriend, Vicky, a CD single she wanted. For Carrie she had got a bright green ski hat just in case Ian *did* teach them to ski when he got back from Canada, and for Ian she had decided to keep a diary of everything that happened while he was away. She would have liked to include photographs but she had lost her camera in the fire. Jenny had found a little silver brooch in a second-hand shop in Greybridge for Mrs Grace. It had been badly tarnished but Jenny had spent a long time cleaning it and now it looked as good as new. Jess's present was the most difficult of all. Jenny hadn't yet found exactly what she wanted and she was hoping she would see the perfect gift on her shopping trip with Carrie.

She looked round the cottage as she worked. Where were they going to put the presents? Fraser Miles and Ellen hadn't had time to think of getting a Christmas tree – but in any case all the tree decorations had been stored in the attic at Windy Hill and had gone up in flames. Jenny sighed. Christmas without a Christmas tree. It just wasn't the same.

Jenny had just finished wrapping her last parcel

when Matt arrived to take her to Windy Hill.

'Ready?' he asked, looking round. 'Has Jess gone already?'

Jenny nodded and Matt ruffled her hair, 'I know you'll miss him, Jen,' he said sympathetically.

Jenny's head came up. 'Maybe I can't have Jess for a while,' she said, 'but I *can* help out with the scanning – so let's go!'

'Good for you,' Matt said, smiling. 'And you can visit Jess whenever you like.'

But Jenny wasn't sure about that. Maybe Fiona wouldn't want her to visit.

The telephone rang that afternoon just as Jenny, Matt and her father got back to the cottage.

'Tim did really well,' Fraser Miles said, walking towards the phone. 'He must have scanned that final batch at an average of eighty an hour.'

'Now all we have to do is get enough feedstuff into the fields before the snow comes,' Matt said.

Jenny smiled at him. 'All?' she said.

'Nobody ever said sheep farming was easy,' Matt joked.

Fraser Miles held the receiver out to Jenny. 'It's Anna McLay,' he said.

'I just had to ring and say how much I appreciate what you've done, Jenny,' Fiona's mother said. 'You've no idea the difference it has made to Fiona already.'

'How is Jess?' Jenny asked.

Anna McLay laughed. 'Oh, he's fine,' she said. 'He seems to have settled in very happily.'

Jenny was silent for a moment. 'So soon?' she said at last.

'He seems to understand that Fiona needs him,' Anna McLay said gently. 'He's a wonderful dog, Jenny.'

'I know,' Jenny said quietly and then, with an effort. 'I'm glad he's helping.' She hesitated. 'Do you think I could come and visit tomorrow, Mrs McLay?'

Anna McLay was silent for a moment. 'I don't know if Fiona is quite ready to see anyone yet, Jenny,' she said.

Jenny swallowed her disappointment. Even one day without seeing Jess seemed a very long time.

Anna McLay was speaking again. 'But I'm sure you could come on Christmas Day – after all, Jess is your dog and Christmas Day is special. I'll warn Fiona and if she doesn't feel up to visitors she can make herself scarce for a while. What do you think?'

'Yes, thanks, Mrs McLay, and happy Christmas.' Jenny tried to sound cheerful.

'And I hope you have a very happy Christmas, Jenny,' Anna McLay replied. 'By the way, Ellen is on her way back and she's bringing a surprise with her. I hope you'll like it.'

'Thanks, Mrs McLay,' Jenny said as she rang off.

So Jess wasn't missing her at all, she thought. She ought to be happy about that but somehow she wasn't.

She was still thinking about Jess when Mrs Grace arrived back. 'Give me a hand with this, Jenny,' she called from the yard.

Jenny went over to the door and opened it. Mrs Grace was heaving something out of the boot of the car.

'A Christmas tree!' Jenny cried excitedly. 'I was wondering where we were going to put the presents.'

'It's just a small one,' Mrs Grace said. 'But then Thistle Cottage is just a small cottage so that's all right.'

'Where did you get it?' asked Jenny.

'From Anna McLay,' Mrs Grace told Jenny. 'She noticed that we didn't have one when she was here yesterday and, when I told her about the tree decorations, she decided that the least she could do was replace them. So now we have a tree and a box of brand-new tree decorations. The cottage is going to be quite festive after all.'

Jenny took an end of the tree and helped Mrs Grace to carry it into the house. Then she went back for the box of tree decorations.

'These are wonderful!' she said, as she opened the box and held up a handful of bright, glittering baubles. Lengths of tinsel followed and a string of tiny white lights. The scent of resin filled the air. Jenny sniffed. 'It smells like Christmas,' she said, her spirits lifting.

Mrs Grace looked at Jenny's gaily-wrapped pile of Christmas presents on the coffee table. 'You've been busy,' she said. 'It *looks* like Christmas too.'

Jenny laughed. Perhaps it wasn't going to be such a sad and lonely Christmas after all. But it would certainly be a strange one without Jess to share it.

5

Jenny jumped out of bed next morning and raced to the window. It was Christmas Eve. She peered out. The sky was heavy with snow clouds but so far it wasn't snowing. Jenny dressed hurriedly and rushed into the kitchen. Mrs Grace had already arrived and was washing up some plates and cups.

'Have Dad and Matt gone out yet?' Jenny asked her.

Ellen Grace nodded. 'They went out early – but

not before I made them a good breakfast. It looks as if we might get snow today.'

Jenny poured herself a glass of orange juice and looked out of the window. 'I hope we don't get cut off,' she said.

'I thought you loved snow,' Mrs Grace said, surprised.

'Not if it means I can't go and see Jess,' she replied. 'Mrs McLay says I can go up to Dunraven tomorrow. How is he, Mrs Grace? Did you see him this morning?'

Ellen Grace dried her hands and reached into her bag. She drew out an envelope and set it down on the table before Jenny. 'This is for you,' she said. 'And don't worry about Jess. He's as bright as a button. He and I had a quick game of tug-of-war with his blanket before I left.'

Jenny laughed. 'Oh, he loves doing that,' she said. 'I wish I'd been there.' She opened the envelope. Inside was a Christmas card – from Fiona. The writing was a little shaky. *Thank you for letting me have Jess*, it said. *I'll look after him, I promise. Merry Christmas, Fiona.*

'I wonder if Fiona plays tug-of-war with him,' Jenny said, suddenly. 'I miss him such a lot.'

Mrs Grace looked at her sympathetically. 'You'll see him tomorrow,' she said. 'And you'll have a nice time out with Carrie today.'

'I'm looking forward to that,' Jenny agreed. 'I feel like haven't seen Carrie for ages. The Turners have been taking their Australian visitors all round the countryside.' She put her head on one side. 'But seeing Jess is different,' she said. 'That's going to be my very best Christmas present.'

Ellen Grace looked at her and laughed. 'You know, with your head tilted like that, you look a lot like Jess.'

Jenny laughed too. 'Now that's what I call a compliment,' she said.

Pam Turner dropped the girls off in Greybridge's busy High Street while she went to find a parking place. The town was bustling with Christmas shoppers. 'We'll meet outside Aston's at two o'clock,' she said.

Carrie nodded, dancing with impatience. 'I've got all my Christmas presents to get,' she wailed as her mother drove off.

'All of them?' exclaimed Jenny, as they made their way through the crowds.

Carrie nodded, her red hair bobbing. 'I just haven't

had time to buy any. We've been driving all over the place. What on earth am I going to get for Mum? And Dad? I can't buy him any more aftershave. He's still got the stuff I bought him last Christmas.'

Jenny took Carrie's arm and dragged her into Aston's. It was the only department store in Greybridge. 'If you can't find it here, Greybridge doesn't have it,' she read as they passed through the swing doors.

'How do you know?' Carrie asked.

Jenny pointed to the sign on the door. 'It says so,' she said. 'Come on!'

While they went round the shop looking for gifts, Jenny told Carrie all about Jess going to Dunraven.

'But that's awful,' Carrie declared. 'Trust Fiona. It's just typical.'

'You know, Carrie, I think she really does like Jess a lot,' Jenny replied.

Carrie snorted but when Jenny told her how she had seen Fiona and Jess together and about the Christmas card her expression became more thoughtful. 'Maybe she has changed after all,' she said. 'She certainly sounds really sick. Imagine feeling that bad at Christmas.'

'Hello, Jenny,' a voice said behind them.

Jenny turned round. It was Marion Stewart. She smiled at Jenny. 'I see you're doing some last minute Christmas shopping too,' she went on. 'You can't have had much time for shopping recently.'

'Hello, Miss Stewart,' Jenny said. 'I'm looking for an extra-special present for Jess.'

'Oh, your dog,' she said. 'He's a sweetie, isn't he?'

Jenny looked curiously at Marion Stewart. She hadn't seemed very fond of Jess when she had met him. Now she was looking around, as if she was searching for someone.

'Did your father bring you into Greybridge?' she asked brightly.

'No,' Jenny replied. 'Carrie's mum did.'

Marion Stewart's face fell. 'Oh, well, then. I must get on,' she said. 'Merry Christmas – and tell your father I'll be in touch.'

'I bet she will,' said Carrie, as Marion Stewart walked away. 'I tell you, Jenny, she's after him.'

Jenny frowned. 'Dad wouldn't be interested in her,' she declared. 'He still misses Mum too much.'

'Whatever you say,' Carrie declared. 'Now I saw some great pottery jugs in the china department. One of those would be perfect for Mum's paint-brushes. Come on, it's this way.' Carrie began to wriggle through the crowds of Christmas shoppers.

Jenny followed her. The shop was so busy that the aisles were crammed with people. The Christmas decorations glittered in the bright shop lights and there were Christmas carols playing over the loudspeakers. Jenny hummed along. 'While shepherds watched their flocks by night,' she said. 'That's my favourite Christmas carol.'

'Why doesn't that surprise me?' Carrie asked, looking innocent.

Jenny laughed. 'Come on,' she said. 'Let's get your jug, then I want to look for something special to take to Jess tomorrow – and I've got to get decorations for the Christmas cake.'

By the time they met Mrs Turner, Carrie was laden with plastic bags and Jenny had found a toy rubber bone with bells inside it for Jess. It was red and green and was called a Jingle Bells Bone. Jenny thought it looked really Christmassy. They squashed themselves and their parcels into the back of Pam Turner's Mini.

'I got a book about the Border reivers for Dad,' Carrie told her mother. 'Do you think he'll like it?'

Mrs Turner looked at her and smiled. 'I'm

sure he will,' she said. 'Did you remember to get wrapping-paper?'

Carrie's hand flew to her mouth. 'Oh, no, I forgot!'

'Just as well I bought plenty them,' Mrs Turner said, laughing. 'Time to go home. I'm exhausted!'

As they were passing the main entrance to Dunraven, Jenny leaned over and tapped Mrs Turner on the shoulder. 'If you let me off here, I can run down the track,' she said.

Pam Turner frowned at the sky. 'It looks as if it's going to snow. Will you be all right?' she asked.

Jenny nodded. 'I go that way all the time,' she said. 'It only takes ten minutes and it isn't dark.'

'Oh, all right then,' Mrs Turner said. 'Merry Christmas, Jenny.'

'Merry Christmas, Jenny,' Carrie said, giving her friend a huge grin.

Jenny clambered out of the car and waved as it disappeared along the Cliffbay road. Merry Christmas, she thought. Would it be a merry Christmas without Jess?

As she turned to walk down the track to the cottage she had an idea. Why couldn't she just take a quick detour to Dunraven and look through the window? It would only take a moment and she might see Jess.

Jenny retraced her steps and pushed open the gate to the farmyard. There was a huge Christmas tree in the corner, its lights already twinkling cosily, although it wasn't yet dark.

Jenny crept across the yard, her eyes on the window. The tree was set slightly back so that she could see inside the living-room. A fire burned brightly in the grate and Fiona was sitting on the hearth-rug with a book in her lap. Her cheeks were faintly flushed from the heat of the fire. But she wasn't reading. There was a smile on her lips and she seemed to be speaking softly to someone. Jenny edged closer still and caught her breath. Jess was lying curled up on the rug beside Fiona, looking up at her. Then Fiona turned back to her book and began reading.

Jenny moved even closer. The Border collie's ears pricked and he looked towards the window. Then, seeing Jenny there, he rose and quietly trotted over. Jenny's eyes pricked with tears as she looked at him through the glass. For a long moment Jess just stayed there, his eyes fixed on hers. He put his head to one side and laid it against the window. Jenny stretched out a hand, then drew it back quickly and stood out of view as she heard a faint voice from inside the room. Fiona was calling to Jess. In a moment she would come to see what he was doing.

Jess gave Jenny one last long look then turned and ran back to Fiona. Jenny caught a quick glimpse of the girl's face as she smiled at the Border collie. There was no doubt about it, Fiona really did love Jess.

Stumbling a little, Jenny turned and slipped quickly back through the gate and on to the track to Thistle Cottage. She had seen Jess, but it hadn't made her as happy as she thought it would. He looked so at home with Fiona. A horrible thought crept into Jenny's mind. Would Jess want to come back to her?

Tears welled up in Jenny's eyes and she dashed them away – but her vision was still blurred. She looked up. Great fat flakes of snow drifted down, blotting out the sky, whirling around her, settling on her hair. The snow had come at last – and it was heavy. Jenny peered at the darkening sky. The snow grew thicker, covering the track, muffling her footsteps, wiping out her footprints as soon as she had made them. Jenny huddled into her jacket and quickened her pace.

★ ★ ★

Jenny was busying herself decorating the Christmas cake, trying to take her mind off her worries about Jess. She had made a whole scene with skaters and sledges and fir trees. There were even two reindeer and a Father Christmas. It was well after five o'clock before Fraser and Matt returned. A blast of icy air swept though the cottage as the front door opened and they came in, shaking the snow from their heavy jackets. Jenny jumped up and ran to her father.

'Oh, Dad, I'm so glad you didn't get stuck in the snow!' she exclaimed. 'Is it still as bad?'

Fraser Miles pulled off his tweed cap and looked at it. The top was encrusted with snow. 'It doesn't look like stopping for a long time yet, lass,' he said. 'We almost went into the ditch on the track up to the top field at Windy Hill. There's talk of a blizzard on the radio.'

'What about the sheep?' Jenny asked. 'Will they be all right?'

'There isn't anything we can do about them at the moment, Jen,' Matt said, collapsing into an armchair. 'The snow is blowing and piling up under the walls and hedges. We managed to get a fair number down on to lower ground. Let's hope that the snow doesn't get too much worse. We'll try to get up there first thing in the morning. There are bound to be a few ewes needing to be dug out.'

Fraser Miles took off his heavy boots and came to sit by the fire. He looked tired.

'Give me ten minutes and I'll have your meals on the table,' Mrs Grace said. 'It's almost ready. Steak casserole and an apple pie to follow.'

'That sounds great, Ellen,' Matt said, as the housekeeper got up to leave the room. 'We've had a hectic afternoon.'

Jenny looked at her father as he sat slumped in his chair. He had closed his eyes for a moment. He must be exhausted, Jenny thought. She went and sat on the rug at her father's feet. He opened his eyes and rested a hand on her hair.

'Dad,' she said, 'will we be snowed in?'

'If this snow keeps up we might well be,' Fraser Miles said. 'And the work on Windy Hill might be held up until well after Christmas, if this weather continues.'

Jenny sighed. She hadn't thought about that. But it was Jess that was worrying her. If they were cut off she wouldn't be able to go and see Jess tomorrow.

'What do you think, Matt?' Fraser asked.

Matt shook his head. 'You saw the Dunraven track, Dad,' he said. 'If the snow keeps up all night I don't think anything could get through there – not until the snow stops at any rate. It might be as well if Ellen spent the night here.'

'She can have my room,' Fraser said. 'I'll sleep in here with you, Matt.'

'Indeed you won't,' Mrs Grace said, as she came through the door. 'I can sleep on the floor in Jenny's room, if need be.'

'I'll sleep on the floor and you can have my bed, Mrs Grace,' Jenny put in. 'It would be a shame if you got stuck at Dunraven on Christmas Day.'

Ellen Grace smiled. 'We'll work all that out later,' she said. 'Now, who's hungry?'

Fraser and Matt rose at once but Jenny followed them more slowly into the kitchen. Her Christmas Day visit to Jess was looking less and less likely.

Jenny rushed to her bedroom window on Christmas morning. She had slept on a makeshift mattress of cushions and blankets and Mrs Grace had used her bed. The housekeeper was up already. Jenny pulled back the curtains and gasped. The snow must have fallen all night. It lay, white and glistening, right up to the cottage door. The fields around were deep in snow and the track had disappeared. But at least it had stopped and that meant there was still a chance that Jenny could get up to Dunraven to see Jess. Jenny pulled on her dressing-gown and made for the kitchen.

As she opened the kitchen door, Ellen Grace turned to her. The housekeeper was stuffing the turkey. A great heap of potatoes and carrots and broccoli lay on the draining-board, ready to be prepared.

'Merry Christmas!' Ellen Grace called. She had the radio on and a church choir was singing Christmas carols.

'Merry Christmas, Mrs Grace!' Jenny replied, going to look out of the window. 'Oh no, it's started to snow again,' she said.

'Well, we're off,' Matt called, as he and his father looked into the kitchen.

They were both dressed in thick jackets and tweed caps with flaps pulled down over their ears.

'We wouldn't win a fashion contest but we're dressed for the weather,' Fraser Miles joked. 'Merry Christmas, lass.'

Jenny went to hug her father and Matt. 'Don't

get stuck in the snow,' she warned them. 'Not on Christmas Day!'

'We wouldn't dare miss Ellen's Christmas lunch,' Matt said with mock seriousness.

'I should think not,' Ellen Grace smiled. 'One o'clock on the dot,' she said putting the turkey into the oven.

Jenny watched through the window as her father called to the dogs and he and Matt got into the jeep. The wheels spun for a moment, then caught and they were off, chugging up the track. Jenny and Mrs Grace waved, watching anxiously as the vehicle negotiated the narrow track.

Jenny smiled. If the jeep could make it then she would get to see Jess later. She turned to Mrs Grace. 'Well, it's definitely a white Christmas,' she said.

Ellen Grace put an arm round her shoulders. 'The best kind,' she said. 'Now, breakfast for you and then we've got a lunch to prepare.'

As the morning wore on, Jenny got more and more worried. The snow kept falling, blotting out the landscape and piling up against the cottage walls. Jenny kept an anxious eye on the track that was slowly disappearing.

When the phone rang, Ellen Grace went to answer it and Jenny followed her into the hall.

'It's Ian,' Mrs Grace said, smiling. 'They've just got up in Canada. I'll have a few words with him, then I'll put you on, Jenny.'

Jenny brightened up. Ian! He would understand how she felt about Jess. Jenny took the receiver eagerly when Mrs Grace had finished her chat with her nephew.

'Ian,' she cried. 'How are you? Happy Christmas!' When Jenny heard her friend's familiar voice, she couldn't help telling him what was weighing so heavily on her mind. 'Jess has gone to Dunraven to help Fiona get better, so I haven't even seen him today and I'm supposed to be going up there this afternoon but it looks as if we might get snowed in—'

She heard a gasp on the other end of the line. 'What?' said Ian. 'Jess is up at Dunraven – and with Fiona? After all that she's done?'

Jenny explained to Ian about just how ill Fiona had become and the doctor's words of warning and Anna McLay coming to Thistle Cottage to ask her if she would let Jess stay at Dunraven for a while. Ian immediately understood the huge sacrifice

Jenny had made and by the time she put the phone down his sympathetic words had made her feel a lot better.

'You look more cheerful,' Mrs Grace said, as Jenny wandered into the kitchen.

'I feel more cheerful,' Jenny announced. 'Would you like me to lay the table?'

'That would be a help,' Mrs Grace replied. 'There's a freshly ironed tablecloth in the sideboard drawer. And don't forget the crackers and the candles.'

'I won't,' said Jenny brightly, taking a pile of blue and white plates from the kitchen shelf. 'At least we have some of our own things,' she said, looking at the plates that used to stand on the dresser in the kitchen at Windy Hill.

'Yes, I'm glad we managed to salvage those,' Mrs Grace agreed.

Jenny pulled out the drop-leaf table in the living-room and spread the snowy-white tablecloth over it. Then she set to work. Even though they couldn't be at Windy Hill, she was determined to make this Christmas special.

Ten minutes later, Jenny stood back and admired her handiwork. Every plate was carefully aligned, the cutlery sparkled and the glasses shone. Jenny laid a Christmas cracker beside each side plate, then she put a bowl of holly and ivy in the centre of the table between the two tall candles.

Just as the twelve-thirty news came on the radio, the door opened and Matt and Fraser Miles came in, looking like abominable snowmen, and letting in a draught of icy air.

'Something smells good,' Fraser remarked, as he slowly removed his wet coat and hat.

'There are plenty of things that smell good,' corrected his son, grinning. 'I suppose you're going to make us go and get all cleaned up before Christmas lunch, Ellen.'

The housekeeper put her hands on her hips and looked at him severely. 'Indeed I am,' she agreed. 'You're *covered* in snow.'

Matt grinned again and clumped off to get tidied up. Jenny turned to her father.

'How are the sheep, Dad?' she asked.

Fraser Miles ran a hand through his hair. 'We had to dig a few out of drifts but we don't seem to have lost any yet, thank goodness. Getting down the track to the cottage was very difficult. I don't think I'd like to try it again until the snow eases.'

'But that means I won't be able to go and see Jess today!' Jenny exclaimed.

Fraser Miles shook his head. 'I think you're going to have to wait until tomorrow, lass.'

Jenny turned away and looked out of the window at the still falling snow. A lump rose in her throat. She was beginning to regret that she'd ever agreed to let Fiona McLay have Jess.

Half an hour later, they sat down to Christmas lunch. Fraser Miles had lit the candles and now they glowed softly. They had a steaming tureen of homemade Scotch broth to start and then Jenny helped Mrs Grace carry in the main course.

'Wow!' said Matt, looking at the laden table as Jenny set down the big dish of vegetables. 'You really have pulled out all the stops, Ellen.'

The turkey took pride of place. Ellen Grace had set it out on a platter in the centre of the table. There were roast and boiled potatoes, sage and onion stuffing, chipolata sausages, bread sauce, a big bowl of broccoli and carrots and a dish of redcurrant jelly.

'There's Christmas pudding and brandy butter to follow,' Ellen told him. 'Then, if you're still hungry, there are mince pies and Christmas cake.'

Fraser laughed. 'After all that, Ellen, I don't think I'll ever be hungry again.'

Jenny looked round the room. It wasn't home and Jess wasn't here but the little living-room looked cosy and festive. The fire burned brightly in the grate and the lights on the Christmas tree twinkled, glancing off the coloured baubles.

'Let's pull the crackers,' she said, picking up the red and gold cracker from her plate.

Fraser Miles reached across and took the other end of Jenny's cracker. 'Maybe there'll be a lucky

charm in this one,' he said as the cracker popped.

Jenny sorted through the little pile of goodies and unfolded a bright yellow paper hat. She put it on, then exclaimed as she saw what had fallen out of the cracker.

'Oh, look, a horseshoe!' she said, handing it to her father.

Fraser Miles smiled. 'Now that's what I call a good omen,' he said.

Jenny smiled back. She hoped he was right.

Jenny sat back at the end of the meal. 'I'm so full I'll probably never move again,' she announced. 'That was wonderful, Mrs Grace,'

Ellen Grace smiled, pleased. 'We've still got our presents to open,' she reminded Jenny. She turned to Fraser and Matt. 'Jenny insisted on leaving them until you and Matt got home.'

Fraser Miles smiled. 'That was thoughtful of you, lass,' he said. 'Let's open them now, then.'

Jenny got to her feet and knelt down beside the Christmas tree.

'I feel like Father Christmas,' she said, as she picked up the presents one by one and handed them out.

'This one is for you from Matt, Mrs Grace,' she

said, looking at the label. 'And this is for you, Dad, from Mrs Grace.'

Jenny distributed the presents and watched with pleasure as the others opened their gifts from her. Then she looked at her own pile. 'This is so exciting,' she said, unwrapping the first. 'Oh, wow, a camera! Thanks, Dad!'

'There's a film in it already,' her father told her, smiling. 'So you can take some pictures today.'

Jenny smiled and raised the camera, getting all of them into the frame. 'Smile!' she said, pressing the button.

As well as the camera there was a personal stereo from Matt and tapes from Mrs Grace. Vicky had sent a box of scented soaps to her via Matt and Ian had left a gift for his aunt to give her – a book about Border collies with lots of colour photographs. Mrs Grace opened a prettily wrapped gift and exclaimed in pleasure, 'Why, isn't that thoughtful? Look what Fiona has given me.'

Jenny looked at the gift Mrs Grace was holding up. It was a patchwork knitting-bag with pockets for wool and needles. Mrs Grace held it out admiringly. 'Of course, Fiona hasn't managed to get out to the shops so she must have decided to make her Christmas presents. Isn't this pretty?'

Jenny fingered the bag. There were patches of every colour and pattern, all jumbled together, but somehow the pattern worked. 'It's great,' she agreed. 'I didn't know Fiona was good at that kind of thing.'

Fiona had put a lot of work into her present for Mrs Grace, but seeing the bag had made Jenny think of Jess again.

She went to the window. 'It's still snowing,' she said, sighing.

Fraser Miles looked at his daughter. 'I don't think you'll get up to Dunraven today, lass,' he said.

Jenny gazed out at the swirling snowflakes. Jess was only ten minutes' walk away but with the snow falling this heavily, it might as well be miles.

As they sat dozing around the fire, dusk began to fall and the snow continued. Jenny looked at the darkening windows still thinking of Jess. She closed her eyes. If she couldn't have Jess with her on Christmas Day at least she could dream about him. She heard Jess barking. Jenny snuggled deeper into her armchair. But the barking got louder and Jenny shook herself awake. It wasn't a dream. It was real. That really *was* Jess. He was outside in the snow, barking to get in.

6

Jenny jumped up from her chair and rushed to the front door, throwing it open so quickly that it rocked on its hinges.

'Jess!' she yelled.

Behind her she could hear the others, roused from sleep, asking what was going on, but she paid no attention. All her attention was on Jess. Covered in snow, the Border collie hurled himself at her, knocking her over with his enthusiastic greeting,

223

soaking her with his wet coat, licking her face and barking excitedly. Jenny laughed and hugged him tightly, not wanting to let him go ever again.

'Oh, Jess!' she breathed. 'Jess, what on earth are you doing here?'

Jess looked up at her, his eyes adoring, his tail wagging. Jenny laughed again and hugged him tighter.

'Well, well, look who it is,' Mrs Grace cried.

'Not even a blizzard could keep him away from you, Jenny,' Fraser Miles said, bending to give Jess a pat. 'Come on, let's get him dried off.'

Matt laughed. 'He certainly is one determined dog,' he said. 'I'll go and get a towel.'

Mrs Grace shivered and stepped across Jenny and Jess to shut the front door. Snow blew in as she closed it. 'There,' she said. 'Now I think we'd better ring the McLays. They must be wondering what's happened to Jess. They would never have let him out in this weather.'

But just as Mrs Grace was reaching for the telephone, it rang.

'It's Anna McLay,' she announced after listening for a moment. 'Yes,' she said into the receiver, 'Jess is here with Jenny. Why don't you have a word with her?'

Mrs Grace handed the phone to Jenny. 'Anna was worried about Jess,' she explained.

'I'm so glad he's safe,' Mrs McLay said agitatedly when Jenny took the receiver. 'I was so worried when I discovered he had gone. Is he all right?'

'He's perfectly fine,' Jenny reassured Mrs McLay. She looked at Jess. Matt was rubbing him dry with a towel. 'He was so covered in snow that he looked more white than black, but Matt is drying him off now and he'll soon get warm. But we can't understand how he got here. What happened?'

Anna laughed with relief. 'Well, Jenny,' she said. 'Fiona ate a full meal for the first time since the fire. She started to fall asleep afterwards, so I suggested that she should go to bed. Anyway, a little while after Fiona had gone up to her room I felt a draught coming from the kitchen and went to investigate. The door was open and Jess had disappeared. I guessed he might have tried to get back to you, Jenny, but I was worried in case he wouldn't be able to find his way to Thistle Cottage in the thick snow.' Mrs McLay laughed, 'I should have known better.' Then she continued, 'Calum is going to clear the track with the tractor so that Ellen can get back to Dunraven tonight.'

Jenny hesitated, her heart sinking. 'Do you want us to bring Jess back straight away?'

'Not at all,' Anna McLay told her. 'Fiona is still asleep and it would be unkind to bring Jess back just as soon as he's arrived at Thistle Cottage. He must have made such an effort to get there. But I wonder if you would mind bringing him back later this evening? I know Fiona will want to see him when she wakes up.'

Jenny looked at Jess fondly. He would have to go back to Dunraven but not just yet. 'I'll get Dad to bring us up when he takes Mrs Grace back after tea,' she agreed. 'That means Jess and I will have a little time together.'

'Whenever you like, Jenny,' Anna McLay told her. 'I think Jess only waited to see that Fiona was all right before going to find you. He obviously missed you, though he was so good with Fiona I would never have guessed. I can't thank you enough for lending Jess to her.'

Jenny looked at Jess. Matt had finished drying him and the collie came at once to her side. She reached down a hand and stroked his head. 'I'm glad Fiona is so much better,' she said gently to Mrs McLay. 'You must be pleased.'

Anna McLay sighed. 'I'm more exhausted than anything else,' she admitted. 'Fiona has been such a worry to me lately but it looks as if she's getting better at last, thanks to Jess. I'm going to put my feet up and have a snooze now that I know she's sleeping peacefully.'

'That sounds like a good idea,' Jenny said. 'Enjoy your rest.'

'I will,' Mrs McLay promised. 'And I'm glad Jess is with you on Christmas Day, Jenny.'

Jenny smiled. 'It's the best Christmas present I could have,' she declared. 'Merry Christmas, Mrs McLay.'

Jenny put down the phone. Jess was looking up at her, his tail wagging furiously. 'Come on, Jess,' she said. 'I've got a Christmas present for you.'

Jess barked back a greeting and wagged his tail even harder, keeping close to Jenny's side.

'He really has missed you, hasn't he?' Matt remarked, looking at Jess.

Jenny's face lit up. 'I thought he wasn't missing me at all, Matt,' she said. 'Mrs McLay told me he had settled in so well that I thought maybe he'd forgotten about me.'

Matt snorted. 'That'll be the day,' he scoffed.

Jenny led Jess towards the fire and sat down with him in front of the blazing logs. She unwrapped his toy bone and laid it down in front of him. Jess picked it up in his mouth and rolled it over. He looked surprised as the bell inside jingled. Jenny laughed.

'Try it again, Jess,' she said.

Jenny watched happily as Jess played with his new toy.

Fraser Miles looked at the Border collie and smiled. 'He's certainly determined,' he said to his daughter and pointing at Jess. 'That's a dog that doesn't give up. Believe me, that's important in a sheepdog.'

Jenny looked at Jess proudly. He couldn't ever be a working dog himself but her father had once said that his pups would be working dogs – and good ones too!

'Oh, I believe you,' Jenny said, hugging Jess. 'And Jess does too, don't you, boy?'

Jess gave a short bark and snuggled closer to her. Jenny laughed softly. It had turned out to be a wonderful Christmas Day after all. She looked round the little sitting-room. The log fire burned brightly in the hearth, the Christmas tree lights

THE SACRIFICE

twinkled, reflecting in the glass baubles and decorations, and discarded wrapping-paper from their presents made bright splashes of colour. Mrs Grace had put on a tape of Christmas carols, which was playing softly in the background. Matt and Fraser Miles were once again dozing in their chairs.

'Shall I start on the washing-up?' Jenny asked Mrs Grace.

Ellen Grace yawned. 'Later, Jenny,' she said. 'Relax for a bit. Enjoy your time with Jess. I'm going to have a nap.'

Jenny played quietly with Jess as the others dozed. She couldn't imagine a better Christmas afternoon – here with Jess in front of a roaring fire, just the two of them awake. When the phone rang she got up reluctantly and went to answer it. It was Anna McLay again.

'Jenny?' Mrs McLay said, her voice shaking. 'Is Fiona with you? She's disappeared. We can't find her anywhere.'

Jenny gasped. Mrs McLay sounded almost hysterical with fear and worry. 'No, she isn't here,' Jenny replied. 'Why should she be? What's happened?'

'I thought maybe she had gone after Jess.' Anna

McLay said. She sounded close to tears.

'No, Mrs McLay,' Jenny answered. 'She hasn't come here. Did she know Jess was here?'

Anna McLay's voice broke. 'No. I mean, I assumed that she was still asleep and so hadn't been up to tell her where Jess was,' she said. 'But she must have woken up and guessed where Jess had gone and tried to come after him.'

'Mrs McLay,' Jenny said as calmly as she could, 'tell me exactly what's happened.'

Anna McLay took a deep breath. 'After I called you, I dozed off. The others were already asleep,' she began. 'Then, when I woke up, I went upstairs to check on Fiona. She wasn't there and then I looked downstairs and found that her boots and coat were gone from the entrance hall. She must have woken up before the rest of us, discovered Jess was missing and started out after him. I'm frightened, Jenny. Fiona has been so ill. She's still weak. Look at the weather! How long can she survive in that if she gets lost?'

Jenny looked out of the window. Snow swirled against it. 'It's snowing again,' she said.

Mrs McLay's voice cracked. 'It's getting worse all the time. She must be out there somewhere,' she said. 'Out in the snow and the cold. She could be anywhere. We've got to find her, Jenny. We've just got to!'

'We will, Mrs McLay,' Jenny promised. 'Just hang on while I get Dad.'

As Jenny went to wake her father, Jess came to her side, sensing her worry and she laid a hand on his head. The collie licked her hand and Jess rubbed his ears. Despite everything Jess had done for Fiona already, he couldn't help her at the moment. Thinking of Anna McLay, Jenny felt a shiver of fear. She had promised that they would find Fiona – but would they? Would they be able to find her in the blizzard that was raging outside?

7

Fraser Miles got to his feet at once when he opened his eyes and saw Jenny's distraught face. 'What's the matter?' he demanded.

'Fiona is missing,' Jenny explained quickly. 'Her mother is on the phone. Can you talk to her, Dad?'

Fraser brushed past Jenny and swiftly lifted the receiver. Jess was still at Jenny's side. She put a hand down and felt him lick her hand but her eyes were still on her father, speaking urgently into the phone.

'Jen?' Matt said enquiringly. 'What's going on?'

Jenny turned to Matt and Mrs Grace and recounted everything that Anna McLay had told her. Ellen Grace and Matt listened quietly, only occasionally putting a question to her here and there. Their faces grew more and more serious as her story unfolded.

'I wonder if they've called the police,' Jenny said, when she had finished telling them all she knew.

Fraser put down the phone, nodding. 'Anna is phoning the police now but I don't think we can wait for them,' he said. 'Dunraven is only half a mile up the road. The police would have to come all the way from Greybridge – and just look at the weather! It would take them ages to get here. We've got to start searching ourselves.'

'Dad is right, Jenny,' Matt put in. 'And it's Christmas Night. There will only be an emergency officer on duty at Greybridge.'

'I'll help, and Jess will too,' Jenny said immediately.

Fraser Miles smiled. 'We'll all do everything we can. We'll start out straight away.'

Mrs Grace nodded and began to move towards the door. 'I'll get the coats and boots,' she said. 'Matt, you look for the strongest torches we've got, and

Jenny run round and switch on every light in the house. If Fiona is lost out there in the darkness she might see the lights and try to make for them.'

'That's a good idea, Ellen,' Fraser Miles said. 'I'll ring the McLays back and tell them to do the same. It's pitch black out there so any lights should be visible from quite a distance.'

Jenny nodded and rushed to do as Mrs Grace suggested. When she came back, leaving the little house blazing with light, her father was putting the phone down.

'The police are on their way,' he told them. 'The McLays are going to start searching at their end and we'll start from here. With luck we should find Fiona somewhere in between the two houses.'

Jenny nodded. 'That sounds like a good plan,' she said.

'Wait a moment,' Matt said. 'We're assuming that Fiona will follow the track but there's so much snow covering it that she could easily have missed her way and be wandering about the fields. We can't afford to ignore the possibility that she's lost.' He looked out of the window. 'With the snow coming down the way it is, she could quite easily lose her sense of direction.'

Jenny glanced out of the window. Matt was right. The swirling, spinning mass of snowflakes would confuse anyone and Fiona was still weak from her illness.

'You're right, Matt,' Fraser Miles said, as Mrs Grace came in with a pile of coats and scarves. He started to pull on a heavy waxed jacket.

'Where is she most likely to wander off the track?' Matt asked.

'It takes a turn about halfway to Thistle Cottage,' Fraser Miles said. 'The edges are unfenced just there.'

'And there are even narrower tracks leading off the main one,' Ellen Grace put in. 'There are two ways she could go if she missed the track. She could go up towards Darktarn or down towards the cliffs.'

Fraser Miles frowned. 'Either of those could be dangerous,' he said, 'There's the river that runs through the gully below Darktarn Keep. She could fall in.'

'And if she heads for the cliffs she could wander too close to the edge,' Matt agreed. 'It looks as if we'll have to split up. Ellen, maybe you could take the track, Jenny and I'll take the cliffs and Dad could take the Darktarn route. Do we need to leave anyone here in case Fiona turns up?'

Fraser shook his head. 'The house is well lit. It's warm and cosy and, if Fiona arrives here, she'll be perfectly safe. We can do much more good going out looking for her. But I don't want anyone out there on their own. We have to go in twos. It's far too dangerous otherwise. We could end up with someone else lost as well as Fiona.'

'That makes sense,' Mrs Grace agreed, as she pulled on heavy boots. 'But it will mean we have to leave one route unsearched for the moment. We'll have to search the road to Dunraven if only to meet up with the McLays — and we'll have to decide which other direction to take. We can't search three routes.'

Matt nodded. 'Why don't you and Dad take the road to Dunraven and Jenny and I will head for the cliffs?' he suggested.

'Why the cliffs?' Jenny asked.

Matt shrugged. 'I don't know. It's just as likely she's headed off in the Darktarn direction.'

'One thing is sure,' Fraser Miles said, as he headed for the door. 'The longer we hang about here talking about it the longer it'll take us to find Fiona.'

Jenny pulled on her woollen bobble cap and thrust her feet into thick socks before putting on her gumboots. She put on her heaviest coat and wrapped a woolly scarf around her neck. 'I'm ready,' she announced.

The moment they stepped outside the front door Jenny's heart sank. 'We'll never find her in this,' she whispered to Matt.

The wind blew her words away, whipping the snowflakes to a swirling mass that danced wildly in the light from the cottage behind them. Beyond the brightness cast by the lights, the countryside lay in deepest blackness. Even the snow showed up only dimly. The moon was obscured by heavy cloud and fast falling snow blotted out landmarks, making it difficult to gauge distance and direction.

'Keep together, you two,' Fraser Miles called back as he and Mrs Grace set out for Dunraven. 'Look after Jenny, Matt.'

'I will,' Matt called back as Fraser and Mrs Grace disappeared up the track.

Jenny watched her father and the housekeeper go. 'Jess will look after both of us,' she said. Beside her, Jess whined and drew close to her legs. 'Oh, Jess,' Jenny said, rubbing his ears. 'It'll be like looking for a needle in a haystack. Fiona could have wandered anywhere off course.'

Matt put his arm through Jenny's. 'Come on, Jen,' he encouraged her. 'Let's get going!'

'I only hope we've made the right decision.' Jenny told him. 'What if she's gone in the other direction? We'll all miss her.'

'It's a chance we've got to take,' Matt said seriously. 'There isn't any way of knowing for certain which way she might have gone.'

Jess licked Jenny's hand and gave a soft bark. 'Oh, Jess, please help us find Fiona,' Jenny said.

Jess put his head on one side and looked up at her. Jenny gazed back at him, then she had an idea. 'Wait a minute, Matt,' she exclaimed, darting back into the cottage.

'Where are you going?' Matt called after her.

'To get the present Fiona gave Mrs Grace,' Jenny called back She dashed into the living-room and picked up the knitting bag. Then she ran back outside to Matt.

'What on earth do you want that for?' Matt asked, puzzled. 'Come on, Jenny, we're wasting time!'

Jenny looked at him, her eyes eager. 'But this could *save* us time, Matt,' she cried. 'Fiona made this knitting bag for Mrs Grace.'

'So?' said Matt.

'So, it'll have her scent all over it,' Jenny explained eagerly.

'But how is that going to help us?' Matt asked.

'It won't help *us*,' Jenny admitted. 'But it'll help Jess. Jess must know Fiona's scent really well by now. With any luck, he can lead us to her.'

Matt looked doubtful.

'It's worth trying,' Jenny insisted. 'Anything is better than just guessing where she might be.'

'All right,' Matt agreed. 'We'll try it. We might as well.'

He reached behind him and pulled the cottage door closed. Jenny bent down and held out the knitting bag to Jess. 'Find the scent, Jess,' she commanded. 'Find Fiona, please, boy!'

Jess sniffed eagerly at the knitting bag.

'How much did Mrs Grace handle that bag?' Matt asked. 'We don't want Jess finding Ellen instead of Fiona.'

Jenny frowned. 'I hadn't thought of that,' she admitted. 'But Fiona must have handled it much more than Mrs Grace did.' She turned once more to Jess. 'Fiona!' she said softly.

Jess sniffed again then looked up at Jenny. He gave a single short bark then bounded away beyond

the range of the light from the cottage windows. Jenny switched on her torch and located him, just scampering under the wire that bounded the field beyond. Jess turned and barked again at them, this time more sharply.

'What do you think, Matt?' Jenny asked. 'Do you think he's picked up Fiona's scent?'

'He certainly seems keen for us to follow him,' Matt said. 'And that isn't the way Ellen went so he certainly isn't following her.' He suddenly made up his mind. 'Come on, Jen,' he said. 'We've trusted Jess before and he's never let us down yet.'

Jenny raced after Jess, slipping and sliding on the snow beneath her feet. She hoped they could trust Jess this time too. If not, they might not find Fiona in time.

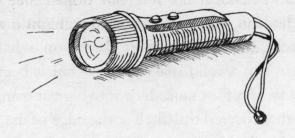

8

Jenny and Matt struggled through the blinding snow. The wind caught the flakes and blew them in great flurries across their path as they tried to catch up with Jess. Their torch beams waved wildly as they lurched across the uneven ground, lighting the huge snowflakes as they fell crazily from the sky. Jenny couldn't see Jess at all now but she knew he was ahead of them somewhere.

'Jess! Where are you, Jess?' she called to him, but

her voice was drowned by the howling wind.

In her eagerness to reach the Border collie, Jenny ploughed on, taking the most direct route across the field. She set her foot down on what she thought was a solid mass of snow but it began to give way. Her foot sank deep into a great trough of snow that covered the ditch at the edge of the field. Jenny lost her balance and put out a hand to the bank that backed on to the ditch. Too late, she realised that it was a snowdrift that had banked itself up against the perimeter fence. Letting out a cry of alarm, Jenny lost her balance completely and unable to stop herself, tumbled into the snowdrift.

At once, the world was blotted out as the soft snow gave way beneath her and closed around her body. Her eyes were tightly shut but she could feel snow begin to fill her mouth as she called out in alarm. She tried to struggle to her feet but it was no good. The more she struggled, the deeper into the drift she seemed to get. She began to panic as she realised that she had no idea which way she was facing. Was she working her way out of the drift or was she digging herself deeper into it? She lashed out, trying to free herself of the clinging, suffocating snow. She couldn't even cry for help. Just as she thought she could stand it no longer, she felt a hand in a thick woollen glove grasp her shoulder and a voice that seemed to come from a long way off, called her name. It took her a moment of confused thought to realise that it was Matt. She grasped the hand that closed over her shoulder, desperate not to lose contact, and felt herself being dragged from the snowdrift. Freezing air and a bitterly cold wind whipped her face as she struggled for breath.

'Are you OK, Jen?' Matt called to her as he worked to free her from the snowdrift.

Jenny clung to him, not wanting to let go, not wanting to be alone again in that dark, cold world beneath the snow. She shook her head and raised her gloved hands to her face, trying to clear her nose and mouth. 'Matt!' she gasped. 'Oh, Matt, it was terrible. I felt as if I was being buried alive.'

Matt put his arms round her and hauled her right out of the snowdrift, hugging her to him. 'It's all right now, Jen,' he reassured her comfortingly. 'I've got you – you're safe.'

Jenny clung to him for a long moment, too glad to feel his arms safely round her to think of anything else.

'Do you think you can get up now?' Matt said

gently. 'It isn't good for either of us to be sitting in the snow like this.'

Jenny managed to get to her knees, still half–buried in the bank of snow. 'I didn't realise I had stepped into a snowdrift,' she told her brother when she got her breath back. 'It looked so solid.'

Matt helped to brush the snow from her clothes. 'Don't let it soak in,' he warned her. 'It would seep through and chill you.'

Jenny nodded and brushed furiously. Then a thought struck her. 'What if something like that happened to Fiona?' she asked, worried. 'You were there to pull me out, Matt. But there wouldn't be anybody to pull Fiona out of a drift like that.' She turned to her brother, her eyes shadowed with worry. 'Oh, Matt. She could be lying in a snowdrift somewhere, suffocating.'

Matt put an arm round Jenny's shoulders. 'Come on.' he said. 'Don't start imagining all the things that might have happened to Fiona.' His words were reassuring but, even as he spoke, he was looking around, his expression worried.

'What is it?' Jenny asked.

Matt frowned. 'I was wondering where Jess had got to,' he said to her. 'He must have heard you call out. It isn't like him to ignore that.'

'Jess!' Jenny gasped. She turned and flashed her
torch beam as far as it would reach.

Matt caught her arm. 'Listen, Jen,' he said. 'I heard
something just then.'

Jenny listened carefully. She was almost sure she
heard a distant bark. Then it came again and there
was no mistaking it. It was Jess, and his bark sounded
urgent!

'Which way?' Matt demanded. 'The snow makes
it really confusing.'

Jenny cupped her hands round her mouth and
called Jess's name. The sound of barking came again,
answering her call, and Jenny whirled round. 'This
way, Matt,' she announced. 'Keep calling him. He'll
lead us to wherever he is.'

Calling and following the sound of Jess's barking,
Matt and Jenny made their way across the snowy
fields, flashing their torches around them as they
went, hoping to catch sight of the Border collie.
They had reached the field above Dunraven when
Jenny stopped for breath. It was hard work, plodding
through the deep, uneven snow. She looked around
the white landscape as she got her breath back. She
could see the lights of Dunraven farmhouse

blazing out across the snow-covered fields that surrounded it.

Mrs McLay had obviously taken Ellen Grace's advice. Every light in the place was burning – as well as all the lights in the outbuildings. If Fiona was anywhere around, she couldn't fail to see Dunraven. That meant that either she was lost somewhere out of sight of the farm or she was injured and couldn't make it back to her home. Jenny's heart sank. Then she drew herself up and pushed on. Worrying wouldn't do any good! And where was Jess? Jenny called his name once more and a dark shape flew at her out of the darkness, tail wagging and eyes bright in the gleam of her torch. 'Jess!' Jenny exclaimed, bending down to him.

But Jess was off, racing across the snow to a spot where the drystone wall bordered the top of the field. A huge mound of hard-packed snow, driven by the wind, was piled up against the wall and Jess was perched on top of the mound. He stood there, barking at them, urging them on. Then he leaped over the wall and out of sight. Jenny shone her torch around the area, tested the strength of the pile of snow, then scrambled up the mound on to the top of the drystone wall. She crouched there, directing her torch beam downward on the far side of the wall. The beam illuminated a dark shape lying at the foot of the wall. The shape was half-covered in snow but it wasn't difficult to make out what it was. It was a body.

Jenny gasped. 'Matt, look! Over here!' she called to her brother.

Matt was already pushing through the deep snow towards the wall. He scrambled up and leaned beside Jenny, looking down at the huddled figure below them. 'I think we've found Fiona,' he announced grimly.

Jenny swallowed hard. The dark shape was very still. Matt leaped down from the wall and began to examine the figure that was lying there. The wind had caused the snow to pile up at Jenny's side of the wall so that the ground on the other side was not so deep in snow – but it was very icy. Jenny saw Matt slip several times. He glanced up at her.

'Is it Fiona?' she asked, although she knew it had to be.

Matt nodded. 'She's conscious but only just,' he said. 'It's very icy down here. She must have slipped and hit her head on the wall. The only thing is,

there's no telling how long ago the accident happened.'

'We'll have to get her back to Dunraven as quickly as we can,' Jenny urged, casting a glance towards the illuminated farmhouse below them.

Matt frowned. 'First I'll have to make sure we don't do more harm than good by moving her,' he warned. 'Can you get down here and give me some light, Jenny?'

Jenny nodded and got ready to jump down from the wall. Jess barked a warning and Matt put out a hand. 'Be careful,' he said. 'It's very slippery just under the wall.'

Jenny thrust her torch in her pocket and lowered herself down cautiously. It wasn't hard to see how Fiona had slipped. She saw Matt bend towards the still form lying on the snow and greeted Jess as her pet rushed up to meet her.

'Good boy, Jess,' she congratulated him. 'Clever Jess to find Fiona.'

Jess wagged his tail but his eyes were on Fiona. 'How is she?' Jenny asked as she approached Matt.

'I'll check if there are any bones broken,' he said. 'Can you give me a bit of light with your torch?'

Jenny pulled out her torch and held it steady

while Matt gently tested Fiona's arms and legs. His hands were sure and gentle. Jenny was reminded of the way Matt handled an injured ewe. She looked at her brother's face, intent on his work, and then she shifted her gaze to Fiona's face. Her eyes were closed and her face was nearly as white as the surrounding snow. There was an ugly dark bruise on one temple and a trickle of dried blood ran from under Fiona's anorak hood to her ear. Jenny held her breath as Matt gently pushed back the hood and felt around the wound. As she watched, Fiona's eyes opened and Jenny leaned forward.

'Fiona,' she said gently. 'Don't try to move just yet. Matt and I are here. You're going to be all right.'

Fiona looked at Jenny with puzzlement in her eyes. Then she licked her dry lips and whispered, 'Jess? Where's Jess? He was here but he went away.'

At the sound of Fiona's voice, Jess moved forward and gently nuzzled the injured girl's cheek, licking her face. Fiona raised an arm weakly and tried to stroke him. 'Oh, Jess,' she said, a tear sliding down her cheek. 'You came back. I thought you had deserted me.'

'He came to find us, to show us where you were,' Jenny explained. 'What happened, Fiona?'

Fiona shook her head from side to side. Jenny could see Matt watching her carefully as he worked, checking her limbs for broken bones.

'I don't know,' Fiona said. 'I wanted to find Jess but I slipped and then I don't remember . . . all I remember is that Jess was here again. Then he went away.' She closed her eyes. Another tear escaped from under her lashes and slid down her cold cheek.

'Don't try to talk any more,' Matt advised her. 'We're going to get you home now.'

'But what about Jess?' Fiona asked hoarsely. 'I want Jess. I need him.'

Jenny swallowed hard as Jess thrust his nose into her hand. 'He's here,' she reassured Fiona. 'He won't go away again,'

'Promise?' Fiona said in a broken voice. Her eyes, fixed on Jenny's, were pleading.

'I promise,' Jenny told her. 'Jess is going to stay with you for as long as you need him.'

Fiona sighed deeply and some of the tension went out of her face as she closed her eyes in relief.

'The important thing right now is to get you home as quickly as possible,' Jenny said firmly.

Fiona's eyes opened again and Jenny winced at the pain in them. 'Home?' she said. 'Nobody likes me there. Why should they? I've been so bad to everybody.'

'Jess loves you,' Jenny said softly. 'He found you. He led us to you.'

Fiona sighed. 'Only Jess, only Jess,' she whispered. Her hand went out to touch the Border collie beside her and Jess looked up at Jenny. Jenny couldn't speak – she couldn't imagine what it must be like to be as unhappy as Fiona. But at least Jess had helped her.

'Fiona, you've got to try to stay awake,' Jenny managed to say as Fiona's eyelids drooped once again. 'Fiona!'

The injured girl's eyelids fluttered and then closed again.

Matt frowned. 'That isn't a good sign,' he said, rubbing Fiona's cheeks. Her eyes opened briefly. 'Fiona, we're going to move you. Try not to go to sleep.' Matt looked at Jenny. 'We don't know how long she's been lying out here. There don't seem to be any bones broken but her breathing is very shallow. She could be in the early stages of hypothermia.'

Jenny knew that hypothermia was when a person's body temperature dropped dangerously low – so low that they could die. She pointed down the hill towards the blazing lights of Dunraven in the distance. 'If I take both torches and light the way, can you carry Fiona?'

'Easily,' Matt announced, bending to pick up the injured girl. He stood up with Fiona's limp body in his arms. Jenny looked at Fiona's face. Her eyes were closed and her skin was deathly pale. She hardly seemed to be breathing at all.

'Come on, Jess,' Jenny called to the Border collie. 'Lead the way.' She turned to Matt. 'If we keep close to Jess this time we should avoid the snowdrifts.'

Matt nodded and they set off towards the lights of Dunraven. Jenny crossed her fingers and hoped against hope that Fiona hadn't suffered any lasting damage.

9

Even though they could clearly see Dunraven in front of them, the journey down towards the farmhouse wasn't easy. The snow was deep and Matt was out of breath by the time Jenny guided him on to the track that led to the farmyard.

'You go on ahead and see if anyone's there,' Matt shouted to Jenny over the howling wind.

Jenny nodded and sped off towards the farmhouse. There were tractor marks on the path.

Calum McLay had made a good job of clearing the track. With Jess at her heels, Jenny ran to the door of the farmhouse and rang the bell. There was a flurry of movement, a bark from inside and Paul, his face pale, threw the door open. Toby, his honey-brown Border terrier, was by the little boy's side.

'Jenny!' Paul cried, as Jess and Toby greeted each other. 'Have you found her? Have you found Fiona?'

'Jess found her,' Jenny told him quickly. 'Are your parents here, Paul? Matt is bringing Fiona in now but she needs a doctor.'

Paul peered past Jenny into the swirling darkness. 'They're still out looking for her,' he said. 'Mum wouldn't let me help in case I got lost too.'

Jenny frowned. Then Jess gave a sharp bark and ran to the edge of the farmyard. He stood there, front legs stiff, and nose pointing down the track. Jenny listened carefully. She could hear voices. Then Toby started barking too and ran towards Jess.

'I think that's my dad's voice,' Jenny said.

'Look!' cried Paul. Jenny looked to where the little boy was pointing.

As she peered into the dark, she saw the lights of

torch beams and heard the voices getting louder.

'Jenny!' called Matt. 'We're here — all of us!'

Jenny ran to meet the party coming up the track into the farmyard. Calum McLay was carrying his daughter now. Matt was rubbing his arms gratefully.

Mrs McLay hovered round Fiona, her face anxious. 'Take her straight to the fire, Calum,' she ordered. 'I'll call the doctor right away.'

The McLays hardly noticed Jenny as they hurried into the farmhouse. Anna McLay went at once to the phone and began to speak urgently into it. Jenny turned to Fraser Miles and Ellen Grace and smiled. 'It's lucky you were all just arriving,' she said.

'We met the McLays halfway up the track between Dunraven and the cottage,' Mrs Grace explained.

'Then we caught up with Matt,' Fraser Miles put in. 'I hear we have Jess to thank yet again.'

'Yes — he found Fiona,' Jenny said proudly. 'She had gone looking for him but she slipped and hit her head.'

'How did you know where to start looking?' Fraser asked as they went into the farmhouse.

Jenny explained about the Christmas present that Fiona had made for Mrs Grace as they all crowded into the porch, taking off their wet coats and boots. Jess and Toby came running into the hall, shaking the snow from their coats and soaking everyone. No one told them off; Jess was a hero.

Anna McLay beckoned them into the warmth. 'We've to take Fiona straight to hospital,' she said. 'Doctor Scott says it would take him too long to get here in this weather and, if we can get down the track in the Land Rover, we'll find the main road isn't so bad. It'll be quicker to take her directly to Greybridge.'

'I'll get the Land Rover started,' Calum McLay said. 'You pack whatever Fiona will need, Anna.'

'I'll do that,' said Ellen briskly. 'Anna, you go and sit with Fiona. And Jenny, you go and get warm. You look half frozen – Matt too.'

Jenny and Matt obediently made their way into the sitting-room where a huge log fire was burning. Fiona was lying on the sofa in front of the fire, Paul beside her. Anna McLay went immediately to her daughter. Fiona looked up and said a few words in a weak voice to her mother. Her short dark hair was pushed back from the bruise on her forehead. There was a little colour in her cheeks now. Jess slipped past Jenny and went at once to the sofa, setting himself where the girl could reach out a hand and stroke him. Fiona laid her hand on Jess's head.

Anna McLay knelt beside the sofa and stroked her daughter's hair. She turned to look at Jenny. 'You and Matt have saved Fiona's life. We owe you and your family such a lot, we'll never be able to repay it. All we can do is try and show you in the future how grateful we are.' Tears stood in Mrs McLay's eyes as she finished speaking.

As she got up Jenny went over to her. 'I think Fiona has been very unhappy,' she said softly. 'If there is anything Jess and I can do to help her we'll be glad to do it.'

Anna McLay nodded silently, the tears coursing down her cheeks. Just then Calum McLay came back into the room. As he put an arm round his wife's shoulders, Jenny noticed how haggard he looked. She could hardly bear to watch as he passed a hand over his eyes.

Mrs Grace came into the room carrying a small overnight bag. 'I've brought a warm blanket too,' she said, holding out a pink woollen blanket.

Anna McLay took it from her with a word of thanks while Calum lifted Fiona into his arms. Anna tucked the blanket round Fiona. Then she paused. 'But what about Paul?' she asked.

'I'll be here,' Mrs Grace pointed out.

Paul slipped his hand into Jenny's. 'Will you stay too, Jenny?' he asked.

Jenny looked down at the little boy's upturned face. She liked Paul best out of all the McLays. 'Of course I will, Paul,' she promised him.

Anna McLay made for the door. 'I'll phone as soon as I know what's happening.'

Jenny, Paul and Mrs Grace stood at the door, watching the Land Rover leave. Jenny put her arm round Paul's shoulders and gave him a squeeze.

Matt and Fraser started out to walk back to Thistle Cottage.

'Don't lose your way,' Mrs Grace called after them.

Fraser smiled at her. 'Don't you worry, Ellen,' he said, looking up at the sky. 'Now the snow has stopped it's a beautiful clear night.'

Jenny looked up. She hadn't noticed that it had stopped snowing. She had been too concerned with Paul, and watching the McLays drive off, to notice the dramatic change in the weather. The snow clouds had cleared away and high above them a bright full moon rode in the sky like a silver coin, casting its light over the countryside. Stars studded the blackness of the sky, like tinsel strewn on black velvet.

'It's beautiful,' Jenny breathed.

'Not a cloud in the sky,' Fraser Miles said softly. 'The weather should improve now.'

Jenny turned to him. 'That means you'll have an easier time with the sheep,' she said.

'It means no more snowdrifts for a start,' Fraser replied.

'And we can get up to the higher ground with extra feedstuff,' Matt put in.

Jenny looked once more at the star-studded sky; it was beautiful. She waved to her father and brother as they marched off down the track and then looked down at Paul.

'Come on, Paul,' she said. 'Let's go inside.'

The phone rang just as they were finishing the supper Mrs Grace had prepared for them. The housekeeper handed the phone to Paul, and Jenny watched the little boy's face carefully.

'Mum says she and Dad are going to stay with Fiona tonight,' he told Jenny. Then he listened carefully again. 'Fiona is all right but she has to stay in hospital for . . . what is it, Mum? . . . observation,' he finished, his face puzzled.

'That just means they want to keep an eye on her,' Jenny put in.

Jenny and Mrs Grace looked at each other in relief as Paul finished his call. 'That doesn't sound too bad,' Ellen Grace said.

Jenny nodded. 'Thank goodness,' she said, yawning. 'Oh, I'm so tired.'

The housekeeper smiled. 'No wonder,' she sympathised. 'You've had quite an evening. Why don't you pop up to bed? You're yawning your head off. You may as well sleep in Fiona's room. It's on the right at the top of the stairs.'

Jenny nodded as she smothered another yawn. 'I think I'll do that,' she said. She looked at Jess. 'Goodnight, Jess,' she said, putting her arms round him. 'I'll see you in the morning.'

Jess followed Jenny to the foot of the stairs and watched her until she got to the top. His head was tilted to one side but he wasn't whining. He knew she would be there the next day.

Jenny switched on the bedroom light and looked around. She had never been inside Fiona's room before. It was nicely furnished with pine units, a desk, and a bed with a bright duvet cover. But it wasn't the furniture that caught Jenny's attention. The room was made cosy by the posters stuck on every wall and the books brimming from the bookcases and the tapes strewn across the desk. It wasn't cold or uninviting or empty. It was just like the kind of room that both she and Carrie had. Jenny was surprised. Maybe she would give Fiona another chance and try to get to know her.

Jenny yawned hugely. But right now she was too tired to think. All she wanted to do was sleep.

10

When Jenny woke in the morning, it took her several moments to realise where she was. She sat up and looked around the room and the memory of the previous evening came back to her. She was at Dunraven, in Fiona McLay's room. She had been so tired the night before that she had forgotten to draw the curtains and the room was flooded with winter sunshine. Outside, the fields were still deeply covered with snow. In the distance, Jenny could see the sea sparkling in the sunlight. It was a beautiful morning.

Jenny reached out to open the window a little. Her hand touched a pile of photographs sitting on top of the bookcase and they cascaded to the floor. Jenny bent to pick them up, shuffling them together. Slowly, she riffled through the photos, her forehead creased in concentration.

There were photographs of birds and wild flowers. But there were also photos of people – of Jenny, Ian and Carrie. Jenny had no recollection of Fiona snapping pictures of her. But why would Fiona want to take pictures of them?

A piece of paper fluttered in the breeze from the open window and Jenny put out a hand to stop it blowing to the floor.

Dear Peter, it began. It was a letter. Jenny put it back on the desk. She had no intention of reading Fiona's letter but she couldn't help wondering who Peter was. There was a Christmas card and a few photographs of people Jenny didn't recognise on the desk too. Jenny looked at the card. *Here are my friends. I'm looking forward to seeing the photos of your friends . . . Merry Christmas from Australia, your penfriend, Peter*, the card said.

Jenny frowned. She looked again at the letter Fiona had been writing, wrestling with herself. Should she read it? She had a suspicion now of what Fiona was doing. Jenny reached out a hand and picked up the letter. A few words jumped out at her. *These are my friends . . . I took the photos, that's why I'm not in them.*

Jenny laid the letter down and turned, looking out of the window. The sun was still shining on the snowy, glittering scene below but Jenny's heart felt heavy. She knew now why Fiona had taken those secret photos. She was pretending to her penfriend that Jenny, Carrie and Ian were her friends.

Jenny remembered how angry Fiona had been about the project their class had been set last term. They'd had to draw a map of their house and the surrounding area, then put in paths from their homes to their friends' houses. But there hadn't been any paths marked on Fiona's map.

Jenny frowned. At primary school Fiona's few friends had all been bullies. Since they had moved on to senior school they were in different classes and had drifted apart. Fiona hadn't made any new friends.

Jenny tucked the letter and the photos under a

pile of papers on Fiona's desk. She didn't want the girl to find out that she knew her secret. She shook her head. Fiona must have been so lonely!

Then a thought occurred to her. If Fiona wanted friends so badly, why couldn't she have them?

Jenny and Jess went home that day and the first thing Jenny did was phone Carrie and tell her all the news.

'How was Christmas?' she asked first of all.

Carrie laughed. 'Chaotic,' she said. 'But great. Aunt Babs and Uncle Mike loved the snow. They'd never had a white Christmas before. Mum was really pleased with her jug and Dad is already halfway through his book – and I got some terrific presents. My Australian relatives gave me a portable CD player. I'm dying to show it to you. How did yours go?'

Jenny launched into the story of her Christmas, telling Carrie all about Fiona and Jess.

'Is Fiona going to be all right?' Carrie asked.

'She has to stay in hospital for a few days, but she can have as many visitors as she likes,' Jenny explained.

'I don't suppose Fiona will have many visitors,'

Carrie replied. 'She doesn't have any friends.'

'I want to talk to you about that,' Jenny told Carrie. 'Can you come over?'

'Sure,' said Carrie. 'The snowploughs have been out so the roads are clear. How about this afternoon?'

'Perfect,' said Jenny.

As Jenny put the phone down she nodded her head in satisfaction and rubbed Jess's ears. 'How would you like to go and see Fiona in hospital, Jess?' she asked.

Jess looked at her and wagged his tail.

'That's what I thought you'd say,' she laughed.

When Carrie arrived, Jenny outlined her plan. 'I thought we could go and see her – and we'll take Jess too. Greybridge Hospital allowed us to take him and Toby to see Paul when he was in hospital, so I'm sure they'll let us bring Jess in to see Fiona.'

Carrie looked doubtful. 'Are you sure Fiona will *want* to see us? She's always been so rude to everyone.'

'Only because she felt that no one liked her,' Jenny said slowly. 'Don't you see? She was so afraid of not being liked that she almost *made* people stay away from her. That way she couldn't get hurt.'

JESS THE BORDER COLLIE

'Only she *did* get hurt,' Carrie put in.

Jenny nodded. 'Can you imagine how lonely she must be to have to invent friends?' she asked. She looked challengingly at Carrie. 'Will you come to the hospital?'

Carrie snorted. 'Of course I will,' she said. 'You don't have to ask. And besides . . .' she stopped.

'Besides what?' asked Jenny.

'Well,' said Carrie, tossing her bright red hair back from her face. 'I was thinking that Fiona would only have herself to blame when we turn up. She's the one that's pretending we're her friends. She can't blame us if we make it come true.'

Jenny and Carrie found Fiona propped up in a chair in the day room. She was quiet, and still looked very pale, but her cheeks flushed when she saw Jess. The Border collie ran to her straight away, making a great fuss of her.

'Oh, thank you for bringing Jess,' Fiona breathed as she hugged the sheepdog.

'Is that your dog, Fiona?' a passing nurse asked. 'He's lovely.'

Fiona flushed a little more. 'No, he isn't mine,' she said. 'He belongs to—'

THE SACRIFICE

'He's mine,' Jenny interrupted. 'I'm Fiona's friend . . . and so is Jess.'

'Thank you for coming to see me,' Fiona said looking down, 'I didn't think I had any friends.'

'Well, you have now,' said Carrie briskly.

'If you want us, that is,' Jenny said more gently.

Fiona flushed deeply and looked away. 'I don't deserve to have you as a friend, Jenny, not after all I've done to you,' she said.

Jenny laid a hand on her arm. 'Let's forget it, shall we?'

Fiona tried to speak but couldn't. Jess laid his head in her lap.

'There,' said Jenny. 'Jess wants to be your friend too and you can't argue with him.'

Fiona looked up and smiled at last. 'I'd love to be your friend, Jenny,' she said. 'And yours, Carrie.'

'And Ian's,' Carrie said with a grin. 'We come as a job lot. Take one, take all.'

Fiona stroked Jess's nose and smiled more widely. 'I'll take you all, please,' she said firmly.

Jenny looked at Fiona as the girl sat, her hand on Jess's neck and her eyes kind and gentle, looking down at the Border collie. Jenny was glad she had discovered Fiona's secret fantasy about having friends. But she would never tell anyone else about finding that letter and those photographs. Jenny felt sure that, from now on, they would see more of the nicer side of Fiona.

11

It was mid-January now and only a thin covering of snow remained on the fields. The repairs to Windy Hill, which had been halted during the worst of the snow, had restarted nearly two weeks ago and were going better than even Fraser Miles had hoped. It was a Saturday and Carrie had come to see Jenny at Thistle Cottage.

'I'm going to collect Jess today,' Jenny announced. 'Do you want to come, Carrie?'

'Try and stop me,' Carrie grinned. 'Let's go right now! I can't wait to see you two back together again.'

Fiona had been taking Jess for walks since she'd come home from hospital, but now she felt she was well enough to cope on her own, so Jess was coming home – at last!

'I can't wait either,' Jenny sighed. 'Even though we've visited him every day at Dunraven, it hasn't been the same without Jess here.'

'You've been really good about letting Jess go and stay with Fiona while she recovered,' Carrie told Jenny as the phone rang.

Jenny picked up the receiver. 'Ian!' she cried. 'How are you? When are you coming home?'

'I'm fine,' Ian replied. 'And I'm having a great time in Canada.'

Something in Ian's voice made Jenny hesitate. 'I'm glad,' she said slowly.

'In fact I like it so much that I've decided I'm going to stay here,' Ian went on. 'That's why I'm phoning. The new house is terrific and Mum and Dad have missed me a lot. I hope you understand, Jenny.'

Jenny swallowed. 'Of course I do,' she said. 'I mean,

I'm really happy you like it so much – but I'll miss you.'

'I'll miss you all too – and Windy Hill, but I'll come back for visits,' Ian assured her. 'How's Jess?'

Jenny told him that she was about to collect Jess. Then she listened while Ian described his life in Canada. When she put the phone down she looked at Carrie.

'He isn't coming back, is he?' Carrie asked sympathetically.

Jenny shook her head. 'He's really happy to be living with his mum and dad again,' she said. 'It's going to seem so strange without Ian.'

'You've got me and all your other friends,' Carrie comforted her. 'And you'll have Jess back today.'

Jenny smiled. 'That makes up for anything,' she asserted. 'Come on, let's go and get him.'

Dunraven came into sight and Jenny and Carrie quickened their steps. As they turned into the farmyard a black-and-white bundle of energy launched itself at them, wagging his tail and nearly knocking Jenny over in his enthusiasm.

'Jess!' Jenny spluttered, hugging him to her. 'I've come to take you home, did you know that?'

Jenny looked over Jess's head at the girl standing in the yard. Fiona's eyes were brighter than they had been for a long time and she smiled widely. 'I think he *did* know,' she said. 'He's been on the lookout for you all morning.'

Jess transferred his attention to Carrie while Jenny stood up and moved towards Fiona. 'Are you sure you're ready to let him go, Fiona?' she asked.

Fiona nodded. 'I'm sure,' she replied. 'He's your dog and he's missing you. I'm so grateful for the sacrifice you both made, Jenny. Having Jess here was the best thing that happened to me. I don't think I could have recovered without him – or you.'

Jenny put out a hand and laid it on Fiona's arm. 'I'm just glad you're better,' she said.

'I don't really deserve it, but you and Carrie – and Jess of course – have really helped,' Fiona said shyly. 'And today I got some cards – from people at school! I even got a class card. But I guess you two must know about that.'

Jenny nodded, smiling to herself.

Jess ran up and began to run circles round the girls. Fiona laughed. 'Oh, someday I would love a dog like Jess,' she said.

Carrie grinned. 'I don't know about that,' she put in. 'Jess is pretty unique.'

Jenny looked at Fiona as the other girl bent to give Jess a cuddle and say goodbye. There would never be another Jess, but one day Jess would have puppies so maybe Fiona would have a dog like Jess after all. It looked as if Fiona might become a good friend of Jenny's too.

Carrie and Jenny waved goodbye to Fiona and turned out of the farmyard.

'Let's go to Windy Hill,' Carrie suggested.

Jenny agreed. She and Carrie had made several visits to Windy Hill to watch the new lambing barn going up. It was completed now and only needed painting. 'Dad says thcy should be finished with the inside of the house soon as well,' Jenny said.

Jess ran ahead of them, chasing imaginary rabbits and scampering back to them when they weren't walking fast enough.

As they reached the track that led to Windy Hill, Jenny felt her heart beat a little faster. Jess ran on and the girls quickened their step, running down the last bit of track towards the gate. Jenny pushed it open and walked into the yard. The farmyard was still littered with ladders and paint pots and lengths of wood but the stables looked as if they had never been damaged at all and the new lambing barn gleamed, its fresh paintwork shining in the sun.

'Oh, look, they've painted the lambing barn dark green – just like the last one,' she cried. 'And, look at the house! All the windows have been replaced.'

Jenny feasted her eyes on the old stone farmhouse. The new red tiles on the roof gleamed in the sunshine and the white-painted window frames sparkled. Mr Thorburn came out of the farmhouse at the sound of Jenny's voice and waved to them.

'I've got a surprise for you,' he said, 'Come on in!'

Jenny caught her breath. Mr Thorburn hadn't allowed anyone to go inside the house while the work was going on because he said it was dangerous. She and Carrie followed him into the house. Jenny sniffed. 'It smells so strange,' she said.

'It smells of new wood and fresh paint,' Carrie agreed as they made their way through to the kitchen.

Jenny stopped to look around. The kitchen seemed very bare without the huge dresser that usually stood against the wall, but that had been salvaged from the fire and would soon be back in its old place.

'The Aga is still all right, isn't it?' Jenny asked, walking over to the big black stove.

'It's working perfectly,' Mr Thorburn agreed. 'Now, how would you like to see your room?'

Jenny's heart skipped a beat. The last time she had seen her bedroom it had been gutted by fire, smoke-blackened and ruined. That was almost two months ago now.

She followed Mr Thorburn upstairs and peered round her bedroom door. 'Oh,' she cried. 'This is just how it used to be.'

Joe Thorburn's eyes twinkled. 'I know,' he said. 'I got strict instructions about this room from your dad and Mrs Grace.'

Jenny walked across the room, touching the bright yellow painted walls, running her hand along the white windowsill and admiring the glossy floorboards.

'We had to put a new floor in here,' Mr Thorburn told her. 'The old one wasn't safe any more. How do you like it?'

'I love it,' Jenny answered. 'Thank you so much.'

'You're welcome, lass,' Mr Thorburn said. 'And when you get new furniture in, it'll look even better.'

Jenny smiled happily. 'Oh, I want furniture that's just like the old stuff,' she assured him. 'I want everything to be just the way it used to be.'

'It really will be just like it used to be,' Jenny repeated, as she and Carrie walked up towards Darktarn Keep. 'Except that Ian won't be here, of course.'

'He'll come and visit,' Carrie said. 'He promised.'

'I hope so,' Jenny replied. 'But right now, most of all, I'm looking forward to going home.'

'Home to Windy Hill,' Carrie echoed. 'It sounds good.'

Jenny lifted her face to the clear, cold air. The sky overhead was a pale clean blue. It looked as if it had been newly washed. The winter sun had little warmth but it sparkled on the waves out to sea, turning the water to silver. Above them, birds wheeled and cried and Jenny could see Windy Hill, its red roofs restored, and the walls of the stables repaired. The new lambing barn, bigger than the one that had burned down, stood next to the stable block. Its glossy dark-green paint shone in the sunshine. Windy Hill. Her home – and Jess's.

Jess gave a short bark and Jenny looked round. The Border collie was standing on top of the

drystone wall that ran round the bottom of Darktarn Keep.

'It's OK, Jess,' she called. 'We're coming.'

Jess barked again and disappeared over the wall. In a moment Jenny saw him running like the wind, winnowing his way through the long grass that covered the hill up to the keep. The wind lifted her hair and blew it about her face. Jenny laughed with delight.

'What a perfect day!' she called to Carrie before turning to follow Jess. 'What an absolutely perfect day!'

THE
HOMECOMING

The Homecoming

Special thanks to Helen Magee

Text copyright © 1999 Working Partners Ltd
Series created by Ben M. Baglio, London W6 OQT
Illustrations copyright © 1999 Sheila Ratcliffe

First published as a single volume in Great Britain in 1999
by Hodder Children's Books

1

Jenny Miles opened her eyes. For the first time in ages she was waking up in her old bedroom. Her spirits soared. 'I'm back at Windy Hill!' she shouted, as she leaped out of bed and went over to the window.

Down in the farmyard, pale February sunshine sparkled on the fresh green paint of the new lambing barn and bounced off the cobbles. Jake and Nell, her father's sheepdogs, trotted across the yard towards the barn, their plumy tails wagging as

289

they followed Fraser Miles. Jenny hugged herself in happiness. It was as if she had never been away.

Her father turned and looked up at her window. He smiled, lifting his hand to wave, his dark hair ruffled by the wind. Jenny waved back, then turned to look around her. She could still hardly believe she was back in her own room. She had pinned a few posters to the newly-painted yellow walls. Her favourite photograph of her mother stood in a frame on a chair next to her new bed, while a new desk filled the space below the window where the old one had been. But the room still looked bare compared to how it had been before last November's terrible fire. The farmhouse had almost been destroyed.

Jenny sighed. Perhaps her room would never be exactly as it had been before, but that didn't matter. 'All that matters is that I'm back at Windy Hill,' she whispered, touching her mother's photograph gently.

'Jenny! Breakfast is almost ready,' called a voice from downstairs.

'Thanks, Mrs Grace,' Jenny called back to the housekeeper, then grinned as she heard barking. 'Morning, Jess!' she added, heading out of the door.

She hung over the newly-painted banister and laughed as she saw Jess, her black-and-white Border collie, gazing up at her as he waited patiently at the foot of the stairs. He'd had a habit of tilting his head to one side ever since he was a puppy. Now, with his white muzzle and a black patch over each eye, he looked adorable.

'I'll be down soon, boy,' Jenny told him, as she rushed into the bathroom.

Jess was still waiting when Jenny hurtled downstairs ten minutes later. He launched himself at her as she jumped the last two steps and she gave him a cuddle. 'Isn't it good to be home?' she said into his soft fur. Jess wagged his tail and licked her ear.

'It certainly is,' Fraser Miles said, coming in through the kitchen door. 'Jake and Nell are glad to be back in their old quarters.'

Jenny smiled up at her father. 'I thought you'd be out with the sheep by now,' she said. Fraser Miles ran a thousand Scottish Blackface ewes on their Borders sheep farm and lambing was only two weeks away – an especially busy time in the sheep farmer's year.

'Marion Stewart is dropping by,' her father

explained, as Jenny went through into the big, sunny kitchen. The walls, newly plastered and whitewashed, looked stark and cold, but Jenny's mother's old blue plates were back on the enormous dresser that stood against the far wall, and that brightened the kitchen up a little. The dresser had cleaned up well from the soot of the fire.

'The insurance company needs just one more signature to confirm that all the restoration work has been completed.' Mr Miles continued.

'And then we can get back to normal,' Mrs Grace said, as she put three plates of bacon, egg and tomatoes on the table.

Jenny nodded eagerly as she sat down to her breakfast. Mrs Grace had come to look after the Mileses after Jenny's mother had been killed in a riding accident almost two years ago. No one would ever take Sheena Miles's place but Ellen Grace had settled in so well that she seemed to belong at Windy Hill now.

'And thank goodness for that, now we're running into the busiest time of year,' Fraser said. 'The first lambs are due at the beginning of March.'

'I can help out as soon as the Easter holidays start,' Jenny offered. 'And Matt will get time off from

college again this year for the lambing, won't he?'
Jenny's brother, Matt, was nineteen and was away at
college studying agriculture. He came home as
often as he could to help out on the farm.

Her father nodded. 'The college treats it as part
of his course,' he assured Jenny. 'I'll certainly be glad
of his help – and yours too if you're serious about
lending a hand.'

Jenny grinned. 'Try and stop me,' she said.

Jess butted Jenny's knee. 'Are you looking for my
leftovers?' she said, rubbing his ears. Jess lifted one
paw and tilted his head to one side. Jenny laughed,
giving him a bit of bacon. Jess wolfed it down and
then, happy that he'd got his titbit, went and lay down
in his basket by the Aga. Mrs Grace shook her head.
'Mind you don't spoil him,' she said with a smile.

'I won't,' Jenny replied. 'He knows he only gets a
treat from my plate after I've finished.' She looked
at her father. 'Maybe Jess could help again this year.
Remember how he wore a harness and took bottles
of milk round to the orphaned lambs out in the
fields last year?'

'That certainly was a sight to see,' Fraser said,
smiling. 'Have you still got the harness you made
for him?'

Jenny shook her head. 'It was lost in the fire. But I could make another one.'

'We'll see,' her father said. 'Things should be a lot easier this year now that we've replaced the lambing barn. There'll be fewer ewes having their lambs out in the fields.'

'You won't lamb all the ewes in the barn though, will you, Fraser?' Mrs Grace asked.

Fraser Miles shook his head. 'No, Ellen. I'll still be lambing in the fields, but I'll use the barn for the weaker ewes and the first-time mothers – and of course I'll be able to keep the orphaned lambs in there in the warming pens.'

Jenny knew that orphaned lambs had to be kept warm and needed to be fed by hand. The warming pens were like boxes with slatted lids. They had heaters underneath so that the tiny creatures wouldn't get a chill. The weather in spring in the Scottish Border hill country could be treacherous and new-born lambs often died of cold.

There was a tap on the door just as they were finishing breakfast and a youngish woman with short dark hair popped her head into the kitchen. It was Miss Stewart, the representative who had dealt with the insurance claim when the farm

THE HOMECOMING

burned down. It had taken a while to get the claim through, and so, over the past few months, Marion Stewart had been a regular visitor at Windy Hill. Jess ran to her, tail wagging. She looked down at him and patted him on the head. 'Good dog,' she said, then briskly brushed a hair that Jess had shed from her skirt.

Jenny called Jess to her. 'Sorry about your skirt, Miss Stewart,' she apologised. 'Jess isn't used to anyone minding about their clothes around Windy Hill.'

Marion Stewart always wore very stylish clothes. Today she had on a bright pink suit and was carrying a smart black briefcase. 'I met the postman as I arrived,' she said, handing Fraser a sheaf of envelopes. 'There seems to be quite a lot of mail.'

'Oh, more cards!' Jenny exclaimed. 'We've had so many to wish us a happy return to Windy Hill. There were six waiting for us when we arrived back.'

'Here's one for you, lass,' Fraser said. 'It's from Canada. And one for Ellen too.'

Mrs Grace poured Marion a cup of tea as Jenny tore open her letter. 'It's from Ian!' she cried, delighted. Ian Amery, Mrs Grace's nephew, had lived at Windy Hill for a time while his parents looked for a house in Canada. Now he had gone to join them. Jenny missed him but she had lots of other friends at school – especially Carrie Turner, her best friend.

Jenny glanced through her letter then looked up as Mrs Grace exclaimed. 'Oh! My sister, Maggie, has invited me out to Canada for a visit at the end of the month . . . In fact, she'd like me to stay until the end of March!'

Jenny felt a swift surge of disappointment that Mrs Grace might go away so soon after they had arrived back at Windy Hill.

'Then you should go, Ellen,' Fraser Miles said. 'It's a long time since you saw your sister, isn't it? And there's no point going all that way for only a few days.'

Jenny smiled and nodded. Her dad was right. 'Yes, Mrs Grace,' she said. 'You deserve a holiday.'

'But March is lambing time – the busiest time of year,' Mrs Grace protested. 'I'd hate to leave you in the lurch.'

There was a short silence, then Marion Stewart spoke up. 'I have a suggestion to make,' she began. 'I have a lot of holiday leave due to me. I could easily take it when Ellen is away and help out at Windy Hill.' She looked at Fraser and smiled. 'I'm sure I could rustle up the odd meal or two. I did a cookery course at evening class in Greybridge last year.'

Fraser Miles raised his eyebrows in surprise. 'That's a very kind offer, Marion,' he said. 'But we wouldn't want to put you to any trouble.'

'It would be a pleasure, Fraser,' Marion assured him. She turned to Mrs Grace. 'So you can go to Canada as soon as you like, Ellen. And perhaps I could move into your room, while you're away, then I'd be on the spot. What do you think, Fraser?'

'That would certainly seem to make sense,' Fraser Miles responded. 'Is that OK with you, Ellen?'

Mrs Grace nodded, looking a little dazed at how quickly everything had been decided.

'Good!' Marion said, looking pleased. 'That's settled, then.' She looked at her watch. 'Now, Fraser, if you could just read and sign this form for me,' she said, taking some papers out of her briefcase, 'I'll have to be on my way.'

'You can open the rest of the cards, Jenny,' Fraser Miles said, handing them to her as Marion put the papers in front of him.

Jenny took the cards. 'This one is from Tom

Palmer, the vet,' she exclaimed, passing it over to Mrs Grace. 'And this one's from Carrie's mum and dad.'

Jenny picked up another card. It was addressed to her. 'It's from Fiona McLay,' she said as she read the message. 'It says, "Happy return to Windy Hill, from your grateful friend, Fiona." '

'That's kind of Fiona,' Mrs Grace said, starting to clear away. 'How is she getting on at school?' Fiona was in the same class as Jenny and Carrie. 'It must have been difficult for her going back after what happened.'

Jenny nodded. 'She's getting on fine now. But then, she's a lot nicer than she used to be.' Fiona McLay lived at Dunraven, the neighbouring farm to Windy Hill. She had bullied Jenny when they were younger and it had been Fiona's fault that Windy Hill had burned down. But the guilt had made Fiona very ill and she had been away from school for a long time. The only thing that had helped Fiona recover had been having Jess as a companion. And, for that, Fiona had been grateful to Jenny. During her recovery, Jenny and Carrie had visited Fiona often and had come to like the changed girl she had become.

Jenny's mind went back to Fiona's first day back at school a couple of weeks ago. The Mileses were still living at Thistle Cottage on McLay land at the time. Jenny had opened the front door on Monday morning to find Fiona and her mother, Anna McLay, standing there.

They had offered Jenny a lift to school. Fiona hadn't felt confident enough to take the bus straight away, and had confided how nervous she was feeling. Jenny had been happy to offer her support. Now she wondered at the change in Fiona McLay. It was amazing to think that this girl, who used to be the class bully, was now seeking help from her! She smiled as she remembered the fuss Fiona had made of Jess, when she'd seen him that morning. She seemed to really love the Border collie and had set off for school a lot more happily after seeing him. Within a few days Fiona had settled back into the school routine – though she did tend to cling to Jenny and Carrie a little now. But Jenny didn't really mind. It was a nice change.

'You're daydreaming, lass.' Her father's voice broke into Jenny's thoughts. 'You'd better hurry or you'll miss the school bus.'

Jenny picked up the last card. 'This one's for you,

Dad,' she said. 'It's marked "Personal".'

'What on earth . . . ?' Fraser exclaimed, as he opened the envelope.

Mrs Grace and Jenny glanced at each other in surprise. 'What is it, Dad?' Jenny asked, as she pulled on her coat.

Fraser Miles coughed, 'Oh, it's just a lot of nonsense,' he said.

Jenny looked over at the card and saw that there was a big red heart on it. She grinned. 'Dad, you've gone all red.' Her eyes lit up. 'Of course! It's February the fourteenth – Valentine's Day. Oh, Dad, have you got a valentine?'

Fraser Miles mumbled and pushed the card over to Jenny. 'I suppose I won't get any peace until you've seen it,' he said.

Jenny opened the card. Mrs Grace leaned over to have a look too. There was no signature, just a big 'M' in one corner.

'It could just be Matt having a joke,' Mrs Grace suggested. But Jenny noticed that she glanced across the table at Miss Stewart, who was busily packing the signed papers back into her briefcase. Jenny caught her breath. Carrie had always said that Miss Stewart had taken a fancy to her father.

Marion Stewart looked up at Fraser and smiled. 'Isn't that romantic?' she said.

Jenny watched her father and Marion as they smiled at each other. Suddenly Miss Stewart didn't seem to be in any great hurry to leave after all!

2

'Well, I reckon it *was* Miss Stewart,' Carrie announced, when Jenny told her and Fiona about the card at school that morning. 'I always thought she was after your dad.'

'Does it bother you, Jenny?' Fiona asked.

'It does a bit,' Jenny admitted. 'It's so weird – my dad getting a valentine card.'

'I can't imagine *my* dad getting an anonymous valentine card,' Fiona said. Jenny couldn't imagine that either. Calum McLay, Fiona's father, was so surly and unfriendly she couldn't imagine anyone ever sending him a valentine.

'I bet my dad would *love* to get a mysterious valentine card,' Carrie announced. 'And it would drive Mum mad. I wish I'd thought of sending one to him.' Jenny and Fiona laughed.

Then Fiona grew serious. 'Is it because of your mum that you don't like the idea of your dad getting a valentine card, Jenny?'

Jenny looked at Fiona, surprised at her understanding. Jenny still missed her mother very much. She nodded and, feeling a little upset, looked away.

Fiona flushed. 'I'm sorry,' she said. 'I've got no right to interfere.'

'No, it isn't that, Fiona,' Jenny replied quickly. 'You're right – thanks. And thanks for your welcome home card, too. It was really nice of you.'

Fiona flushed even more. 'You're welcome,' she murmured.

'I guess we're a threesome now,' Carrie said, sliding an arm through Jenny's and the other through Fiona's. 'Look, Dad has asked if we'd like to go out to Puffin Island on Saturday. Is everyone keen?' Carrie's dad ran boat trips to Puffin Island, a nature reserve just off the coast.

Jenny shook her head. 'I'd love to, but Matt is coming home this weekend and I promised I'd help with the sheep, now it's so close to lambing time. His girlfriend, Vicky, is coming to help too.'

'Oh, well,' said Carrie. 'We'll just have to be a twosome this weekend!' she joked to Fiona.

'I'm really looking forward to it,' Fiona said excitedly. 'I've never been before.' Jenny and Carrie had been surprised to discover that Fiona was interested in wildlife.

'Well, I'm sure you'll have a great time,' Jenny said. Though it did feel odd that Carrie would be spending the weekend with Fiona and not her.

When Jenny arrived home from school that afternoon, there was another surprise waiting for her.

'I've booked my ticket to Canada,' Mrs Grace said. 'The only flight I could get was next Monday.'

'But that's so soon,' Jenny protested.

Mrs Grace nodded. 'I've got so much to do before then,' she said worriedly. 'I have to pack up Ian's things and do some shopping for myself. It's just as well Marion Stewart is coming to help out. She's even offered to cook dinner for all of us on Saturday, so I can get on with other things.'

'That's nice of her,' Jenny agreed, then added, laughing, 'It sounds as if we'll be in good hands while you're away!'

Mrs Grace smiled back. 'I can't disagree with that!' she replied.

Marion Stewart arrived just after lunch on Saturday. She was wearing jeans and a very expensive looking sweater instead of her usual smart suit. Mrs Grace had gone into Greybridge for a couple of hours to do some last-minute shopping and to pick up her tickets for Canada.

'I'll take Jess for a walk this afternoon if you're helping with the sheep, Jenny,' Miss Stewart offered.

'Thanks,' Jenny replied. 'I'm sure Jess would love that.'

'You don't know what a help this is, Marion,' Fraser Miles said, shaking his head. 'How can I thank you for it?'

'You could take me out to dinner one evening,' Miss Stewart replied, smiling up at him.

Fraser Miles smiled back. 'That would be a

pleasure,' he said. 'Just name the day.'

Now Jenny was *sure* that Miss Stewart had sent that card! But before she could dwell on this development any further, she heard the sound of Matt's motorbike turning into the yard and everything else was forgotten. She whirled round, dashing out of the front door, Jess barking excitedly at her heels.

Her brother was helping his girlfriend Vicky off the bike. 'Matt!' she cried.

'Hi, Jen!' Matt responded, picking her up and swinging her round. He put her down again, his blue eyes laughing at her. Jess leaped up at him, wanting his share of Matt's attention, and he bent towards the Border collie to ruffle his coat. Jess licked his face.

Jenny turned to the slim, fair-haired girl who was unfastening the luggage from panniers on the side of the bike. 'Hi, Vicky!' she said. Vicky was doing the same course as Matt at agricultural college.

'Hello, Jen. It's nice to see you again – and Jess!' Vicky replied as Jess jumped up at her. She looked up at the farmhouse. 'I can't wait to see inside!'

'Let's go in then,' said Matt.

'Wait a minute, Matt,' Jenny said. She had to ask,

just to be sure. 'Did you send Dad a valentine card?'

'No way!' Matt laughed. 'I only sent one valentine card.' He grinned, looking at his girlfriend.

'It was very romantic,' Vicky said, blushing.

'So does that mean Dad's got a secret admirer?' Matt asked, surprised.

Jenny nodded. 'Mrs Grace and I think Marion Stewart sent it. The card was signed with a big M.'

Matt gave a low whistle. 'The next few weeks should be interesting, then,' he said, an amused glint in his eye.

Mrs Grace arrived home from Greybridge late that afternoon, loaded with carrier bags. Fraser Miles was pulling into the farmyard with Jenny, Matt and Vicky in the back of the jeep. Jess shot out into the yard.

'Hello, boy!' Jenny cried as the Border collie threw himself at her, almost knocking her over. 'Have you been waiting for us? Did you have a good walk?' She hugged him. The young sheepdog wagged his tail so hard he overbalanced and sat down heavily beside her. Jenny laughed. 'That reminds me of when you were a puppy,' she said. Jess had been the smallest puppy in the litter – the runt, her father had called him. He had been born with a twisted leg and had to have it in a plaster cast for weeks to straighten it. He had always been falling over then. But the treatment had worked and now no one would guess there had ever been anything wrong with him.

'Come on, boy!' Jenny urged, taking one of Mrs Grace's bags. 'Let's get this stuff inside.' Jenny offered a small plastic bag to Jess and he took it gently in his mouth, then trotted across to the kitchen door.

Mrs Grace laughed. 'Good boy, Jess!' she called. Jess wagged his tail proudly and disappeared into the house.

'We'll be right behind you,' Fraser called, as he and Matt strode across the yard with Jake and Nell. 'I want Matt and Vicky to give me a hand shifting some sacks of concentrate.' Jenny nodded. The ewes were very near to lambing now and needed extra feeding.

As Jenny followed Mrs Grace into the kitchen, a delicious smell met her. Marion Stewart stood at the oven. Her normally tidy hair was a little ruffled.

'That smells wonderful,' said Mrs Grace.

'How has Jess been, Miss Stewart?' Jenny asked, as Jess trotted across the kitchen floor and gave her the plastic bag he'd been carrying.

'I took him up to Darktarn,' Marion Stewart replied. 'We had a great time, didn't we, boy?' She held out her hand to pat Jess but the Border collie scampered out of reach.

Jenny looked at Jess in surprise.

'What's wrong with Jess?' Mrs Grace asked.

Jenny bent down and ruffled Jess's ears. 'I don't know,' she said. 'He's usually so friendly.'

'Maybe he doesn't trust me yet,' Miss Stewart said brightly. 'But he'll get used to me.'

Jenny frowned. Jess was usually such a friendly dog. She turned to Miss Stewart, a little embarrassed at Jess's behaviour. 'Thanks again for taking Jess out,' she said. 'He loves going up to Darktarn. That's one of my favourite places too. And I'm sure you're right – he'll soon get used to you.'

Miss Stewart nodded. 'Now,' she said. 'Sit down, Ellen. Everything is done.'

Ellen Grace sat down at the table. 'This is very kind of you, Marion.'

Marion Stewart smiled. 'I might as well start as I mean to go on,' she declared.

At that moment the door opened and Fraser came in with Matt and Vicky.

'How was the shopping?' Vicky asked.

'Exhausting,' Mrs Grace replied.

Fraser Miles walked across the kitchen and lifted the lid of a saucepan. 'That smells delicious,' he said.

Marion smiled. 'It's carrot and ginger soup,' she said. 'And breast of chicken in a herb crust to follow.'

'Wow!' said Matt. 'We don't usually have such fancy cooking.'

Marion smiled again. 'Oh well, I hope you enjoy it,' she said.

Mrs Grace laughed. 'I'm sure we all will,' she said.

'It will be quite a treat! I'm rather a plain cook,' the housekeeper explained.

'But a good one, Ellen. I love your cooking!' Matt said, putting his arm round Mrs Grace.

'Flatterer!' Mrs Grace replied. But she seemed pleased. 'I'll just put these things away,' she said, picking up some carrier bags.

'I'll help,' Jenny offered. 'Come on, Jess.' The Border collie scampered after them.

'Mrs Grace,' Jenny said, as they unpacked the bags of shopping, 'I'm going to miss you while you're away.'

Ellen Grace smiled. 'I know that, Jenny,' she said. 'And I'll miss you too – but you'll have Marion here.'

'Yes, I know,' Jenny replied. 'And she seems really nice. But I'm *used* to you. I can come home and tell you everything that happens at school – and I know Jess is happy here with you – and I don't even know if I *like* carrot and ginger soup,' she finished, breathlessly.

Mrs Grace laughed. 'Give it a try,' she said. 'You might love it.'

Mrs Grace was right. Jenny did love Marion

Stewart's cooking. 'That was delicious,' she said as she put down her soup spoon.

Marion put the main course in front of them. Jenny looked at the small piece of chicken in the centre of her plate. There was a small heap of garden peas and a few tiny potatoes beside it. It looked lovely, but there was so little of it! She looked over at Matt.

He sat there, open-mouthed, then said, 'Is this all there is?'

'Er, it looks delicious, Marion,' Mrs Grace said. 'But I usually make quite a hearty meal – a roast dinner or a shepherd's pie – in the evening. A day out in the fields works up the appetite,' she explained apologetically.

'Now, don't be so ungrateful, Matt,' Fraser chided. 'We can always fill up with bread and jam afterwards, if we're still hungry.'

Matt nodded and cheered up a little. Vicky smiled. 'I know it sometimes seems as if Matt's got hollow legs,' she said ruefully, as a rather deflated Marion turned away to fetch the water jug. 'But even *I* feel ravenous after a day in the fields.'

'What there is really does taste great, Marion,' Matt complimented her, as he tucked in.

'I hope you like it too, Fraser,' Marion said.

Fraser looked down at his plate. He had nearly finished. 'I must do,' he said. 'It's almost all gone!' he joked.

Jenny giggled. Her father usually ate at least twice as much when he came in from the fields.

'Perhaps we could go out on our dinner date tomorrow, Fraser,' Marion suggested.

'But it's Mrs Grace's last evening before she goes to Canada,' Jenny protested.

'That's true,' Fraser Miles put in. 'But I'm sure you and Ellen would like a cosy evening together before she flies off to Canada. What do you say, Ellen?'

'I can't think of anything nicer,' Mrs Grace replied, smiling.

'Thanks, Ellen,' Fraser said, looking pleased. 'That's a date then, Marion.'

Marion smiled up at Fraser and flicked a tiny speck of fluff off his sleeve. 'I'll look forward to it,' she said.

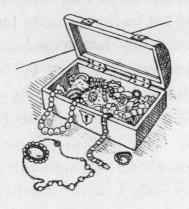

3

Matt and Vicky had gone back to college the following evening, when Fraser Miles came downstairs dressed for his dinner date with Marion. He looked very smart.

'You look really nice, Dad!' Jenny exclaimed, as Jess ran to meet her father.

'I hardly recognised you, Fraser,' Mrs Grace joked. 'It's quite a change from your usual farming clothes. Now, be careful Jess doesn't get dog hairs all over your trousers. Marion wouldn't like that.'

Jenny called Jess to her and gave him a cuddle. She had forgotten how handsome her father could look when he was all dressed up. Then Jenny noticed that her father was carrying a box under one arm. She recognised it. It was her mother's jewellery box.

'I found this when I was rearranging my things upstairs,' Fraser said. 'I think it's time you had it, lass.'

Jenny felt tears prick her eyes as she took the box from her father and opened it. She looked inside at the familiar earrings, bangles and necklaces. In her mind's eye, Jenny saw her mother wearing them. She missed her so much. 'Thanks, Dad,' she whispered.

Jenny turned to Mrs Grace. 'Sometimes Mum used to let me try her jewellery on,' she said. 'She laughed when I decked myself out in all her bangles and necklaces.' Jenny took out her favourite necklace, a delicate gold chain interlined with aquamarines. She clasped it round her neck.

There was a sound at the door and Marion Stewart looked into the room. 'I hope I'm not early, Fraser,' she said brightly.

'Not at all, Marion,' Fraser replied. 'Come in.'

As Marion came into the room Jess immediately moved away. Jenny couldn't understand it. Jess was still uneasy around Miss Stewart.

'My goodness, Jenny, that's a lovely necklace!' Marion Stewart exclaimed.

'It certainly is,' Mrs Grace agreed. 'It was Jenny's mother's. Sheena had some lovely things.'

Jenny put her hand to the necklace and looked up at Marion. 'Mum's grandmother left it to her. Great-Grandma left Mum all her jewellery.'

Marion Stewart smiled. 'Your father has told me a little about your mother. She sounds like a wonderful person.'

'Oh, she was,' Jenny said, taking off the necklace and putting it safely back in the box.

'Ready, Fraser?' Marion asked, reaching up and straightening his tie.

Fraser Miles nodded and gave Jenny a quick pat on the shoulder as he escorted Marion to the door.

'Enjoy yourselves,' Mrs Grace called after them as they left, then she turned to Jenny and smiled. 'Your father seems to like Marion a lot,' she said thoughtfully.

★ ★ ★

When Jenny ran downstairs on Monday morning, Jess launched himself at her in his usual boisterous fashion. She found her father and Mrs Grace in the kitchen. 'How was your date, Dad?' she asked.

Fraser Miles flushed slightly. 'I wouldn't call it a date, lass,' he said.

'Marion called it a date,' Mrs Grace teased.

Jenny looked curiously at her father. He seemed embarrassed.

'We had a very nice meal,' Fraser admitted. Then he looked at his watch. 'Marion should be here again, soon.'

As he spoke, the door opened and Marion came in, two large suitcases in her hands. 'Good morning, everyone,' she said, smiling.

'Here, let me help you with those,' Fraser said, and he took the suitcases upstairs.

'I've cleared out my room ready for you, Marion,' Mrs Grace said. 'I hope you'll be comfortable.'

'I'm sure I shall be, Ellen,' Marion replied. She reached out to pat Jess. But, as before, Jess shied away.

'Jess!' Jenny exclaimed, embarrassed at Jess's behaviour. 'Say hello to Miss Stewart.'

'Don't worry about him, Jenny,' Marion said

brightly. 'He'll have plenty of time to get to know me while you're at school. After I've settled into Ellen's room, I'll take him for a walk.'

Jenny nodded. 'Thanks, Miss Stewart. I hope you had a good time last night.'

Miss Stewart smiled. 'Wonderful,' she said, smiling at Fraser as he came back into the kitchen.

Ellen Grace went to the window. 'That's Anna now,' she said. Anna McLay had offered to take the housekeeper to the airport.

A moment later Mrs McLay came in. 'We'll have to go, Ellen,' she said. 'We don't want you to miss your plane.'

Fraser Miles picked up Mrs Grace's suitcases and went with them out into the yard. Jenny and Miss Stewart followed.

'Oh, Ellen,' Mrs McLay said, as they loaded the boot. 'I've been meaning to ask you. Did you ever come across my diamond and ruby ring while you were working at Dunraven?' For the time that Windy Hill was being repaired, Mrs Grace had divided her time between the McLays' house, Dunraven, and Thistle Cottage, where the Mileses had stayed.

Ellen Grace frowned, then shook her head. 'I

remember the ring,' she said. 'You wore it at Christmas and I remember remarking how nice it was. But I would have told you if I'd found it lying around. Have you lost it?'

Anna McLay nodded. 'It's worth quite a lot of money,' she said. 'But it has even more sentimental value. I've looked for it everywhere.'

'I'm sorry I can't help, Anna,' Mrs Grace said. 'It really is a lovely ring. I hope it turns up.'

Anna McLay smiled and closed the car boot. 'Don't worry about it. Now we'd really better go.'

'Have a good trip, Ellen,' Fraser said, giving her a hug.

Mrs Grace smiled, then turned to hug Jenny. 'Goodbye, lass,' she said. Jenny hugged her back, hard.

Then Mrs Grace turned to Marion Stewart. 'Thanks again, for helping out, Marion,' she said. 'With you here to look after things, I don't suppose they'll even notice I've gone!' she joked.

But Jenny was quite sure she would miss Mrs Grace – and so would Jess.

'So they went out on a date!' Carrie exclaimed on the school bus half an hour later. Jenny had just told Carrie and Fiona about her weekend.

Jenny nodded. 'I think Dad really likes Miss Stewart,' she confided.

'Well, we had a great time at Puffin Island,' Fiona said. 'Didn't we, Carrie?'

Carrie nodded enthusiastically. 'And we're going to the cinema next Saturday afternoon. You will come, won't you, Jen?'

Jenny shook her head. 'The first lambs are due soon,' she explained. 'I want to give Dad a hand.'

'Oh, Jenny!' Carrie said frustratedly. 'We'll hardly ever see you out of school if you're going to spend every weekend helping with the sheep!' She turned to Fiona. 'Shall we go and have a burger after the cinema? There's a new place just opened in Greybridge.'

Jenny listened to them discussing their plans and sighed. Carrie seemed quite happy with just Fiona's company nowadays. They didn't seem to need her at all.

But a couple of weekends later, Jenny got a surprise. Early on the Saturday morning, Vicky turned up with Matt.

'So if you want a day off, I can take your place,' Vicky said to Jenny.

'That's a good idea,' Miss Stewart put in. 'You could take Jess for a walk, Jenny. I want to get some serious cleaning done today.'

'He looks as if he needs a walk,' Vicky agreed, going over to Jess. Jess licked her hand and wagged his tail.

Jenny looked at the Border collie lying in his basket. She'd noticed he spent a lot of time in his basket when Miss Stewart was around. He still hadn't accepted her. 'I'll phone Carrie, then,' she said. 'We can take Jess to Cliffbay. He loves a run along the beach.'

But when Jenny rang Carrie, her mother, Pam Turner, told her that Carrie wasn't there. 'She stayed overnight at Dunraven,' Mrs Turner explained. 'You'll get her there.' Jenny put down the phone, disappointed.

'What's wrong?' asked Miss Stewart.

'Carrie's staying with Fiona,' Jenny replied. She frowned. 'She didn't mention she was doing that this weekend.'

'She probably forgot,' Miss Stewart said reassuringly. 'Why don't you ring her at Dunraven?'

Jenny hesitated. 'I don't want to butt in if I'm not wanted.'

'Oh, Jenny, surely Carrie wouldn't think you were butting in,' Miss Stewart replied. 'She probably thinks you're too busy to see her.'

But still Jenny didn't want to phone Dunraven. After all, Fiona hadn't invited her.

'Why don't you take Jess for a walk up to Darktarn and then you can go and help out in the fields this afternoon,' Miss Stewart suggested. 'I'll be here so Jess won't be lonely.'

Jenny jumped up. 'Good idea!' she said. 'Come on, boy!'

* * *

Going to Darktarn *was* a good idea. The old Border keep had been a favourite place with Jenny and her mother and going there always made Jenny feel better. As Jess ran ahead, Jenny stood and let the wind blow through her hair. From up here she could see the whole of Windy Hill laid out below her and, far in the distance, the sea sparkled in the sunshine.

By the time Jenny returned to the farm she was feeling a lot better.

'You've changed your mind, have you?' Fraser Miles asked, when he, Matt and Vicky popped home for lunch.

'We'll be glad of your help,' Matt added. 'We're going to check the first-time mothers to see if any of them are likely to give birth early and we'll pen the ones that look like lambing first in the lambing barn.'

When it was time to leave, Jenny looked around for Jess. He was in his basket again. She walked over and gave his ears a rub. She was almost certain that Jess was spending so much time in his basket because he didn't like Marion. But why?

'What's on the menu tonight, Marion?' Matt asked, as he and Fraser made for the door.

Marion gave him a brilliant smile. 'It's a surprise, Matt,' she said.

Matt nodded. 'Oh, well, it's sure to be good – and the more the better, by the way,' he added cheekily.

'Come on, Matt,' said Vicky, pushing him out of the door. 'See you later, Miss Stewart.'

The young ewes were nervous and skittish. Jake and Nell had to work hard, rounding them up without scaring them.

'Away to me, Nell,' Fraser said to his dog, as Matt sent Jake far out across the field in the opposite direction. Jenny watched, fascinated, as the two dogs raced across the short grass, their plumy tails streaming out behind them.

'Jake will get behind them,' Fraser Miles explained. 'He'll make sure none of them bolt. Then Nell will round them up so that we can get them into the holding pens.'

Jenny nodded. Jake was the outrunner, able to hear and obey commands from a long distance while Nell was best close in to the sheep, driving them on towards the pens.

'Get the gate, Jenny,' Matt said, as the flock began to move. Jenny hauled open the gate of the holding pen while Nell picked off the ewes Fraser had selected and shepherded the sheep into a column, guiding them through the gate. Matt and Vicky got behind them, driving them towards the pen.

As the last ewe of the group entered the pen, Jenny closed the gate and watched while her father and Matt examined the ewes, judging which ones were likely to give birth first. Then those were separated off into another pen and the process began again. By the time they had finished they had more than fifty ewes to drive down the track to the lambing barn and Jenny was kept busy with the gates and rounding up the odd straggler. It was getting dark by the time they got the last of the young ewes safely housed in the lambing barn and made their way towards the house.

Jenny called to Jess and the Border collie came running towards her.

Marion was taking a roasting pan out of the oven and Matt looked at it in amazement. 'Roast beef!' he said. 'And roast potatoes.'

'And Yorkshire puddings,' Marion added proudly. 'I thought you would approve!'

'How right you are, Marion,' Fraser said, coming into the kitchen. 'I don't suppose Matt's hints had anything to do with it, did they?'

'Sit down and rest, Fraser,' Marion laughed, as

Matt turned red. 'You look tired.'

'Not a bit of it,' Fraser insisted, going towards her. 'Let me help you, Marion.'

As Miss Stewart bustled about, putting the food on the table, Jenny looked at her father, helping Marion carry plates and serving spoons to the table. Her father and Marion seemed friendlier than ever.

'Is anything wrong, Jen?' Vicky asked softly.

Jenny shook her head. 'Not really,' she said slowly. Then she turned to the other girl. 'Vicky,' she said, lowering her voice, 'do you think Dad and Miss Stewart are in love?'

Vicky looked a little surprised. She frowned. 'I think Miss Stewart is definitely interested in your father,' she said at last. 'But love — I don't know, Jenny.'

Jenny sighed. She didn't know either.

4

When they'd finished eating, Jenny offered to do the washing up. Matt and Vicky had gone out to the stable to see Mercury, Matt's horse. Jess was scampering around the kitchen.

'He's very lively tonight,' Fraser Miles remarked, as Jess ran past Marion, who was clearing the table, and over to Jenny, leaping up at her.

'*Down*, Jess,' Jenny said, as she took the washing-up liquid from its shelf. Her hand brushed against a clear plastic packet and it fell on to the counter, spilling some of its powdery contents. 'Oops!' she said, looking at the packet. 'What's this? Is this yours, Miss Stewart?'

Marion went quickly over to the counter and picked up the packet, putting it back on the shelf. 'Yes,' she replied, sweeping the spilt powder into her hand and into the sink. 'It's from the herbalist – for my headaches.'

'I didn't know you got headaches,' Fraser Miles said, surprised.

'I don't like to complain,' Marion replied. Then, suddenly, Jess ran up to her, barking sharply and snapping at her hand.

'Jess!' Jenny cried, shocked.

Marion snatched her hand out of the way.

Fraser Miles leaped up. 'Jess! Basket!' he bellowed. Jess immediately ran to his basket and lay down. Then Fraser turned to Marion. 'Are you OK?' he asked.

Marion nodded. 'He didn't hurt me.'

'He shouldn't have snapped,' Fraser Miles said seriously.

Jenny looked at Marion. Suddenly she remembered another time when Jess had acted so strangely. It was with Fiona McLay after the fire last November. Jess had been in the house when Fiona had set it on fire and had tried to tell them who was to blame. But it was ridiculous to think that Jess knew anything bad about Marion!

'I don't see why he should have taken against you like this,' Fraser Miles went on to Marion. 'You've been looking after him and feeding him for the last two weeks.' He held out his hand to her. 'Let's go and relax in the living-room.'

As her father and Marion passed Jess's basket to go to the living-room, Jenny saw Jess draw back. Something was definitely bothering him.

Jenny dried her hands and went across to him, kneeling down. She stretched out her hand and stroked his head. 'What is it, boy?' she asked. As she looked carefully at him, Jenny drew in her breath. Jess was trembling. Jenny laid her hand on his side. She could feel tremors running right through him. Suddenly Jess's chest heaved, and he yawned widely. Then he began to shake violently and uncontrollably.

'Dad!' Jenny yelled. 'Dad! Come quickly. There's something wrong with Jess!'

Jenny rushed to the door but her father had heard

her shouts and was already there as she opened it. He went swiftly over to the Border collie, as Matt and Vicky arrived.

'We heard the shouting. What is it?' Matt asked, alarmed.

Fraser Miles turned, his face serious. 'Jess is having a fit,' he said. 'Ring the vet, Matt. Tell him it's an emergency.' Wrapping Jess's blue blanket around him, he picked the Border collie up and carried him over to the Aga, calling, 'Jenny, get another blanket. And Vicky, bring Jess's basket.'

Jenny rushed to the dresser and heaved open the bottom drawer. She pulled out a blanket and raced over to Jess. Behind her, she could hear Matt's urgent voice speaking to Tom Palmer, the vet.

Vicky scooped up the basket and placed it on the rug in front of the Aga. Fraser Miles laid Jess down in it gently. 'We must keep him warm. Shivering like that can mean his body temperature is dropping.' Jenny wrapped the extra blanket tightly round Jess.

Fraser turned to Jenny. 'Has this happened before?' he asked.

Jenny shook her head, too upset to speak.

Fraser turned to Marion Stewart who was

standing by the kitchen table. 'Has anything like this happened while you've been looking after him, Marion?' he asked.

Marion shook her head. 'But he has snapped at me before,' she admitted. 'I didn't want to say anything, but I do find his aggressiveness worrying.'

'Aggressive!' Jenny echoed, horrified. 'Jess has never been aggressive.'

'He must be ill,' Matt said firmly.

Fraser nodded. 'But you should have mentioned Jess's aggressiveness to me, before, Marion,' he said.

'I didn't like to,' Marion Stewart explained. 'After all, I'm not used to dogs. I thought it was my fault that he just didn't like me – and besides, you've been so busy with the sheep, I didn't want to worry you.'

'That was very thoughtful of you, Marion,' Fraser said. 'But the sooner Tom Palmer sees Jess the sooner we'll know exactly what's wrong with him.'

Jenny bent over Jess again. The shaking was becoming less violent and gradually, as Jenny watched, it began to fade away, leaving Jess lying limply in his basket. His eyes began to focus again and he looked up at Jenny pitifully.

'Oh, Jess, what's wrong with you?' Jenny

whispered, putting her arms round him. Even through the blankets, she could feel occasional tremors running through him. She looked at her father. 'He won't die, will he?'

Fraser Miles put his arm round her shoulder. 'Of course not,' he said reassuringly.

'Maybe he's got a bug,' Matt put in. 'Let's just wait and see what Tom Palmer has to say.'

The next half-hour seemed the longest of Jenny's life as she sat by Jess and watched the tremors slowly fade away altogether. At last Jess's eyes drooped and he fell asleep. By the time Mr Palmer arrived, Jess seemed to be breathing more easily.

As Tom Palmer examined him, he shook his head. 'I don't quite know what has happened here,' he said. 'His breathing is a bit shallow and his heart rate is a little erratic but that's only to be expected after a fit.' He looked at Jenny. 'This hasn't happened before?'

Jenny shook her head.

'No, but he *did* seem a bit excitable tonight. And he's also been aggressive with Marion recently,' Fraser Miles said quietly.

'He's snapped at me a few times now,' Marion Stewart confessed. 'And he's seemed a bit nervous – jittery, I would call it. But then I'm not an expert.'

'You don't have to be,' Tom Palmer told her. 'You're being very helpful. If Jess has been aggressive, I need to know about it.'

Jenny looked at her father. 'You know Jess is the best-tempered dog in the world,' she protested.

Fraser Miles put an arm round Jenny's shoulders. 'We have to tell Mr Palmer everything we know, lass,' he said. 'How else can he make a diagnosis and help Jess?'

'Your father is right,' the vet agreed, his face sympathetic. 'The more I know, the better the chance of curing Jess.'

Jenny nodded miserably. 'It's just that Jess is usually so good. He would never bite anyone.'

'He's ill,' Tom Palmer said. 'Some illnesses can change a dog's character.'

Jenny swallowed her tears. She knew what it would mean if Jess was branded an aggressive dog – and she couldn't bear to think of it.

'Of course, he *was* the runt of the litter,' Fraser Miles said. 'There's often a flaw in the smallest pup. He didn't have an easy birth. I suppose there could have been other damage besides his leg.'

'You mean brain damage,' Tom Palmer said, looking serious. 'That certainly is a possibility. He could have been suffering from a weakness from the very beginning and something has triggered it – perhaps a virus. That's most likely.'

'So what can we do?' asked Matt.

Tom Palmer spread his hands. 'If it's a virus there isn't much to be done except wait for it to work its way through. I'll take a blood sample and run some tests to see if anything shows up. We'll also have to wait and see whether the fits recur. Perhaps the problem will sort itself. If it doesn't and there's a permanent tendency to aggression, then we'll have to think again. But we need to give it time before we consider doing anything drastic.'

'What do you mean by "drastic"?' Jenny asked, horrified. Tom Palmer looked at her, his eyes full of compassion. Jenny turned pleadingly to her father. When Jess had been a newly-born pup Fraser Miles had thought the best thing would be to destroy him. Was that what Mr Palmer was suggesting now? 'But, Dad, Jess has always been perfectly healthy apart from his leg.'

Fraser Miles didn't say anything for a moment. 'He's always *seemed* healthy,' he said at last. 'This illness could just have been waiting to happen.'

'Poor thing,' Marion Stewart sympathised. 'Does this mean he'll have to be put down? I know I'm not an expert on dogs but I wouldn't have thought you could afford to keep an aggressive dog on a sheep farm.'

Jenny drew in her breath sharply. Miss Stewart had voiced the thought that had been in all their minds. Jenny turned to Tom Palmer desperately. 'No!' she cried. 'You saved his leg, Mr Palmer. You operated on him when he was just a puppy. You can't put him down just because he's had a fit.'

'Now, now, Jenny,' Tom Palmer said. 'Don't get yourself so worked up. This might never happen again. Let's just wait and see.'

'But if it does happen again?' Jenny insisted.

Mr Palmer looked at her seriously. 'Well, lass, if the fits keep recurring, Jess wouldn't have much of a life. And he might become a danger — to people and other animals. He wouldn't be the Jess you know and love any longer.'

Jenny looked at the vet, horrified. 'You mean if Jess goes on having fits you might really have to put him to sleep?'

'For his own sake,' Tom Palmer said gently.

Marion Stewart leaned across and touched Jenny on the shoulder. 'It would be kindest to Jess,' she said.

The tears streamed down Jenny's cheeks. How could it ever be kind to kill Jess? 'I'll love Jess whatever he does,' she said through her tears.

5

Jenny woke early next morning and slipped quietly downstairs, pulling on a dressing-gown as she went. No one else was up yet and Jess was still fast asleep in his basket. Jenny settled herself down beside him, but she didn't touch him. She was afraid to disturb him.

It was an hour before anyone else appeared. Her father walked softly into the kitchen and found her still sitting silently beside Jess's basket.

Fraser looked down at Jess. 'He seems to be breathing normally,' he said.

Jenny nodded.

Her father gave her a hug. 'I remember finding you down here with Jess when he was just a tiny pup,' he said. 'You'd got up to feed him and you were both fast asleep.'

Jenny brushed a hand across her eyes. Jess had needed to be hand-fed for the first few weeks of his life but Jenny had never minded getting up in the middle of the night to feed him. 'He *will* be all right, won't he, Dad?' she asked, desperately.

'Tom is a good vet,' her father said. 'He'll look after Jess. Now you go and get dressed.'

Jenny rose reluctantly and went back upstairs. When she returned, Jess was still sleeping. Matt and Vicky were in the kitchen and Miss Stewart was preparing breakfast.

'Vicky and I are going out to the fields with Dad soon,' Matt told Jenny. 'Are you going to stay with Jess this morning?'

Jenny nodded. She couldn't bear to think of leaving him while he was so ill.

'Come and have some breakfast, Jenny,' Miss Stewart said.

But Jenny could hardly eat for worrying about Jess. She forced down a piece of bacon and tried to listen to her father talking about the lambing to Matt and Vicky.

Suddenly there was a sound from Jess's basket and Jenny shot out of her seat and bent down beside him, her heart thudding. Slowly, Jess opened his eyes. Catching sight of Jenny, he licked her hand then went to sleep again. Jenny breathed a sigh of relief. At least he had woken up briefly. She had begun to think he might sleep for ever.

'We'll have to be off,' Fraser Miles said. 'I think we'll have our first lambs soon.'

Matt and Vicky rose from the table and, as Vicky passed, she gave Jenny a sympathetic smile, bending down to stroke Jess. 'I hope he gets better soon,' she said softly.

Jenny nodded, tears pricking her eyes. 'So do I, Vicky,' she said fervently. She picked up Jess's food and water bowls to take them to the sink. 'Maybe he'll feel like something to eat and drink when he wakes up properly,' she said. 'I'll wash these out.'

There was a powdery mark on the floor where Jess's food bowl had been. Vicky grabbed a cloth and wiped it.

Jenny smiled her thanks as Vicky grabbed her coat and ran out to join Matt and Fraser in the jeep. Nell and Jake were in the back, their plumy tails wagging. The dogs loved their work. Jenny waved as her father drove out of the yard.

'If you want to go out with your father this afternoon, I'll look after Jess,' Miss Stewart offered.

Jenny shook her head. 'I'll stay here with Jess today,' she replied. 'I couldn't leave him the way he is.'

'You'll have to leave him to go to school tomorrow,' Miss Stewart warned.

'I know,' said Jenny. 'But maybe he'll be better by then. Maybe if he eats and drinks something, it'll help.'

During the afternoon Jess woke up properly and managed to drink a whole bowl of water and eat some finely minced meat that Jenny prepared for him. And by the time Fraser, Matt and Vicky came home at the end of the day, the Border collie seemed almost back to normal, though he was still a little tired.

'That's good news, Jen,' Matt said, as he and Vicky got ready to go back to college.

Jenny smiled up at him from her place by Jess's basket. 'Let's hope he'll be even better tomorrow.'

★ ★ ★

With a heavy heart, Jenny tore herself away from Jess to go to school next day. As soon as she got on the school bus, Carrie noticed something was wrong. 'What is it?' she asked. 'You look upset.'

Jenny sat down in the seat in front of Carrie and Fiona. 'Jess had some kind of fit on Saturday,' she explained.

Carrie and Fiona both looked shocked. 'Oh, poor Jess,' Carrie cried.

'Has the vet seen him?' Fiona asked.

'Of course,' Jenny replied, slightly irritated by the

question. Fiona sometimes seemed to act as if Jess was hers. 'He says the fit might just be a one-off,' Jenny continued. 'But . . . if not, if he starts to bite . . .' she couldn't go on.

'What?' asked Fiona, then her eyes darkened in horror. 'Oh, no, Jenny. You don't mean he would have to be put down?'

Jenny nodded wordlessly. Carrie laid a hand on her arm. 'It won't come to that, Jen,' she said.

'It can't. Not Jess,' Fiona added.

Jenny looked at Fiona. The girl's eyes swam with sudden tears. She had grown very attached to Jess during her illness – almost too attached. At one point Jenny had thought she might lose Jess to Fiona altogether.

'He could come to Dunraven,' Fiona offered. 'Mum would look after him while you're at school, Jenny.'

'No,' Jenny said quickly. 'Miss Stewart is there to look after him. And Jess is happier in his own home.'

'That's true,' Carrie agreed. 'Can we come and visit him, Jenny?'

Jenny nodded. 'Of course.' She swallowed hard. 'This morning was the first time he's ever stayed in his basket when I left for school. Usually I have to shut the gate on him to make sure he doesn't follow me.'

Carrie leaned towards her. 'Try not to worry,' she said. 'Maybe it was just something he ate.'

'I suppose it could have been that,' Jenny said. 'Oh, I hope that's all it is.' Carrie's words made her feel a little better.

'And, if it was, then he'll be better soon,' Carrie continued. 'You can bring him to our next sleepover. Fiona and I had good fun but it would have been even better with you and Jess.'

Jenny looked at Fiona and Carrie, sitting together as if they had always been friends, and couldn't help feeling a little left out. Then she flushed, remembering that she had avoided phoning Dunraven, thinking that they might not want her around. As it was she was glad she'd been at home when Jess had fallen ill. But Jenny couldn't help wondering whether Fiona would really have wanted her there over the weekend. Perhaps she enjoyed having Carrie to herself . . .

Jenny spent the day worrying about Jess, but when she got home he seemed back to his old self, running to her as soon as she got in the door.

'Carrie thought it might have been something he ate,' she said to Marion, as she hugged Jess. 'You aren't feeding him anything different, are you, Miss Stewart?'

'I hope I know how to feed a dog,' Miss Stewart said sharply.

'Sorry,' Jenny said quickly. 'I think Carrie was just trying to make me feel better,' She sat back on her heels and let Jess lick her face. 'Anyway, I don't care what it was so long as it's over,' she said, looking at Jess's bright eyes.

Even so, Jenny woke early next morning and ran downstairs to check on Jess. The Border collie leaped up from his basket and scampered over to her, wagging his tail. Jenny opened her arms to him, relieved that he still seemed well.

'Maybe Carrie was right,' she whispered in his ear. 'Maybe you ate something you shouldn't have. I hope so.'

By the time her father came down, Jenny and Jess were playing happily on the floor, Jenny tossing a ball for him. 'Up early again, lass?' he said.

'I was still worried about Jess,' Jenny explained. 'But he seems fine.'

'He certainly does,' Fraser agreed, smiling. 'And

I've got a surprise for you,' he said. 'I went out to check on the young ewes last night before I went to bed. We've got our first lambs – twins.'

'Oh, Dad, can I see them?' Jenny asked excitedly. 'And can Jess come too?'

Fraser bent and rubbed Jess's ears. 'Of course he can.'

Jenny dressed in double-quick time and followed her father out to the lambing barn, a lively Jess at her heels.

'There,' said Fraser, as he opened the door.

Jenny looked into the nearest pen. There were two tiny black-faced lambs snuggled into their mother's side, fast asleep.

'Oh, Dad, they're beautiful,' she said. 'Look, Jess.'

Jess poked his nose through the bars of the pen and snuffled as Jenny gazed at the new-born lambs.

'That's only the start,' Fraser Miles said. 'We've got a busy time ahead of us.'

Jenny smiled. She knew her father didn't mind the hard work. The lambs were worth it.

Carrie and Fiona came home with Jenny after school the next day. Jess raced out to meet them.

Jenny felt uncomfortable as she watched Fiona

fussing so much over Jess. She was glad Fiona loved Jess, but Jess was *her* dog, not Fiona's.

Anna McLay called in some time later to pick up the two girls. She was going to drive Carrie home on the way to Dunraven. 'It's good to see Jess looking so much better,' she smiled. 'Fiona was very worried about him. She couldn't love him more if he was her own dog.'

'What's wrong?' Carrie asked, seeing Jenny frown as she heard this.

Jenny shrugged. 'Nothing,' she replied. Her feelings were too complicated to explain, even to Carrie.

Just then, the phone rang. It was Mrs Grace. She was shocked to hear of Jess's illness and rang again the following evening to see how he was doing. Ian said he was sending a get well card to Jess even if he couldn't read it! And Matt rang home every day too.

Marion Stewart was surprised by all this attention. 'Jess certainly seems to be a popular dog,' she said to Jenny.

Jenny smiled. 'Everyone loves Jess,' she said.

Marion nodded thoughtfully. 'So it seems.'

The phone rang again and Jenny picked it up.

This time it was Tom Palmer. 'I got the results of the blood tests, Jenny,' he said. 'Nothing significant showed up, so it's my guess it was a virus. How is he?'

'He's back to his old self,' Jenny told him.

'That's very encouraging,' Mr Palmer said. 'Let's hope that's the last we'll see of it then.'

Jenny rang off and sighed with relief. Then she remembered that she hadn't asked the vet if it could have been something Jess ate. She put it out of her mind. Jess was well again. That was the important thing.

But when Jenny arrived home from school on Thursday there was no Jess running to meet her. Jenny's heart skipped a beat. 'Jess?' she called, as she dumped her schoolbag in the porch. There was no answering bark.

Jenny rushed into the kitchen. Marion was standing by the Aga looking serious. 'I'm afraid Jess has had another fit, Jenny,' she said.

Jenny ran to Jess's basket. The Border collie lay there, twitching slightly. He looked up at her and tried to raise his head but it seemed too much of an effort for him. He dropped his head heavily back down on his blanket.

'Oh, Jess,' Jenny said miserably. 'I thought you were better.'

'The fit didn't last long,' Marion said. 'But he *was* very agitated. He snapped at me.' Miss Stewart looked down at her hand.

Jenny drew in her breath as she saw the dressing that covered the woman's wrist. 'Did Jess do that?' she asked.

Marion nodded. 'But it hardly bled,' she assured Jenny. And, luckily, I've just had my anti-tetanus jabs renewed.'

Jenny turned back to Jess. 'Oh, Jess,' she said softly. 'What's happening to you?'

Marion Stewart came to stand over her. 'Perhaps we should call in Tom Palmer again,' she suggested.

Jenny looked up at Marion Stewart, tears standing in her eyes. She shook her head. 'I don't want to tell Mr Palmer about it – not yet. You said you weren't badly hurt. Can't we give Jess another chance – a chance to get well?'

Marion put her hand on Jenny's shoulder. 'I know what you're afraid of, Jenny,' she said. 'But you must think of what's best for Jess. If these fits go on, his life will be miserable. And you have to think of the consequences. What if he bit a child?'

Jenny bent over Jess again and stroked him. His eyes were closed now and he was sleeping, his breathing regular. 'Mr Palmer says he doesn't know what's causing the fits,' she continued desperately. 'But if this fit wasn't so bad, maybe he'll just grow out of them. Mr Palmer says the only thing to do is wait and let him rest. He'll get better. He's *got* to get better.'

Marion Stewart sighed. 'Let's hope so, Jenny,' she said. 'For his sake.'

'So you won't send for Mr Palmer?' she asked.

'Not this time,' Marion Stewart promised.

Jenny looked up at her. 'Oh, thank you, Miss Stewart,' she said. 'You'll never know how grateful I am to you for giving Jess another chance.'

'Why don't you call me Marion?' Miss Stewart said. 'We're friends, aren't we?'

Jenny nodded. 'Oh, yes,' she said. 'And just wait. Jess will get better soon and then you'll see what he's really like. He's the friendliest dog in the world and he'll just love you – once he's better.'

Marion didn't say anything for a moment. 'Don't get your hopes up too much,' she said at last. 'Sometimes it's best to be prepared for the worst.'

But Jenny wouldn't allow herself to do that – she couldn't imagine life without Jess.

When Fraser Miles arrived home he took Miss Stewart's injury very seriously. 'Let me have a look at it, Marion,' he said. 'Maybe you should see a doctor.'

Marion put her hand behind her back. 'Don't fuss, Fraser,' she said, smiling up at him. 'It was only a scratch.'

Fraser looked worried. 'We can't have Jess biting,' he said. 'And we certainly can't ask you to look after him now, Marion.'

'Nonsense,' Marion said briskly. 'I'll be more careful how I handle him now. Don't worry.'

Jenny looked at Marion gratefully, wondering why she was still so keen to look after Jess. She must really like him, Jenny thought.

Jenny could hardly concentrate at school next day.

'At least the Easter holidays start tomorrow,' Carrie comforted her. 'You'll be able to spend lots of time with Jess then.'

Jenny nodded. 'But I've promised to help Dad with the lambing, and I don't want to let him down.'

'I could look after Jess for you,' Fiona offered.

Jenny knew Fiona was trying to help but she shook her head. 'Thanks, but I couldn't bear to think of him anywhere but at Windy Hill,' she said. 'And if he is really ill, Dad won't expect me to leave him.'

Jenny ran all the way down the track from the bus stop after school and rushed into the kitchen, hardly able to ask the question that was hovering on her lips. 'Has he been all right?' she asked Marion, as she went at once to Jess's basket.

'He hasn't had another fit but he's been very sleepy,' Marion informed her.

'He didn't try to bite you, did he?' Jenny asked anxiously, as she bent over Jess and stroked him. Jess slowly opened his eyes and groggily lifted his head to lick Jenny's hand. Then, after a few seconds, he heaved himself up and clambered out of his basket, wagging his tail.

'He didn't have the energy to bite,' Marion said. 'That's the first time he's moved all day.'

Jenny gathered Jess into her arms. 'Gently, Jess,' she whispered. Jess licked her face again. He might be ill but he was still glad to see her.

And, the following morning, his tiredness of the previous day seemed to have gone. Jess scampered across the kitchen floor to Jenny. She bent down and threw her arms around him. 'Oh, Jess, you're so much better!' she cried, burying her face in his neck. 'And I won't have to leave you to go to school for a whole two weeks.'

'Jess certainly is a lot livelier this morning.' Fraser Miles said, coming in at the kitchen door with Marion. Jenny smiled up at them, overjoyed at Jess's improvement. 'And there's another surprise,' her father continued. 'Look who's here.'

Jenny leaped up as Matt walked through the door. 'Matt!' she cried.

'I got away earlier than I'd hoped, Jen,' Matt said. Then he bent to pat Jess who was standing patiently, tail wagging. 'How are you, boy?' he asked, as he rubbed Jess's ears. He looked up at Jenny. 'He looks well.'

'He's much more like his old self today,' Jenny told her brother. 'I'm beginning to see a pattern. He has a fit, then he's really tired the next day, and then it's as if nothing has happened – he's back to normal.'

'So are you coming to give us a hand with the lambing today?' Fraser asked.

Jenny hesitated. 'I'd like to,' she said. 'But I hate to leave Jess.'

'We'll take him with us,' her father announced. 'That'll give Marion a break from looking after him. He can stay in the jeep but you'll have to keep him on the lead if you want to walk him. I don't want him running loose in among the sheep.'

Jenny nodded. She knew her father couldn't take any risks where the pregnant ewes were concerned. 'I'll take him for a walk up to Darktarn at mid-morning break,' she said, delighted. 'You'd like that, wouldn't you, boy?'

Jess gave a short bark and wagged his tail. Jenny put her arms round his neck and gave him another cuddle.

'But I don't mind looking after Jess if you want to leave him here with me,' Marion said.

'I know,' Jenny replied. 'And I really appreciate that after Jess snapping at you the way he did. But maybe some fresh air will do him good.'

Marion looked a little disapproving. 'Well, I'm not sure about that,' she replied. 'Be careful you don't overtire him. That could bring on the fits again.'

'I won't,' Jenny assured her, as she followed her father and Matt out of the door.

'Marion is being really understanding about Jess,'

Fraser Miles remarked, as they made their way across
the yard. 'You like her, don't you?'

Jenny nodded. 'Of course I do,' she replied.

Her father looked pleased, and again Jenny
wondered what was happening between him and
Marion. She turned to Jess and smiled as he ran to
her, his eyes bright once more. 'Come on, Jess,' she
called. 'We're going lambing!'

6

'Oh, isn't it gorgeous?' Jenny exclaimed, as the just-born lamb struggled to its feet.

Matt laughed softly. 'I never get used to this,' he said. 'It'll always be a miracle.'

Jenny watched as the ewe licked her little black-faced lamb all over, stimulating his blood supply, then the tiny creature nuzzled at his mother and fastened on her teat, beginning to suck.

Jenny turned to Matt. 'That birth went well,' she said.

Matt nodded, then he looked up. 'Dad is waving to us,' he said. 'Let's see what he wants.'

Jenny and Matt made their way across the field. Fraser Miles was bending over a ewe. The sheep was lying on the ground, her legs stiff, and her body heaving with effort. As Jenny watched, the animal began to strain even more, raising her head and curling back her top lip.

'This one is going to need some help,' Fraser Miles said.

Jenny looked at her father in concern. She knew that he would never interfere unless it was necessary. 'What's wrong, Dad?' she asked.

'This ewe is quite an elderly lady now,' Fraser said. 'This will be her last lambing and it's a bit of strain for her. I reckon we've got twins here.' He laid a hand on the ewe's flank. 'There, there, old girl, it won't be long now.'

Matt opened his lambing bag. 'What do you need, Dad?' he asked.

'The lambing oil,' his father answered, rolling up his sleeves.

Matt handed the bottle to his father and Fraser

358

rubbed the oil on his hands and forearms. 'Can you hold her head, Jenny?' he asked.

Jenny went to the ewe's head and took it in her arms. She had done this before. When a ewe had trouble giving birth she needed help to guide the lamb out of the birth canal, but it was a frightening experience for the animal.

Jenny talked gently to the frightened animal as her father and Matt worked.

'I thought so,' Fraser said. 'There are two lambs in here and I don't think she has any strength left to push them out. We'll have to pull them out for her, Matt.'

Jenny held her breath as her father gently eased out the first lamb and laid it on the grass. Matt immediately began to scrape away the membrane of the birth sac so that the lamb could breathe. A tiny black nose appeared, followed by two black front legs.

As he worked, Matt checked the lamb over. 'This one is all right,' he said.

Fraser Miles looked at Jenny. 'How's she doing, Jenny?'

Jenny looked down. The ewe's eyes were closed and her body was trembling. Suddenly she gave a jerk and was still. Jenny looked up. 'Oh, Dad,' she said, suddenly frightened.

Matt leaned over and put his hand on the ewe's side, his face serious. 'You'd better hurry, Dad,' he said, his voice strained. 'I'm afraid we've lost this one.'

Fraser Miles looked up, his eyes dark with sorrow. 'She was a good ewe,' he said softly. 'This is her fifth season. I never get used to losing a ewe.'

Jenny looked down at the sheep. The creature lay still, its head heavy in her arms. 'Poor thing,' she said with a break in her voice.

Matt looked at her sympathetically. 'It's hard, Jenny,' he said. 'But we've got to try and save the other lamb.'

Jenny nodded and blinked the tears away. Lambing could be very sad sometimes.

Fraser Miles set to work. Jenny looked across at him. His face was beaded with sweat as he eased and pulled at the lamb, trying not to damage the little creature still inside its mother's womb.

At last he gave a final pull and another little bundle slithered out on to the grass. At once Fraser began to tear the birth sac away, then reached into his lambing bag again, bringing out a rough towel to rub the tiny body in order to stimulate the blood supply. Jenny knew that usually the mother would do this by licking her lamb. She looked down sadly at the ewe for a moment, then took a deep breath. The ewe was beyond help but her lambs would need all the care and attention they could get if they were going to live.

'We've got to get these two into the lamb warmer as soon as possible, Matt,' Fraser said. 'They'll need to be hand-reared.'

'Matt can take me down in the jeep and I'll look after them,' Jenny said.

Fraser nodded. 'Be as quick as you can, Matt,' he said.

Matt and Jenny carried the new-born lambs to the jeep and wrapped them in a blanket to keep them warm, before tucking them safely in a box in the back. Jess sniffed them interestedly, then licked Jenny's hand. 'We're going back now, Jess,' Jenny said, as she got into the jeep.

Matt dropped Jenny off at the farm, turning straight back to the track. 'See you later,' he called as he drove off.

Jenny nodded as she carried the lambs in their box towards the lambing barn, Jess at her heels.

'There there,' she said as the tiny lambs bleated weakly. 'You'll soon be warm and fed.'

Jenny pushed open the door of the lambing barn, carefully shutting Jess outside. 'I know you wouldn't harm the lambs, Jess,' she said to him as he looked up at her. 'But I promised Dad I wouldn't let you in among the sheep.'

Jenny left Jess whining outside the door and moved down the barn. One end was taken up with pens housing young ewes that were about to give birth for the first time. Her father and Matt would come down later to check on their progress and make sure the ewes bonded to their lambs. That meant putting mothers and lambs in individual pens until the lambs were feeding regularly and the new mothers had got used to looking after them.

Jenny went over to the warming pen, and lifted the lid. She smiled as three furry black noses peeped out at her and the little Blackface lambs bleated piteously up at her. There would be a lot more orphaned and abandoned lambs in here before the lambing was done, but the warming pen was safe and cosy, and in a few days these lambs would be strong enough to come out into ordinary pens. She gently laid the new lambs in the pen and took an old rough towel from a hook on the wall. One at a time she rubbed the lambs down and breathed a sigh of relief as she saw them struggle to their feet, falling over almost at once but trying again.

'You're going to be all right,' she whispered to them. 'I'll be back in a minute with a bottle for each of you.'

With Jess at her heels, Jenny ran for the kitchen. 'I need to make up feeds for two new lambs,' she said as she rushed in.

Marion Stewart turned to her and smiled. 'Why don't you show me? Then, any time you're busy, I can help out.'

Jenny showed Marion the little bottles they used to feed new-born lambs, 'Dad keeps a supply of frozen colostrum to give to new-born orphaned lambs too,' she explained. 'That's the milk that the ewe produces immediately after she gives birth. The lambs need that for the first twenty-four hours so that they get all the antibodies they need to protect them against infection. We have to feed them every four hours at the beginning. Sometimes, if they're very weak or aren't sucking properly, it's every two or three hours.'

'That sounds like hard work!' Marion exclaimed,

looking rather less enthusiastic.

'It is,' Jenny agreed, 'but it's worth it. I would have been coming down soon anyway to feed the lambs that are already in the warming pen. I'll feed the newest ones first, then do the others. Can I leave Jess with you?' she asked.

'Of course you can,' Marion replied, moving towards Jess. The Border collie backed away, growling low in his throat.

'Jess!' Jenny exclaimed.

Marion shrugged, then backed away, looking at the bandage on her hand.

Jenny flushed. 'Maybe he's still got traces of that virus,' she said. She turned to Jess. 'Here, boy!' she said. 'Into your basket.'

Jess scrambled into his basket and looked up at her. 'Stay!' Jenny commanded.

Jess lay down, his head pillowed by his front paws, looking at Jenny pleadingly as she made up the feeds. Jenny tried to ignore him but it wasn't easy to avoid his big dark eyes and he whined when she made for the door.

'No, Jess,' Jenny said firmly as he tried to follow her. 'Stay!'

Jess crouched down in his basket again but his

ears were pricked and Jenny noticed that his hackles were slightly raised. She ran over to him and stroked his neck. 'There, boy,' she said softly. 'I'll be back soon.'

'He'll be all right,' Marion assured her. 'After all, he'll have to get used to me, won't he?'

Jenny smiled. Marion was so understanding. 'Thanks,' she said. 'I won't be long.'

Jenny hurried across to the barn and went immediately to the warming pen to offer the bottles to the new arrivals. They fastened on the bottles and began to suck. Jenny sat back on her heels, feeling the lambs pulling at the teats on the bottles.

She thought of their mother in the top field. It was sad when a ewe died but her two new lambs were healthy enough. She smiled. 'You'll be all right,' she whispered to them, as they finished their feed. 'I'll look after you.'

Jenny raced back to the kitchen and looked in at the door. Marion smiled at her. 'Your dad rang on the mobile,' she said. 'He and Matt are coming down to check the ewes in the lambing barn so he says you're to wait here for them.'

Jenny nodded and called to Jess. The Border collie ran to her and she hugged him. 'He's been good, hasn't he?' she asked Marion hopefully.

'I just left him alone,' Marion said. 'He seemed a little agitated after you left so I thought it was best.' Jenny rubbed her face against Jess's neck. She had a feeling that Marion had left Jess alone because she didn't trust him. 'You go and attend to the other lambs,' Marion went on. 'I'll feed Jess and, if he'll let me near him, I'll take him for a walk later.'

But Jenny saw her glance worriedly at Jess. Marion definitely didn't trust him.

Jenny spent the afternoon helping her father and Matt in the lambing barn. There were five new mothers and their lambs settled in pens by the time Fraser Miles called a halt.

'Let's see if Marion will give us a cup of tea,' he said.

'I could do with one,' Matt agreed.

'And I want to see how Jess is,' Jenny said, giving a new-born lamb a cuddle before she put it into the pen with its mother. The ewe immediately began to nuzzle the little creature, nudging it towards the farthest corner of the pen and settling down with the lamb sucking on her teat.

'That one seems happy enough,' Fraser remarked. 'I reckon we've earned our break.'

But when they pushed open the kitchen door, Jenny knew at once that something was wrong as soon as she looked at Marion Stewart's face. 'Is it Jess?' she asked.

Marion nodded. 'I was just coming to get you,' she said, turning to Fraser.

Jenny hurried over to Jess's basket and knelt down. 'It's just like before!' she cried.

Jess was lying shivering uncontrollably in his basket. Jenny ran to get another blanket from the dresser and wrapped it round him, trying to comfort him.

'What exactly happened, Marion?' Fraser asked.

Marion shook her head. 'I don't really know,' she said. 'I was busy upstairs and when I came down he was like this. I've only just found him.'

Jenny looked up, tears stinging her eyes. 'I don't understand it,' she said. 'He was all right earlier on.'

'This can't go on for ever, Jenny,' her father said seriously.

'I know that,' she said miserably. 'I know it can't go on.'

Next day was Sunday and Carrie phoned early. 'Can you take a day off from the lambing, tomorrow?' she asked. 'Dad's taking Fiona and me out to Puffin Island again. Do you want to come?'

'I can't, Carrie,' Jenny replied. 'We're so busy,'

'You sound worried,' Carrie said. 'Is Jess all right?'

'He's very sleepy this morning,' Jenny told her. 'He had another fit yesterday.'

'Oh, no! Was it the same as before?' Carrie asked, concerned.

'I wasn't there,' Jenny explained. 'Marion was looking after him.'

'Did you ask her if she was feeding him any differently?' Carrie asked.

'Yes,' Jenny replied. 'I asked her that, but she got quite annoyed with me. She seemed to think I was implying that she didn't know how to feed Jess properly.'

'So it's not something he ate,' Carrie concluded.

'No,' Jenny agreed. 'How could it be?'

But as Jenny said goodbye to Jess before going lambing with Matt and her father she wondered. Something had to be causing Jess's fits – but what was it?

By evening, Jess seemed to be getting a little better.

Fiona phoned, anxious about him. 'Carrie told me about the latest fit,' she said. 'How is he?'

'He's getting better again, now,' Jenny answered. 'There seems to be a pattern to it. He has a fit, then he's sleepy next day, then he's completely back to normal the day after. So I'm hoping he'll be fully recovered again tomorrow.'

And sure enough, the following morning, Jess was back to normal.

Fiona called again to ask after Jess. 'So he's all right now,' she said, sounding relieved. 'Are you going lambing today?'

'I expect so,' Jenny replied. 'Jess will be all right with Marion.'

'Would it be all right if I came to see him soon?' Fiona asked.

'Of course,' Jenny replied.

'If you change your mind you can always come to Puffin Island with us – Jess too,' Fiona offered, before she rang off.

Jenny had a good day helping her father and Matt out in the fields. But when they returned to the farmhouse late that afternoon, Jess didn't race out to meet them. Alarmed, Jenny jumped down from the jeep and ran into the kitchen. She looked at Jess's basket. It was empty. There was no sign of the Border collie anywhere. Her heart in her mouth, Jenny ran into the hall, up the stairs, calling Jess's name. There was no answering bark and Jenny ran back downstairs, stumbling in her rush.

'What's happened?' Matt asked, catching her as she hurtled out into the farmyard.

'It's Jess,' Jenny told him, her face white. 'He's gone!'

Fraser Miles walked across the yard, Jake and Nell

at his heels. 'Now, Jenny, are you sure?' he asked. 'Where's Marion?'

'She isn't here either,' said Jenny.

'Maybe she took Jess for a walk,' Matt said.

Jenny's heart began to slow down. 'Maybe she did,' she said. Then she looked around. 'But her car isn't here. She wouldn't take Jess for a walk in the car.' She looked at her father in alarm. 'What if he had another fit? What if Marion's taken him to the vet? What if Mr Palmer decides to put him down?'

Fraser Miles put a hand on her shoulder. 'Tom Palmer would never do that without talking to you about it first,' he said. 'Calm down, lass. There's probably a perfectly rational explanation.'

Matt strode into the kitchen and reappeared a moment later. 'There's a note from Marion,' he announced. 'She forgot to mention she had a hairdresser's appointment in Greybridge. Supper's in the oven.'

'Does she say anything about Jess?' Jenny asked.

Matt shook his head. 'No,' he replied. 'She doesn't mention him at all.'

Jenny looked around the farmyard as dusk crept around them and shivered. Where was Jess?

7

'Have you looked in the stable?' Matt asked.

Jenny shook her head. 'The door's closed,' she said, but she ran across and heaved open the stable door anyway. 'Jess!' she shouted but there was no answering bark, only the sound of Mercury, whinnying from his stall.

'Jenny! He's here!' her father called.

Jenny whirled round and the breath caught in her throat. Fiona McLay was coming in at the farmyard gate. Beside her was Jess.

'Jess! Oh, Jess, I thought you were lost!' Jenny cried, racing towards him.

Jess launched himself at Jenny and she hugged him tightly, rubbing her cheek against his head. Jake and Nell ran up, butting Jess, and the young sheepdog wagged his tail.

'Carrie and I took Jess with us to Puffin Island,' Fiona said, smiling. 'We had a great time. Jess loved every minute of it.'

Jenny stood up, furious. 'You took him without asking me first?' she demanded. 'How *dare* you? You've no right to do that. Jess is *my* dog, not yours!'

Fiona flushed deep red. 'But I didn't think you'd mind,' she began.

Jenny interrupted her. '*Mind?* Of course I mind!' she cried. 'Jess has been ill. How was I to know where he was? I thought he had run off and had a fit. I thought I'd never see him again. Just leave Jess alone, Fiona!'

'Wait a moment, Jenny,' Fraser Miles said, walking over to them. 'Let's hear what Fiona has to say.'

Fiona shuffled uncomfortably. 'Miss Stewart said an outing would be good for him,' she said hesitantly. 'Didn't she tell you?'

'Marion isn't here,' Matt said.

'It's no good trying to blame Marion,' Jenny put in. 'You're just trying to turn me against her, to make trouble. You've always been a troublemaker! You should never have taken Jess away in the first place – and neither should Carrie.' And, breathless, she turned on her heel. 'Come, Jess!' she called.

Jess trotted at her heels into the house. Once inside, Jenny realised she was shaking. She'd really let rip at Fiona. She bent down and gave Jess another cuddle, then looked up as she heard her father and Matt come in.

'Fiona's gone,' Fraser Miles said. 'She was pretty upset.'

'Well, so was I!' Jenny said mutinously. 'Ever since Fiona had Jess to help her over her illness she acts as though Jess is *her* dog.'

'Now, that isn't true, Jenny,' Fraser Miles said gently. 'It was a misunderstanding.'

Jenny flushed. Now that she had Jess back she was beginning to feel calmer. 'Maybe I did fly off the handle a bit,' she admitted. 'But she shouldn't have taken Jess without asking me.'

'She had permission from Marion,' Matt put in.

Jenny didn't say anything for a moment. 'Marion

wouldn't have let her take Jess without leaving a note or something,' she said.

'There's a car,' Matt said, going to the window. 'That's probably Marion now.'

Fraser turned as Marion's car drew into the yard. 'Let's ask her what happened, shall we?' he said.

Marion Stewart opened the kitchen door a moment later. Her short dark hair was newly cut and styled. 'Sorry I had to rush off like that,' she said. 'I completely forgot my hair appointment.' Then she saw Jenny's flushed face. 'Is anything wrong?' she asked.

'Did you tell Fiona she could take Jess to Puffin Island?' Jenny blurted out.

Marion looked taken aback at her tone. 'I said a run in the open air would do Jess good. He was so much better this morning and when Fiona arrived, he was so pleased to see her it seemed a pity to stop him going with her. After all, the poor thing hasn't had much fun recently.'

Fraser looked at Jenny. 'You see,' he said. 'The explanation is perfectly simple. Marion was only thinking of Jess.'

Jenny put her hand on Jess's neck and the Border collie moved closer to her.

'Why, what's wrong?' Marion asked. 'Has Jess had another fit?'

Jenny shook her head. 'He wasn't here when I got back,' she said. 'I was worried about him.'

Marion looked sympathetic. 'Oh, I'm sorry, Jenny,' she said. 'I should have thought.'

'It isn't your fault,' Jenny said. She looked at her father and Matt. 'Sorry I shouted.'

'You were upset,' Fraser said. 'But I think you owe Fiona an apology, don't you?'

Jenny nodded and put her arms round Jess again. 'Just as long as Jess is safe, that's all I care about,' she said.

Jess kept close to Jenny's side all evening, sitting under the table at her feet while they ate. Jenny and Marion had just finished the washing up when the phone rang. Fraser answered it. 'Ellen!' he exclaimed. Jenny watched her father's face as he talked with Mrs Grace. As he listened, his expression grew serious. 'Are you sure that's what you want to do?' he asked.

There were a few moments of silence as he listened, then he said, 'I think you'd better tell her yourself, Ellen.' He signalled to Jenny to come to the phone.

Jenny walked across and took the receiver from her father. 'Mrs Grace?' she said. 'Is anything wrong? Is Ian all right?'

'Hello, lass,' Mrs Grace's familiar voice greeted her. 'Everything is fine and Ian sends you his love. How's Jess?'

Jenny told Mrs Grace about the most recent fit. 'But he seems all right again now,' she finished. 'I don't understand it, Mrs Grace. I'm so worried about him.'

'You must be, lass,' Mrs Grace replied sympathetically. 'And now I'm afraid I've got something difficult to tell you. I've made up my mind to stay in Canada.'

'What?' said Jenny. 'But you can't. You belong here!'

There was a pause before Mrs Grace spoke again. 'It hasn't been an easy decision, Jenny,' she went on. 'I've thought about it a lot. But I don't think you'll be needing me back, not now you have Marion. She and your father seem to get on very well and I'm happy for them.' Mrs Grace sighed. 'My sister has been wanting me to come and live near them for a while now,' she went on. 'Perhaps that would be the best thing. My family is out here in Canada.'

Jenny swallowed hard. Did Mrs Grace think her father and Marion were going to get married? She could hardly ask with her father and Marion in the room. 'Oh, Mrs Grace, I will miss you,' she said.

Ellen Grace's voice was soft. 'And I'll miss you, lass,' she replied. 'But two women in a house is one too many. I'll ring again soon. Take care.'

Jenny said goodbye and handed the telephone back to her father. When he had said goodbye to Mrs Grace, she turned to him. 'Can't you persuade her to come back?' she pleaded.

Fraser Miles smiled and shook his head. 'I'm sorry, lass,' he replied. 'But Ellen is a grown woman. She's entitled to do as she likes. I've asked her to think it over but she must do what she feels will make her happy.'

Jenny sat down beside Jess and stroked his head. The Border collie licked her hand and thumped his tail on the floor.

'It'll be strange not having Mrs Grace at Windy Hill,' Matt said with a sigh. Then he rose. 'I'd better go and check Mercury is all right for the night.' He looked at Jenny as he went out. 'Canada isn't that far away,' he said kindly. 'Maybe you could go and visit Ellen and Ian some day, Jen.'

'That's a good idea,' Marion put in. 'I'm sure you'd love to spend a summer in Canada, Jenny.'

Jenny shook her head. 'I wouldn't be able to take Jess,' she said. 'I'd hate a summer without him.'

Marion looked thoughtful. 'I wouldn't dismiss the idea of a trip to Canada, Jenny,' she said. 'As Jess's future is a little uncertain, you might be glad to get away for a while.'

Jenny looked at Marion miserably. She didn't have to say it – what she meant was that Jess might not be around this summer.

'I thought you had some furniture catalogues you wanted to show me, Marion,' Fraser said quickly, to change the subject.

Marion smiled. 'They're in the car,' she told him. 'Can you come and help me get them? There's a whole pile.'

Jenny watched as the two of them went out of the room together. She looked down at Jess. 'Do you think Dad will marry Marion?' she asked him.

Jess licked her ear and Jenny smiled. Everything seemed to be changing around her. She was still afraid Jess might have another attack but his eyes were bright and clear. Maybe his day at Puffin Island really had done him good.

Her father and Marion approached the kitchen door, talking in low voices. But the kitchen window was open and Jenny could hear their conversation quite clearly.

'I know how much you had come to rely on Ellen, Fraser,' Marion was saying. 'But haven't you wondered what made her decide to stay in Canada?'

'What do you mean?' Fraser replied, sounding surprised. 'Her family's there.'

Marion laughed softly. 'I think it might be more than that,' she said. 'Didn't you think Ellen seemed a little uncomfortable about Anna McLay's ring going missing? Perhaps she thought Anna suspected her of stealing it.'

'That's ridiculous,' Fraser replied. 'Ellen would never do a thing like that.'

Marion spoke slowly. 'I don't know. I suppose it would be very tempting. And it isn't fair to put temptation in people's way. Have you checked Sheena's jewellery recently?'

'It never occurred to me,' Fraser said, his voice shocked. 'You can't seriously believe that Ellen is a thief!'

The voices faded slightly as Marion and Fraser entered the porch. Jenny caught her breath and sprang up as her father and Marion came through the kitchen door. 'Of course Mrs Grace isn't a thief,' she exclaimed.

Fraser Miles looked at her, his face stern. 'Have you been eavesdropping, Jenny?'

Jenny flushed but she stood her ground. 'I couldn't help overhearing you,' she said. Then she turned to Marion Stewart. 'You don't know Mrs Grace or you wouldn't say such a thing,' she protested.

Marion raised her eyebrows. 'I certainly wouldn't like to believe it of Ellen,' she said. 'But the fare to Canada *is* quite expensive . . .'

Jenny took a deep breath. 'You can't just accuse her like that. Mum's jewellery has never been locked up all the time Mrs Grace has been working here and nothing has ever gone missing. Mrs Grace wouldn't touch it. We all trust her absolutely.'

Marion shrugged.

Jenny looked at her for a moment. 'We can check if you like,' she said. 'We can do that now.' She rushed out of the kitchen and into the hall, running up the stairs two at a time, flinging open the door of her room. Switching on the light, she moved swiftly to her wardrobe and took out her mother's jewellery

box. She laid out the contents on top of the desk. Light glanced off the shiny stones and she began to go through the things. Jenny's heart began to beat faster as she lifted out the last piece of jewellery.

Her father and Marion had followed Jenny upstairs and stood in the doorway, watching.

'The aquamarine necklace isn't here!' Jenny cried. She turned to her father. 'You don't believe Mrs Grace took it, do you, Dad?'

Fraser looked at Jenny then turned to Marion and shook his head. 'You can't accuse someone without proof,' he replied.

'But you must admit, it looks suspicious,' Marion put in. 'Anna's ring has disappeared and so has Sheena's necklace – and Ellen is in Canada, intending to stay there. It would certainly make *me* think . . .'

'What's going on?' said Matt, coming up the stairs. 'I heard you from the yard, Jenny. And just listen to Jess.'

Jenny suddenly realised that Jess was barking. She ran out of the room and hung over the banister. Jess was at the bottom of the stairs, tail erect, barking loudly.

'Hush, Jess!' Jenny commanded. 'It's all right.'

Jess lay down at the foot of the stairs and gazed up at her, keeping watch, sensing that she was upset.

Jenny turned back to her father. 'You don't believe that Mrs Grace is a thief, do you?' she asked.

Matt looked shocked and his father quickly explained the situation. 'Not Ellen,' Matt concluded. 'I can't believe it of her.'

Fraser Miles looked uncomfortable. 'She's been such a help to us in the past,' he said. 'I think of her as one of the family.'

Marion just smiled. 'Perhaps you're too trusting, Fraser,' she said, laying a hand on his arm.

Fraser ran a hand through his hair. 'Now I don't know what to think,' he said.

'What are you going to do, Dad?' Jenny asked. 'Are you going to ask Mrs Grace if she stole Mum's necklace?'

Fraser shook his head. 'I couldn't do that,' he said. 'But perhaps it's for the best that she's decided to stay in Canada . . .'

Marion slipped an arm through his. 'That's more than generous, Fraser,' she said.

Jenny watched as they both turned away and went downstairs. Jess sprang up and sidled round them, coming to lie down at the foot of the stairs again.

Matt turned to Jenny and shook his head in amazement.

Jenny sighed heavily and began to walk downstairs. Jess leaped up at her and she hugged him, looking back at Matt. 'I'll never believe Mrs Grace is a thief – no matter how bad it looks for her.'

8

Over the next week Jenny had more to worry her. Jess had another fit on Thursday afternoon and on Friday morning, Jenny decided to stay at home. Jess had just woken up and was still a little drowsy.

'I'll help with the lambing,' Marion offered.

Jenny looked at Marion gratefully. 'And I'll wash up the breakfast things while you're out. It's just that I can't bear to think of Jess getting ill again while I'm away from him,' she said.

'That's all right, Jen,' Matt put in. 'We'll manage. You look after Jess. See you later.'

'Why don't you give Carrie a ring and ask her over?' Fraser suggested. 'You've been so busy helping me you haven't seen her for ages, have you?'

'That's a good idea,' Jenny agreed.

When the others had gone, Jenny filled Jess's bowl with water and set it down beside him. He raised his head and lapped at the dish and Jenny heaved a sigh of relief, then rang Carrie.

'I'll be right over,' Carrie promised.

Jenny settled down on the floor beside Jess. The Border collie was resting again but he had managed to drink all of his water. 'Maybe you could try eating something in a little while, Jess,' Jenny whispered to him.

When Carrie arrived, Jess opened his eyes and licked her hand.

'He's had a drink,' Jenny told Carrie. 'I thought I'd see if he wanted something to eat.'

'Good idea,' Carrie said.

'And I said I'd do the washing-up for Marion,' Jenny continued, as she picked up Jess's food bowl.

'I'll get started on that,' Carrie offered, reaching for the washing-up liquid. 'Oh, my mum uses this for her headaches,' she said, noticing Marion's packet of herbal remedy on the shelf.

Jenny nodded. 'So does Marion.' She looked at the packet. 'She'll have to get some more soon. That packet was nearly full last time I saw it.'

'But Marion hasn't been here that long,' Carrie said, looking puzzled. 'My mum's powder lasts for months and months. She only uses a tiny pinch at a time.'

Jenny put some food in Jess's bowl and went to place it back on the floor. She froze as she looked at the place where the bowl had been. There again, was the powdery mark. 'I've noticed that before,' Jenny said slowly, pointing it out to Carrie.

Still holding the packet, Carrie came to stand beside her. Jess stared at the packet in Carrie's hand and growled.

'Jess, what is it?' Jenny said, bending down to him.

Jess continued to stare at the packet. Carrie reached down and touched a finger to the powder on the floor then held it against the clear plastic of the packet. 'It looks like the same stuff,' she said slowly. Carrie tipped a little of the powder from the packet into her hand. 'It *is* the same,' she concluded.

Suspicion began to dawn in Jenny's mind. 'That powder has been sprinkled over Jess's food,' she said.

'It certainly looks that way,' Carrie replied quietly.

'Oh, Jess!' Jenny cried. 'Is this what's been making you ill? You were right, Carrie. It *was* something he ate.' She turned to the other girl. 'But why would Marion do a thing like this?' Jenny asked, unwilling to believe Marion could be so cruel. 'Maybe Jess ate some accidentally.'

'But accidents like that don't happen more than once, do they?' Carrie replied. 'Look, Jenny, I think we should take this stuff to show to Mum. She'll be able to tell us more about it.'

Jenny nodded. 'The sooner the better,' she agreed. 'Let's go!'

'I know the powder is dangerous unless taken in exactly the right quantity,' Mrs Turner said when the girls showed her the packet. 'I can't imagine Marion having used so much of it for headaches. Mine lasts for ages. Maybe she spilt it,' Mrs Turner went on. 'You would have to ask a herbalist exactly what effect it would have if taken in large doses. I get my supply from the herbalist in Greybridge.'

Jenny nodded. 'We'll do that. Thanks, Mrs Turner. We'll go right now.'

'I'll phone Fiona,' Carrie said. 'She can meet us at the bus stop.'

'Fiona?' Jenny echoed.

'You don't mind, do you?' Carrie asked. 'We'd planned to meet this afternoon anyway, and as it's about Jess, she'll want to come along. She's been phoning me to ask how he is because she didn't like to phone you.'

Jenny looked at Jess, standing by her side. Fiona really did love him and Jenny regretted the things she had said to Fiona the last time she had seen her. 'OK,' she said. 'Fiona too.'

An hour later Carrie pushed open the door of the herbalist's shop in Greybridge.

'I'll stay outside with Jess,' Fiona offered.

Jenny nodded and gave Jess a quick pat before following Carrie into the shop. Jars and bottles lined the shelves and there was a huge glass flask on the counter filled with dark liquid. The shop smelled of herbs and spices. A woman in a white coat smiled at them from behind the counter. 'How can I help you?' she asked.

Jenny took the packet out of her pocket and handed it over nervously. 'We wondered if you could tell us about this,' she said.

The woman took the packet and tipped some of the contents on to the palm of her hand, then looked at them curiously. 'Where did you get this?' she asked. 'I wouldn't sell this to children.'

Jenny opened her mouth to answer but Carrie interrupted. 'We found it,' she said quickly. 'The label had your shop's name on it and we were worried in case it might be dangerous so we brought it in to see what it was.'

Jenny looked at Carrie in surprise but the herbalist was smiling. 'You did the right thing,' she approved. 'Taken in the right quantities this substance has remarkable healing properties. A very small amount can be effective for pain relief. But if the dosage is wrong it can have very dangerous side effects.'

'What kind of side effects?' Jenny asked, her heart beating a little faster.

The woman shrugged. 'That varies,' she said. 'Very often it causes extreme drowsiness – but that's only if the dosage is wrong. And it can cause sickness and fever – even fits. It was very sensible of you to bring this in. I'll just hold on to it. We wouldn't want anyone taking it accidentally.'

Jenny swallowed. 'I suppose if an animal found it and took some it would be really dangerous,' she said.

The herbalist nodded seriously. 'A dog or a cat could suffer a great deal if they took this by accident. It could eventually kill them.'

Jenny swallowed again and Carrie touched her arm. 'Come on, Jenny,' she said.

The herbalist smiled. 'Thank you,' she said. 'You did the right thing bringing this in.' She frowned slightly as she looked at Jenny. 'Are you all right? You look a little pale.'

Jenny managed to nod and smile until she was outside. She put her arms round Jess and he licked her face. 'Oh, Jess, you might have died,' she said.

Carrie told Fiona what had happened in the shop. 'It's really hard to think Marion would poison Jess deliberately,' she continued as they walked down the street.

'Let's go for a walk down by the river and think this out,' Jenny suggested.

They turned on to the river walk and Jenny let Jess off the lead. He scampered ahead of them, snuffling at the bushes and barking at the ducks on the water.

'He looks all right now,' Fiona said. 'Maybe he *did* get hold of the stuff by accident.'

'Every time he had a fit?' Jenny asked. 'No, it can't be that. He always had the fits when Marion was looking after him. She must have put that stuff in his food. Why else would there be some on the floor round his dish?'

'Why would Marion want to poison Jess?' Carrie asked. 'I thought she liked Jess.'

'But Jess doesn't like *her*,' Jenny replied.

Fiona looked worried. 'I don't think Marion is as nice as she pretends, Jenny,' she said. She flushed. 'I know you thought I was trying to turn you against her that day we took Jess to Puffin Island but it was Marion who told me to take him. I just dropped in to see if you had changed your mind about coming. Marion said you were too busy helping with the lambing and you wouldn't mind us taking Jess. . . . And there's something else I haven't told you.'

Carrie picked up a stick and threw it for Jess. The Border collie raced after it.

'What?' asked Jenny.

'When I arrived I knocked on the kitchen door but nobody answered,' Fiona went on. 'The door was open slightly so I just assumed you were upstairs.'

'Go on,' Jenny said.

'Of course, you weren't there,' Fiona said. 'But Marion was.' Fiona stopped.

'You'll have to tell us the rest now, Fiona,' Carrie urged.

Fiona flushed slightly. 'I went upstairs, thinking that you might be in your room, Jenny.'

'Then what happened?' Jenny asked.

'Marion was coming out of your bedroom,' Fiona told her. 'She was stuffing something into her pocket, but she was so surprised to see me she dropped it on the floor.'

'What was it?' Jenny asked, shocked.

'A necklace,' Fiona replied.

Jenny gasped. 'A necklace! One of Mum's necklaces is missing. Marion said Mrs Grace must have taken it. Can you remember what the necklace was like?'

'It was a gold chain with pale blue stones set in it,' Fiona replied.

'But that's it. That's the one that's missing!' Jenny cried.

'So *Marion* stole it!' Carrie put in. 'But why on earth would she want to steal one of your mum's necklaces?'

'Perhaps she wanted to get Mrs Grace into trouble,' Fiona suggested. 'The way she got me into trouble with Jenny for taking Jess away.'

'It looks to me like Marion was trying to turn you against Mrs Grace as well, Jenny,' Carrie said.

Jenny thought for a moment. 'You've always said that Marion wanted to marry Dad,' she said to Carrie. 'And Mrs Grace thinks they will get married. I think that's why she's decided to stay in Canada.'

'And Miss Stewart wanted Jess out of the way too,' Fiona put in, 'because she doesn't like him, and Jess can sense that.'

'And she knows that I wouldn't be friends with her if I thought Jess had a problem with her. So by poisoning him she's been able to put Jess's hostility down to his illness!' Jenny exclaimed. 'But why didn't you tell me all this before?'

Fiona shook her head. 'I didn't think you would believe me,' she explained. 'You seemed to be getting on so well with Marion and after I brought Jess back you were so angry. And anyway, why should anyone believe me? Especially you, Jenny. After all, I set fire to Windy Hill and I've been really rotten to you in the past.'

Jess scampered up and offered his stick to Jenny. Jenny bent and rubbed his ears, taking the stick. 'I'm sorry I lost my temper like that,' she said to Fiona. 'I should have listened to you.'

'And I should have told you about Marion and the necklace sooner,' Fiona said. Her face grew distressed. 'Maybe if I had spoken out earlier Jess wouldn't have got so sick. Marion would have been forced to stop poisoning him.'

Jenny frowned. 'Well, she can't poison him any more,' she said. 'She doesn't have the herbs.' She shook her head. 'I should have taken more notice of Jess. He saw the danger in Marion.' Jenny jumped up.

'Where are you going?' Carrie asked.

'Back to Windy Hill,' Jenny replied. 'Marion isn't going to get away with this.'

'You mean you're going to accuse her?' Fiona asked. 'But you don't really have any proof – and, according to what you told me, the herbalist said that those herbs *could* be used for headaches.'

'I don't care. I'm going to tell her I know what

she's been up to,' Jenny said firmly. 'Then she won't dare to try and harm him again.'

Fraser, Matt and Marion were back by the time Jenny got home.

'Where have you been?' Matt asked, rubbing Jess's ears as the Border collie ran to him.

'Greybridge,' Jenny replied, looking at Marion.

'With Jess?' said Marion. 'He certainly seems to have recovered well.'

Jenny looked at her smiling face and reminded herself that this woman had tried to poison Jess. Looking at Marion's pleasant expression, it was hard to believe. 'If he *is* better it's no thanks to you, Marion,' she said.

Fraser Miles looked up from the newspaper he was reading. 'What did you say, Jenny?' he said as if he couldn't believe his ears.

'I said it was no thanks to Marion that Jess is better,' Jenny insisted. She turned to Marion, then took a deep breath. 'I took your headache powder to the herbalist in Greybridge. She told me what happens if it's given in the wrong quantities. And I know you've been giving it to Jess. You've been poisoning him!' At the sound of

Jenny's strained voice, Jess ran to her, pressing against her leg.

'Jenny!' Matt exclaimed, his face shocked.

Jenny lifted her chin and looked at Marion, her hand protectively on Jess's head.

Marion opened her eyes wide. 'How dare you accuse me of that? I'm shocked at you, Jenny.'

Jenny flushed. 'You were giving those herbs to Jess,' she said quietly. 'That's what made him sick.'

Marion put her hand to her head. 'Oh, Jenny, I wish you hadn't stolen my herbs,' she said. 'All your shouting has brought on another headache. Fraser, I must go and lie down.'

Fraser turned to Jenny. 'Jenny, go to your room,' he said.

'But, Dad,' Jenny protested. 'I'm telling the truth! She really has been trying to poison Jess. You've seen how Jess behaves around her.'

'Jenny!' her father thundered. 'Do as you're told! I think you've caused enough trouble for one day with your ridiculous accusations. Look what you've done to Marion.'

Jenny looked at Marion standing behind her father. She had her hand to her head but, as her eyes met Jenny's they were steely and cold. 'Don't be hard on her, Fraser,' she said. 'All you have to do is phone the herbalist. She'll tell you those herbs are a headache remedy. Jenny is so upset about Jess needing to be put down she doesn't know what she's—'

'Jess *doesn't* need to be put down!' Jenny interrupted hotly.

'Jenny!' her father warned. He turned back to Marion. 'It's very good of you to look at it that way,' Fraser said to Marion. 'Is this true, Jenny? Are the herbs a headache cure?'

'Yes, but . . .' Jenny began.

'That's enough,' her father said. 'Go to your room.'

Jenny looked helplessly from her father to Marion. He didn't believe her. And if he didn't believe her about this then he would never believe her about the necklace. Marion stared back, her eyes triumphant. She knew she had won. She knew Fraser was on her side. Jenny looked once more at her father. 'Dad?' she said desperately.

Fraser Miles regarded her coldly. 'I told you to go to your room, Jenny,' he said. 'We'll talk about your behaviour tomorrow when you've calmed down.'

Jenny turned, defeated. Fiona had been right. She had no proof and she had failed – she had failed Jess.

9

Jenny was up early next day, determined to try to talk to her father before Marion came downstairs. As she entered the kitchen Jess ran to her and she bent to pat him, not at all surprised to find him so well.

'Of course you're well, Jess,' she whispered to him. 'Marion hasn't got her herbs any more, has she?' She smiled in spite of her worries. Jess's eyes were bright and he wagged his tail furiously as she hugged him.

Matt was stacking plates from the table on to the worktop by the sink. He turned to her. 'You know, you really should try to get on with Marion,' he said. 'She's doing her best to help us.'

Fraser Miles came into the kitchen as his son finished speaking. 'I want you to apologise to Marion when you see her,' he told Jenny. 'She's spending the morning in bed. She still has a headache but she's coming out with us this afternoon to help with the lambing.'

Jess moved closer to Jenny, warned by Fraser Miles's tone that she was in trouble. Jenny reached a hand down and buried her fingers in the soft fur at his neck but she said nothing. It was obvious that her father was still very angry with her.

'Well?' he said. 'You will apologise, won't you?'

Jenny swallowed. 'But, Dad, you don't understand . . .' she began.

Fraser looked at her impatiently. 'I understand that you don't like Marion and that you're determined to push her out of Windy Hill,' he said. 'It isn't good enough, Jenny. We've got trouble with the lambing and I'm too busy to put up with any more nonsense from you.'

'What trouble?' Jenny asked, alarmed.

Fraser ran a hand through his hair. 'We have a rogue ewe,' he told her. 'I've found several lambs dead — killed.'

Jenny gasped. She knew that sometimes a ewe would kill her lamb for no apparent reason — but several!

'You mean this ewe is killing other lambs — lambs that aren't her own?'

Matt nodded. 'We're going to try and weed her out but it could take days to cover the whole flock. Don't make any more trouble, Jen.'

Jenny nodded. 'I thought I'd go over to Dunraven today,' she told her father. 'I'll take Jess with me.'

Fraser gave her a brief nod. 'That would be best,' he said. 'But when you come back I'll expect you to apologise to Marion. Think it over, Jenny. I'm serious about this.'

Jenny watched as her father and Matt left, calling to Jake and Nell. If any sheepdog could find a rogue ewe, it would be Nell, she thought. Jenny hoped she could do it. Losing lambs was a serious business.

Jenny turned from the window and put some bread in the toaster. She wished she could be out in the fields, helping — but not if Marion Stewart was going to be there.

★

Fiona came out to meet Jenny as she arrived at Dunraven. Carrie had already arrived. Jess jumped up and Fiona made a fuss of him. 'What happened when you got home yesterday?' she asked, as they made their way into the kitchen.

'Did Marion confess?' Carrie asked eagerly.

Jenny shook her head. 'Dad didn't believe me and Marion denied everything, then said that Jess really should be put down. It was terrible.'

Fiona looked at her with concern. 'But she can't have Jess put down,' she said.

'She won't,' Jenny said determinedly. 'I'm going to keep him with me all the time so she'll never get another chance to poison him. If he doesn't have any more fits, he'll be safe. But I'm scared. What happens after the Easter holidays when I'm at school?'

'Mrs Grace will be back by then,' Carrie assured her.

'No she won't,' Jenny said desolately. 'Marion has turned Dad against Mrs Grace too, remember? So he's not going to encourage her to come back from Canada.'

Anna McLay appeared at the door. 'Hello, Jenny,'

she said as Jess trotted over to meet her. 'Did I hear you saying that Ellen was staying in Canada?'

Jenny nodded. 'All her family is out there now,' she said. 'And besides . . .' she stopped.

Anna McLay looked concerned. 'What is it, Jenny?'

'Miss Stewart thinks that Mrs Grace stole your ring,' Jenny blurted out. 'She told Dad that was why she had decided not to come back.'

Anna McLay looked shocked. 'But that's ridiculous!' she said. Then she flushed. 'Oh, this is my fault. I'm so sorry. I should have remembered to tell you. I found my ring.'

'What?' said Jenny. 'When?'

'A few days ago,' Mrs McLay replied. 'I was taking a pair of trousers to the cleaners and I found it when I was clearing out the pockets. I must have slipped it in there when I was doing some housework and forgot all about it. I really should have mentioned it before.'

'That's all right,' Jenny said excitedly.

Mrs McLay left and Jenny turned to the others. 'This makes all the difference. If I tell Dad that, then he'll know that Mrs Grace isn't a thief.'

'And maybe he'll realise that Marion could be wrong about other things too,' said Carrie.

'Lying about them, you mean,' Fiona put in.

Jenny nodded and called Jess. 'Wait till Dad hears what I've got to tell him, Jess,' she said, bending to give him a cuddle.

'Would you mind if I came back to Windy Hill with you later on?' Fiona asked.

'Of course not,' Jenny replied. 'But why?'

Fiona flushed slightly. 'I still feel guilty about not mentioning seeing Miss Stewart with your mum's necklace,' she said. 'If I could tell your dad what I saw, then it might help.'

Jenny smiled. She still couldn't quite get used to the idea that Fiona would want to help her. 'That's really thoughtful of you, Fiona,' she said.

Jess reached up and laid his head in Fiona's lap.

'Jess trusts you, now,' Jenny said. 'And so do I.'

Fiona blushed even more. 'It's time I did something for you,' she said awkwardly. 'You've done such a lot for me.'

'I'll come too,' Carrie announced. 'After all, you might need some moral support.'

Jenny laughed. 'I reckon I'll need all the support I can get, Carrie.'

Carrie looked at her, for once serious. 'You only have to ask,' she said.

Jenny nodded. 'I know that,' she said. She knew now that she and Carrie would always be friends – and Fiona was proving to be a good friend too. How could they fail to persuade her father they were telling the truth?

When Jenny pushed open the kitchen door at Windy Hill late that afternoon, her heart sank a little. Her father and Matt were sitting opposite each other at the kitchen table with Marion between them – and they looked exhausted. Fraser Miles's head was down and he was staring into his coffee cup, his thoughts obviously far away. Marion looked round as the girls came in and gave them an unfriendly look. Her usually immaculate hair was windblown and untidy and she had a smear of mud across one cheek.

Matt looked up and smiled but he looked utterly weary. 'Hi, Jen. Hello, girls,' he said. 'I hope you've had a better day than we've had.'

Jenny sat down at the table and Carrie and Fiona followed her. 'Did Nell manage to find the rogue ewe?' she asked.

Fraser shook his head. 'Not yet,' he said shortly. 'We found four more dead lambs today.' He ran a hand through his hair. 'That sort of thing has never happened at Windy Hill before. I can't help but think it's a bad omen.'

Marion laid a hand on his arm. 'Sheep farming is such hard work, Fraser,' she said sympathetically. 'Have you ever thought of giving it up? Windy Hill would fetch a good price. You'd probably never have to work again. You could relax, take holidays, do something else if you wanted to.'

Jenny gasped. 'No!' she burst out. Seeing the shocked expression on Matt's face, she turned to watch her father's response. His face too seemed frozen with shock, then he moved his arm so that Marion's hand was no longer resting on it. 'Leave Windy Hill?' he said. 'Sell it? I don't think you understand what the farm means to us, Marion.'

Marion flushed slightly but she recovered quickly and stretched over to lay her hand on his arm again. 'Oh, I know you love farming,' she said. 'But surely there are less demanding jobs? You're so talented, you could do anything.'

Fraser gave an incredulous laugh. 'That's very complimentary of you, Marion,' he said. 'But you don't understand. Sheep farming is my life. I could never give it up. And besides, Windy Hill isn't mine to sell.'

This time, Marion drew back her hand. 'What do you mean?' she said, her voice sharp. 'I thought you owned it.'

'I do own it during my lifetime,' Fraser said. 'But Windy Hill belonged to my wife's family. It's held in trust, to be handed down to Matt.'

Jenny smiled at Carrie and Fiona in relief.

'You!' Marion exclaimed, turning to look at Matt.

Matt frowned. 'Why should that upset you, Marion?' he asked. 'If you're interested, I can assure you that I would never sell Windy Hill either. There will always be Mileses at Windy Hill. It's our home.'

Marion tried to smile, but couldn't quite manage it. 'Oh well,' she said, 'it's been a hard day and I feel one of my headaches coming on.' She rose and turned away. 'In fact, I think I had better go home. I have a feeling my headaches are going to prevent me coming to Windy Hill – for the foreseeable future. I'm not sure all this hard work is for me.'

Fraser looked concerned, then his eyes hardened as he realised what Marion was really saying. 'I think I understand, Marion,' he said. 'Don't let us keep you.'

Marion nodded. 'I'll go and pack,' she said, making for the door.

Jenny looked at her father. He looked even more weary than he had earlier. 'I thought she was interested in me and my family – not in how much the farm might be worth if she could get me to sell it,' he said, shaking his head sadly.

Jenny was concerned at the disappointment she could see in her father's eyes. Had he really liked Marion so much?

A few minutes later, Marion appeared again, carrying her two suitcases.

'I'll see you out,' Fraser said quietly. 'Thank you for everything you've done.' He took the cases from Marion and followed her out to her car.

Suddenly Jess darted after them. Jenny leaped up. 'Jess!' she called.

Carrie and Fiona followed Jenny to the door and Matt came up behind them.

Marion was at the boot of her car, changing out of her wellingtons into shoes. Jess bounded over to the boot, hackles up, growling.

'Jess! Here, boy!' Jenny called again.

Jess ignored her. He was pulling at a rolled–up scarf that was hanging over the edge of the boot.

412

'Jess!' Fraser Miles called sharply.

Jess turned at once, the scarf caught in his teeth. It unravelled slowly and, as Jenny watched, something glinted as it fell to the ground. 'It's Mum's necklace!' she exclaimed, running over and picking it up. She held it out to show her father.

Fraser Miles's eyes were flinty as he looked at Marion. 'What are you doing with this necklace?' he demanded.

'I don't know how it got there,' Marion protested. 'I've never seen that scarf in my life.'

'So what was it doing in the boot of your car?' Fraser asked frostily.

Marion flushed. 'I don't know,' she stammered. 'Unless Ellen Grace put it there. I wouldn't put it past her. After all, that woman's a thief.'

Jenny clutched her mother's necklace in her hand and turned to face Marion Stewart. 'Mrs Grace isn't a thief – *you* are!' she cried. 'Mrs McLay *found* her ring. Nobody stole it. Mrs McLay just mislaid it. But you stole Mum's necklace and tried to put the blame on Mrs Grace!'

Marion looked down her nose at Jenny. 'Don't make accusations you can't prove,' she snapped.

'But she *can* prove them,' Fiona said, stepping forward. 'At least, I can! I saw you coming out of Jenny's bedroom with that necklace the day you told me to take Jess to Puffin Island. You were stuffing it into your pocket.'

'This is outrageous!' Marion blustered. 'How dare you call me a thief?'

'You aren't only a thief,' Carrie declared, taking a step towards Marion Stewart. 'You tried to poison Jess.'

'You wanted us all to think that Jess was dangerous,' Jenny said, her voice strained. 'You

414

wanted him put down. You wanted him dead – either poisoned or destroyed.'

Marion snatched her scarf from Jess, wrenching it out of his mouth. Her hand caught against his teeth and the dressing she had worn on her wrist for so long flapped loose. Jenny's eyes widened as she saw the clear, unblemished skin beneath the dressing. 'Jess didn't bite you at all, did he?' she breathed. 'You put that bandage on your wrist just to make us think he was dangerous.'

Fraser looked at Marion in disgust. 'You weren't interested in me or my family at all, were you, Marion?' he said. 'You didn't care about the things we think are important. You just wanted me to marry you, then sell Windy Hill to provide you with an easy life.' He shook his head. 'To think I nearly fell for it. You had me convinced that Ellen was a thief. You even tried to turn me against my own daughter.' He cast a quick look at Jenny and she put her hand in his. He grasped it tightly then turned once more to Marion Stewart. 'It's time for you to leave,' he said shortly. 'And please don't come back!'

Marion slammed the boot shut and strode round to the front of her car. Without a backward glance, she got into the driver's seat, started the engine and roared off.

Fraser squeezed his daughter's hand. 'I should have listened to you, lass,' he said wearily.

Jenny bent and called Jess to her. The Border collie came running and she hugged him fiercely. She could hardly bear to think how close she had come to losing Jess.

10

As Marion Stewart's car disappeared into the distance, Fraser Miles turned to Jenny and Matt. 'Come on,' he said. 'We've got something to do.'

'What's that?' asked Jenny.

'I'm going to phone Ellen to ask her to come back to us,' Fraser replied.

Jenny smiled up at him. 'Do you think she will?'

'I hope so, lass,' her father said, striding towards the house. 'I certainly hope so.'

Carrie grinned. 'Fingers crossed,' she said.

'Mum has been missing her a lot, too,' Fiona agreed, as they all followed Fraser inside.

Everyone crowded round the telephone as Fraser rang Canada. 'Ellen?' he said when someone answered. 'I've rung to ask you to come back. We need you.'

Jenny heard a surprised exclamation on the other end of the line and listened carefully as her father explained about Marion Stewart, then he handed the phone to her. 'Ellen wants to speak to you,' he said.

Jenny took the phone and smiled as Mrs Grace's voice came over the line. 'Oh, Jenny, what a terrible time you've been having,' the housekeeper said. 'I must say, I never liked that Marion Stewart, but I thought your father was very taken with her. In fact I expected to hear they were getting married and there would be no room for me at Windy Hill any more. So I thought the best thing to do was to make a life for myself out here in Canada.'

'But you'll come back now, won't you?' Jenny asked anxiously.

'Your father certainly seems to want me back,'

Mrs Grace replied. 'He says he misses my cooking,' she laughed.

Jenny looked up at her father. 'It isn't just your cooking,' she said. 'We miss *you*. We all miss you.'

There was a short silence before Mrs Grace spoke again. 'You don't know how glad I am to hear that,' she said at last.

'And you'll come home?' Jenny asked again.

'Home,' Mrs Grace repeated. 'That sounds nice. Yes, Jenny, I'll come home.'

Jenny passed the phone back to her father and turned to the others, beaming. 'She's coming home!' she said.

Matt grinned. 'Thank goodness for that!' he said. 'I don't know about anybody else, but I'm starving!'

Jenny laughed and Carrie made for the fridge. 'Come on, Fiona, let's cook a celebratory tea for us all,' she said.

Matt rolled his eyes. 'What have I done?' he asked. 'Thank goodness Vicky is coming tomorrow. At least she can cook!'

'She can help with the lambing too,' Jenny said happily. 'And Mrs Grace will be home soon.'

'I can't wait,' said Matt.

★

'She's picked something up,' Matt said three days later as Jenny stood beside Vicky, watching Nell. The sheepdog moved forward, body close to the ground, creeping in among the flock. Jenny had Jess on his lead by her side. The Border collie's ears were pricked, all his attention on Nell.

'Do you think she's found the rogue ewe?' Vicky breathed.

Fraser Miles stood watching his dog, his eyes intent. Jake was waiting patiently by his side while Nell searched, combing the flock, separating one sheep from the rest, then rejecting it. But this time the dog seemed to be on to something.

'I think she might have,' Fraser said, moving forward. 'Stay here, you three. Keep Jess with you, Jenny.'

Jenny put her hand on Jess's neck and watched, fascinated, as her father walked towards Nell with Jake at his heels. Nell was among the flock now, moving quietly so as not to disturb the ewes and their lambs.

Then Jenny saw Nell crouch down and fix her eyes on one particular ewe. It stood there for a moment as if mesmerised, then it slowly began to move towards the dog. Nell rose swiftly and nudged the ewe out of the flock, herding it towards Fraser Miles. Fraser murmured to Jake and the sheepdog moved behind the ewe, ready to turn it if it bolted. Fraser reached out and caught it by the scruff of the neck, then he turned briefly. 'Bring the rope, Matt,' he said.

Matt walked slowly forward, a rope in his hand. He slipped it round the sheep's neck and secured it.

Fraser Miles bent and rubbed Nell's ears. 'That'll do, Nell,' he said softly. 'Good dog!'

Jenny raised her hand from Jess's neck as Jake and Nell trotted over. Jess nuzzled the bigger dogs, wagging his tail.

'Isn't Nell wonderful?' Jenny said to Vicky.

Vicky smiled. 'Jake and Nell are both wonderful sheepdogs in their own way,' she said.

Fraser Miles nodded. 'You're right, Vicky,' he agreed. 'But Nell is a bit special. Jake is a good outrunner, the best I've ever had, but Nell can pick a bad one out of a whole flock. Not many dogs can do that.'

'Jess is like Nell,' Jenny said thoughtfully. 'He picked out Marion Stewart, didn't you, boy? He knew she didn't belong at Windy Hill.' Jess butted

Jenny's hand and licked it, looking up at her adoringly.

'So he did, Jenny,' Fraser Miles replied, smiling. 'Jess is a grand dog too.'

Matt led the ewe over to the jeep at the edge of the field and loaded it on to the trailer.

'What will happen to it, Dad?' Jenny asked.

'It will have to be destroyed,' Fraser Miles told her. 'Once a ewe starts trampling lambs there's nothing else for it.'

The afternoon was growing dark and the wind was rising off the sea. Jenny looked around the fields. They were dotted with ewes and tiny Blackface lambs. 'It's been a good lambing hasn't it, Dad?' she asked.

Fraser smiled. 'Even better than last year,' he said, his eyes moving over his flock.

Jenny lifted her head and let the wind blow through her hair. Then she looked down at Windy Hill, lying snug and safe in the valley below.

'Come on,' said her father. 'Let's go home.'

They were halfway down the track to the farm when Jess sat up, ears pricked, and began to bark.

'What is it, boy?' Jenny asked, as Matt slowed down for a corner.

Jess continued to bark, scrabbling at the door of the jeep.

'He wants out,' Vicky said. 'You'd better stop, Matt.'

Matt stopped the jeep and Jess leaped out. 'Wait for me!' Jenny called, jumping out after him.

Jess ran round her feet, then raced away from her, turning to make sure she was following.

'Go on, Jenny. We'll follow,' her father said, as Matt started the engine again.

Jenny raced the last few metres towards the farm gate and hurtled through it. Jess was already at the kitchen door, still barking. Jenny stumbled in surprise. Light was flooding out of the door, spilling into the yard and, as she ran again towards the house, a figure appeared in the doorway. Jess leaped up at the figure, his tail wagging furiously.

'Mrs Grace!' Jenny yelled, throwing herself across the doorstep. 'Oh, it really *is* you. You're back!'

Ellen Grace caught Jenny in her arms, hugging her as Jess tried to climb up the housekeeper's legs. Mrs Grace bent down, gathering Jess to her. 'I managed to get an earlier flight,' she said breathlessly as Jess licked her face.

Jenny looked at the familiar face. Mrs Grace's hair

JESS THE BORDER COLLIE

was tousled and her cheeks were flushed. 'We didn't expect you yet,' she said, hugging her again as she stood up.

There was the sound of a vehicle pulling up and Jenny turned to see her father, Matt and Vicky getting out of the jeep.

'Ellen!' said Fraser, his face breaking into a smile as he came towards the housekeeper.

Mrs Grace went to meet them. Matt threw his arms round her then looked up, his eyes going to the kitchen door. He sniffed. 'I smell something cooking,' he said.

Vicky laughed. 'What a welcome, Ellen,' she said.

Ellen Grace laughed back. 'It's the best welcome I could have,' she replied.

Jenny laughed and bent to hug Jess. 'Jess likes having you home too, don't you, Jess?' she said. Jess barked and licked Jenny's ear.

'We *all* do,' said Fraser Miles, shepherding everyone into the kitchen. 'Welcome home, Ellen.'

Jenny closed the door on the darkening afternoon and turned towards the cosy warmth of the kitchen. 'Now we really are *all* back at Windy Hill,' she said. Then, turning to her Border collie, added, 'And it's all thanks to you, Jess!'

PORPOISE IN THE POOL
Animal Ark Holiday 12

Lucy Daniels

Mandy and James are spending their summer holiday at Sennen Cove in Cornwall. The Cove is a home to a school of porpoises but also popular with jetskiers. On their second day on the beach they spot an injured porpoise hemmed in by rocks. Mandy and James need to help the poor creature get better and back in the water. But can they also stop the jetskiers endangering the porpoises again?

Another Hodder Children's book

POLARS ON THE PATH
Animal Ark 53

Lucy Daniels

Mandy Hope is having an Arctic adventure!
She can't wait to meet the amazing animals
that live amongst the snow and ice.

The Hopes are in the small town of
Churchill to watch polar bears migrating
north. It's a spectacular sight. But when
one of the cubs strays from his mother,
Mandy fears for its safety. Can she help
reunite the cub with his family before winter
sets in?

DOG IN THE DUNGEON
Animal Ark Hauntings 1

Lucy Daniels

Mandy and James will do anything to help an animal in distress. And sometimes even ghostly animals appear to need their help . . .

Skelton Castle has always had a faithful deerhound to protect its family and grounds. But Aminta, the last of the line, died a short while ago. So when Mandy and James explore the creepy castle the last thing they expect to see is a deerhound – especially one which looks uncannily like Aminta . . . Could it possibly be her? And what does she want with Mandy and James?

CAT IN THE CRYPT
Animal Ark Hauntings 2

Lucy Daniels

Mandy and James will do anything to help an animal in distress. And sometimes even ghostly animals appear to need their help . . .

Mandy is haunted by dreams of a mysterious cat. Could it be because she is worried about Bathsheba, the vicarage tabby who has run away? Or does the strange, stone-coloured cat of her dreams have something to tell her?